Uncooperative Characters

Pete Simons

D1522754

Cover design by Rosie Simonse

For my children,
Jimmy, Katie, Petey, and Rosie.

And for Milo and any future grandkids
who may arrive after the time of this writing.
Welcome!

Also by Pete Simons

The Coyote
White as Snow

Table of Contents

"If we don't all row, the boat won't go."
— Unknown

William: "I'm sure we can all pull together, sir."
Vetinari: "Oh, I do hope not. Pulling together is the aim of
            despotism and tyranny. Free men pull in all kinds of
            directions."
— Terry Pratchett, *The Truth*

"Be who you are
and say what you feel
because those who mind don't matter
and those who matter don't mind."
— Theodor Seuss Geisel (aka "Dr. Seuss")

1

𝔓rologue

𝕴n the beginning, there was nothing but God. Time did not exist at that point, but if it had, it would have been extremely bored for an exceptionally long interval of timelessness.

Finally, God got fed up with nothing and said, "Let there be light." And because He was in a generous mood, He simultaneously created space and time at no additional charge.

And there was a big bang, even though no one was around to hear it except God. Which kind of settles the whole "tree falling in a forest" thing because if the big bang hadn't happened, the universe wouldn't exist.

And the light was good, assuming you were comfortable with 100,000,000,000,000,000,000,000,000,000,000,000 degrees Celsius, or 180,000,000,000,000,000,000,000,000,000,000,032 degrees Fahrenheit for you fellow Americans.

And because light cannot exist without its opposite, there was darkness. The darkness wasn't exactly evil, but you wouldn't want to buy a used car from it.

And God created Heaven and Earth and something like two trillion galaxies, give or take a few hundred billion. And each galaxy had something like a hundred thousand million stars. And most of the stars had planets. But Earth was the best, of course.

Truth be told, this took longer than a day, but no one was counting.

Once He was finished with the infrastructure, God created the angels. And some were light, and some were dark, and many were shades of gray.

And He produced many forms of life on Earth. He tweaked and tinkered with each of his creations until one day He concocted man. And now that He was getting the hang of this thing, He created woman, which was even better.

Then God said, "Let's play a game and see whether man becomes good or evil."

So He created Satan.

And Satan said, "Would Your Holiness like to make a little side wager on this?"

And God did. They agreed upon a price.

And while God was looking elsewhere, Satan whispered into man's ear, "Free will."

And then all hell broke loose.

2

Behind the Eight Ball

oy Bottoms handed over his last twenty-dollar bill in exchange for a slip of paper documenting his bet on the tenth race at Meadowlands, then he wandered off toward the viewing stands. Given how his luck had soured tonight, he wasn't even sure that he wanted to watch the event. *I might just as well have flushed that twenty down the toilet,* he thought.

He sat down heavily on the bench, wondering how he was going to explain the theft of the five hundred dollars to his mother. He'd fully intended to replace the money using this evening's winnings, a plan that would have worked beautifully had there been any winnings.

Roy glumly watched the thoroughbreds line up at the gate. Last Gasp, the horse he had bet on to win, was an extreme longshot at 50 to 1, but it was the only chance he had to recover his mother's money and save himself from (at best) a severe tongue-lashing and (at worst) an eviction notice, which his asshole brother-in-law would be only too happy to enforce. Not that he'd mind moving out of his mother's house, except for the fact that he had no money and no place to go.

Head hung low, Roy noticed a pink card on the ground that was partially covered. It appeared to read, "You're going to win, roy." He picked it up, and on closer inspection it said:

Having a hard time lately? Don't despair!

You're going to win royally with the advice of
Dr. Iko Sahedron!
Mystic and seer from the East!
Ask your burning questions and be answered!
Your good luck begins now!

The loudspeakers suddenly blared with the sound of a prerecorded trumpet.

"And they're off! Eat My Dust, the favorite, takes an early lead! He's followed by Soggy Biscuits and Tweet This, with Last Gasp running fourth in surprisingly strong form. As they circle the bend, Over Confident passes Last Gasp and challenges Tweet This for third. Busted Radiator is coming up now from the outside, putting pressure on Last Gasp.

"Rounding the first turn, Eat My Dust is in trouble! Yes, he seems to be slowing down considerably and has developed a distinct limp. He's out of it now, for sure. Soggy Biscuits takes the lead, followed closely by Over Confident and Tweet This. Last Gasp is back in fourth again but looking tired, with Busted Radiator fast on his tail.

"But what's this? Busted Radiator is trying to bite Last Gasp in the butt. His jockey doesn't know what to do. And there's the bite! Last Gasp suddenly lurches forward, almost throwing his jockey from the saddle. He passes Over Confident and bumps Tweet This against the rail. He's in a panic, folks! Be glad you're not in front of that horse right now. They're approaching the finish and it's going to be close. Last Gasp and Soggy Biscuits are nose-to-nose. I can't tell who's ahead.

"And that's it! The race is over! A surprise win by Last Gasp! Soggy Biscuits is second and Over Confident takes third. Oh, my! Last Gasp has fallen! He's down. Luckily his jockey was able to jump free before the horse trapped him underneath. It's pandemonium out there, folks! The veterinarians are rushing to the scene ...."

Roy was no longer paying attention. He couldn't believe his good fortune. He'd now be able to replace his mother's money and clear a $500 profit for himself. Being of a superstitious nature, he kissed Dr. Sahedron's card and placed it in his pocket. Then he set off to collect his winnings.

Roy looked again at the address on the reverse side of the card.

Dr. Iko Sahedron
888 Spheroid Road
(Behind the *Eight Ball Pool Hall*)
By Appointment Only – 1-800-888-8000

The streets in that part of town were haphazard and confusing, but Roy finally found the address and noticed a rotting wooden sign with a picture of a number eight pool ball. He entered the building and walked through the billiards room toward the back stairs. Climbing to the second-floor landing, he approached the only door. It was covered with black lacquer, upon which were painted three question marks in bright red, green, and blue. Next to the door were a button and a small card that read, "Dr. Iko Sahedron – Please ring." Roy reached up to press the buzzer, but before he could touch it, the door opened by itself.

The elderly woman behind the reception desk stared at him in an oddly fixated manner, making Roy uncomfortable. "Um, hello? M-m-my name is …" he stuttered.

"Roy Bottoms," finished the woman. "We know. You have a one o'clock appointment with the doctor. Have you prepared your questions?"

"My questions?"

"Didn't I explain this when you made your appointment? Oh, I must be getting senile. You get to ask him three yes-or-no questions for five hundred dollars. There are some questions that he either cannot or will not answer. If you ask one of these, you'll be permitted to ask another question. The doctor will tell you how many questions you have left. Phrase your queries carefully because he will answer them literally. Once you have asked and received answers to three questions, your session is over. There are no refunds. Don't complain if the answers aren't what you want to hear, or if you didn't ask the right questions. We don't care. You must pay up front—now, please. No personal checks."

Although Roy wasn't sure that he'd made the right decision in coming here, he took his $500 winnings out of his pocket and placed them on the counter. The woman counted the money and put it in the safe behind her desk.

Smiling, she said, "Thank you. You may go in now." She pushed a button on the wall, and the inner door opened. Roy entered, and the door closed behind him.

"No way!" he exclaimed as he passed the threshold.

The room was empty apart from a red and gold carpet, upon which was a leather armchair, presumably meant for him. Dr. Iko Sahedron sat cross-legged in the middle of the room, facing the chair. But he wasn't seated on a chair. Or upon the floor. Or upon anything. The man appeared to be floating in midair. He was white-haired and bearded, dark-skinned, and dressed in an Indian robe and turban. He smiled and pointed toward the chair. Roy sat down.

"Wow. That's got to be a trick with mirrors, right?"

Dr. Sahedron closed his eyes. When he opened them, he said, "My reply is no. You have two questions remaining." And he smiled.

"Damn it. Seriously?"

Dr. Sahedron closed his eyes.

"No, wait, I didn't mean ... Crap."

The doctor opened his eyes and said, "It is decidedly so. You have one question remaining." He smiled.

All right, thought Roy. *I've got to make this good.*

"Which horse will win the first race at Meadowlands tomorrow?"

Dr. Sahedron frowned and said, "You must ask only yes-or-no questions. You have one question remaining." And he smiled.

Roy sat quietly for a few moments. Then he asked. "Will Apple go up tomorrow?"

Dr. Sahedron closed his eyes. He reopened them and said,

"Concentrate and ask again. You have one question remaining."
He smiled.

Exacerbated, Roy rephrased the question. "Will the stock price of Apple Corporation increase tomorrow?"

After the same routine, the answer returned. "You may rely on it. You have no questions remaining." Dr. Sahedron smiled and disappeared in a puff of smoke.

Roy jumped out of his chair and ran toward the spot where the doctor had been levitating. He waved his arms around. Nothing but air. He scanned the room for hidden projectors but saw nothing.

"What the hell?" he exclaimed.

A disembodied voice responded, "I said that you have no questions remaining." The door swung open.

Roy walked out of the room, stunned. He approached the receptionist and asked, "Was that for real back there?"

The receptionist said, "Yup. He's the real deal."

Roy rushed out to place a buy order for $50,000 of Apple stock, using his mother's account. He'd sell it at the end of the day tomorrow and pocket the profits. She'd never even know it happened.

Except it didn't quite work out that way. After an initial rise in Apple's stock price, the Federal Reserve announced an unexpected hike in interest rates, and the stock market tanked. At the end of the day, Apple stock was down 10 percent.

Roy was livid. He ran back to the doctor's office and demanded his money back. The receptionist folded her arms and said, "No refunds."

"But he was wrong! He lied to me!"

The receptionist didn't budge. "He's never wrong, and he doesn't lie. You simply asked the wrong question, or you misunderstood the answer."

"I just asked him if Apple stock would go up today. It went down 10 percent!"

The receptionist sighed. "Did the stock price increase at any point *during* the day?"

"Yes, but …"

"Then his answer was correct. I warned you to be careful with your phrasing, Mr. Bottoms. He answers all questions truthfully, *exactly as asked.* And as I said yesterday, there are no refunds. Now, would you like to make another appointment and see if you can get it right this time?"

Roy debated with himself. This seemed like a scam, but he'd seen the guy disappear into thin air! That had to mean he was on the level, didn't it? He'd just have to be super careful with his questions next time. Then he thought of the perfect thing to ask.

"Okay. Yeah. When's his next opening?"

Later that week, Roy again stole his mother's $500 and used it to pay for another session. As before, the doctor floated in the middle of the room. His steadfast smile was beginning to get on Roy's nerves, but Roy was resolved to say nothing except for the three questions he had carefully prepared.

"Am I named in my mother's last will and testament?"

Eyes closed. Eyes open. "Yes. You have two questions remaining." Creepy smile.

"If my mother were to die, would my sister and I inherit her money equally?"

Eyes closed. Open. "As I see it, yes. You have one question remaining." Questioning smile.

"If I were to kill my mother, would I get away with it?"

Closed. Open. "Better not tell you now. You have one question remaining." Concerned smile.

"If I were to kill my mother, would I go to jail?"

Closed. Open. "My sources say no. You have no questions remaining." No smile. At all. With a puff of smoke, he was gone.

After Roy left the office, the receptionist got up and went into the inner room. "Will he be returning?" she asked.

"Don't count on it," the doctor's voice replied.

She nodded and went back to her desk.

Roy finished applying the coat of furniture oil to the wooden landing at the top of the stairs, leaving some room along the left edge where he intended to plant his own feet. With any luck, he wouldn't even be in the house when the accident happened. He'd be careful to talk to as many people as he could while he was out, to solidify his alibi.

He stood up and carefully stepped to the left before descending the stairs. *Mother should be pleased*, he thought. *She's always telling me I need to help clean the house.*

A few minutes later, he shouted up the stairs, "Mother? I'm going out now. I left some scrambled eggs on the stove for you."

There was no answer. That was unusual.

"Mother?" he called. "Are you okay?"

No response. Roy shrugged and climbed the stairs, stepping to the side as he reached the landing. He knocked on her bedroom door. "Mother?"

Not a sound.

He entered and approached the bed, knowing she was dead even before he touched the cold body to check for a pulse. *This is brilliant*, he thought. *Death by natural causes. I'll be in the clear for sure. All I have to do is clean up the furniture oil at the top of the steps and call 911.* He went downstairs to get some turpentine and a scrub brush.

Whistling an old show tune, he returned to the landing, swung around, and crouched in front of the slippery floor. "I hope she's in a better place now," he said to himself. "I wonder if she is?"

"Without a doubt," a voice behind him replied.

Roy took in a sharp breath and swung his head back to see Dr. Sahedron floating in the hallway. Reflexively, he jumped up and stepped back, slipping on the oil. He was too shocked to even register any pain as he tumbled down the hard steps. *I guess the pain will come later*, Roy thought as he neared the bottom. He would have been correct in that assumption had his neck not snapped when he reached the hardwood floor.

The next thing Roy knew, he was floating in midair and looking down at his prone body. *My head should not be facing in that direction*, he thought. "Well, that sucks for me," he said.

"Yes, definitely," Dr. Sahedron replied, floating beside him.

"This is all YOUR fault! So what's next? Am I supposed to float around here forever?"

"Very doubtful," the doctor stated.

"Okay, then what happens to me now?"

"Outlook not so good," said Sahedron.

Roy felt his soul being tugged downward. "Wait! I didn't even kill her! I can't be punished for just *thinking* something, can I?"

"Signs point to yes."

And Dr. Sahedron laughed loudly as Roy's soul was sucked through the floor and into darkness.

3

Teapot

Yeah, I'm a little teapot, short and stout, but if you try to make anything out of that I'll kick your ass. We can't all grow up to be stainless-steel coffee urns. Yet what I lack in physical stature, I more than compensate for in sheer gumption. So don't mess with me. You've been warned.

I was relaxing in my office that morning with a nice cup of Earl Grey spiked with Jack Daniels when this classy scoop walks through the door. She was a real ladle, alright. Not your usual flatware, that's for sure. She had curves in all the right places and was extremely well polished. My water started bubbling as soon as I saw my face reflected in her shiny silver bowl. They don't make 'em like that anymore. Her beautiful oval head tapered down to the most attractive handle I'd ever seen. *That dame can spoon with me anytime*, I thought.

"Mr. Kettle, I presume? I understand that you are a private detective, is that right?"

Even her voice was attractive. As steam started coming out of my spout, I tried like hell not to whistle at her.

"That's what it says on the door, gorgeous. Yeah, I'm Kettle, but you can call me Sam. What can I do for you?"

"I am Lady Portmeirion. I have a case that I'd like you to work on for me."

I'd like to work on her case for sure, I thought. *I'll bet it's a very nice case. Smooth burgundy felt. Solid wood framing. Just the two of us, rubbing against the …*

"Mr. Kettle? Sam?"

I snapped out of it. "Yeah, as it happens I have some time right now. Please take a seat, and tell me what you need, Lady Portmeirion."

She sat, and I reached for a rag to wipe the condensation from my lid. I'd swear the temperature in the room had increased at least fifty degrees in the last minute or two. I waited for her to speak.

"It's my husband, Mr. Kettle. I'm sorry, I mean Sam. My husband. Lord Portmeirion. I think that ... he's seeing someone else."

"If he's seeing anyone else, he's an idiot, Mrs. Portmeirion. If you don't mind me saying."

"Thank you, Sam. But I'm afraid it's true." She broke down in tears.

I let her cry for a minute, then I handed her a silver polishing cloth that I kept in my desk drawer for moments like these. She dried her eyes and buffed herself, handing me back the towel with a sad little smile. *I'm never gonna wash that cloth again*, I thought.

"And what would you like me to do, ma'am?" I asked.

"I need photographs, Sam. Proof of his infidelity. Without that, he could divorce me and leave me with nothing."

I nodded sagely, but a little too far. A few drops of hot water escaped my spout. She was kind enough not to comment on it.

"One more thing," she purred. "We need a cover story."

"What's that?" I asked.

"It's a believable lie used to cover our tracks. I'm surprised you didn't know that, particularly in your line of work."

"I know what a cover story is. I'm asking why we need one."

"My husband ... he pays people to follow me. He may track you down and ask why we met."

"I see. Sure. How about this: You hired me to find your long-lost twin sister, who ran off with a guy who plays the spoons."

"No," she replied. "That won't do. My husband is quite aware that my sister settled down with a nice man who manages a dinner service. Instead, we'll say that I asked you to guard these valuables for me." She handed me a box. I looked inside and let off some steam. *Damn*, I thought. *I'd hate to be walking down a dark alley and suddenly meet the oysters those pearls came from.* Underneath the pearls was a slip of paper with some numbers written on it. I didn't know what they meant, and I didn't care.

That was my first mistake.

I closed the box and gazed at her perfect form. The windows began to steam up. She waited.

Finally getting hold of myself, I said, "Okay. I get $500 a day plus expenses. If I get you the proof you need, I get an extra two grand at the end of the job. That sound okay to you, ma'am?"

She agreed and I placed the box of pearls and her cash advance in my safe while my secretary brought in the usual contract for her to sign. When our business was concluded she got up and headed for the door. Then the dame suddenly turned and whispered in a sultry voice, "If you need me, Sam, just whistle. You know how to whistle, don't you? You just put your lips together and blow."

Oh, I knew how to whistle. I was boiling over as she closed the door behind her. You could hear the sound five blocks away. Dogs started to howl. It took a full three minutes for me to cool down enough for the tooting to stop.

The dame wasn't kidding about her hubby. Walking home that night, a car drove up on the curbside and before I could react two mugs jumped out and grabbed me. The first mug smelled of stale coffee and told me we were going for a ride. The second one had more of a pilsner aroma. He said nothing and shoved me into the back seat. They got in on either side of me and the driver took off.

I started to boil and felt the muzzle of a gun push into my side. Coffee Mug muttered menacingly, "Keep the lid on, Kettle, or I'll plug you." Beer Mug just looked out the window and smirked.

Deciding I'd better keep chill until I found out just what the deal was, I sat back and enjoyed the ride. We drove past a guardhouse and through some gates onto the Portmeirion estate. It was the kind of place you generally only see in the movies, built by people who had more money than sense and who probably didn't even know how many rooms it had—forget about using them all. Several of the chimneys were belching smoke. Probably burning money, I figured, and I seriously considered raising my fee. At a minimum, I'd be heavily padding my expenses. Baby needed a new tea cozy.

We stopped in front of the main doors. "Get out," Coffee Mug instructed. "His Goblet wishes to have a word with you."

I got out. The door to the mansion was being held open by a stunning dish. She was hard, smooth, and pleasingly round, wearing a dress that provided just the right amount of embroidery around the edges. Her perfume smelled of elderberries. She took my coat and directed me to the library.

"Have a seat. His Goblet, the Lord Portmeirion, will be with you in a few moments. Is there anything I can get for you while you wait?"

I refrained from making a lewd comment, which was unusual for me, and instead I asked, "What are you supposed to be, honey, his butler?"

"Of course not. I'm his cutler."

"His cutlet? I'll bet you are."

"Not his cutlet, wise guy. His cutler. A person who makes, deals in, or repairs cutlery. Look it up. Gosh, it's cold in here. Do me a favor and stoke that fire a little, would you?"

I went over to the fireplace and threw another log on, then adjusted its position using the iron poker.

"Much better," she smiled. "Thanks."

With that, the sexy dish departed, presumably to polish the dinnerware. I closed my eyes and imagined I was made of heavily tarnished silver.

Lord Portmeirion entered a few moments later. His Goblet had a stately bearing and crystalline features. He seemed a bit in his cups, and I wondered how much wine he could hold. It seemed like quite a lot.

"I understand my wife came to see you earlier today, Mr. Kettle," he said, sloshing around as he paced back and forth. "I'd like you to tell me why."

"I'm afraid that my relationship with my clients is confidential," I replied.

"It's good that you're afraid, Mr. Kettle. Very good, indeed. Because there is a man who works for me who can be very

14

persuasive. Shall I call him in?"

"You mean Coffee Mug or Beer Mug? We've already met. They don't seem so tough to me."

"Ah, no. Not them. I was referring to Mr. MacKenszie Carver, otherwise known as Mack the Knife."

I'd heard of the Knife. He was no joke. Sharp as a razor, he would come straight to the point in an interview. I sure wouldn't want him to take a stab at questioning me, particularly if he was on edge.

So I backtracked. I'm tough, but I'm no fool. "There's no need to be unpleasant, Your Gobletness. As the lady's husband, I'm sure it will be fine if I tell *you*. She asked me to guard an item for her. A string of pearls."

"Now why would she do that? We have a perfectly serviceable house safe and a well-trained security staff."

"I wouldn't know, Your Carafe. Perhaps you should ask her. I just do as I'm paid."

Lord Portmeirion nodded and reached for the half-empty wine bottle on the side table, tipping it up and emptying it into his orifice. I wondered again how he could hold so much wine without toppling over.

"Alright, Mr. Kettle, you're free to go. I do hope I shan't find out that you've been fibbing to me. That would be most … unhealthy." With that, the good lord turned on his stem and wobbled out.

The sexy dish returned with my coat and saw me out the door. There was no car waiting, so I walked out the main gate. When I was out of the guard's line of sight, I circled back toward the house and hopped over the fence, hoping like hell that they didn't employ attack dogs on the estate.

Finding a nice spot in the tree line overlooking the house, I settled in and steeped for a while.

Around 11:00 p.m., another car arrived, and a young woman entered the house. Through the lighted window, I could see Lord Portmeirion embrace her. I raised my camera, thinking "paydirt." I was so focused on my camera that I didn't hear anyone creeping up behind me until it was too late. I got the briefest whiff of elderberries, and then something struck the back of my head.

I'd been iced. I was out cold.

I woke with a crushing headache and reached up to find that my lid was bandaged. It was a few minutes before I trusted myself enough to open my eyes. The light made my head hurt even more, but I squinted until I realized that I was lying in a filthy jail cell. A cop grinned at me from the other side of the bars.

"Officer Pott," I moaned, "what an unexpected pleasure."

"We finally got you dead to rights this time," Pott sneered. "You'll hang for this, Kettle."

I rubbed my lid, then decided that was a bad idea. "What are you talking about, Pott? You gonna hang me for taking some pictures of a guy?"

"Ha! Taking pictures! That's a good one." He unlocked the cell and pushed me toward the interview rooms. "Let's go, Blackie."

He knew I hated that nickname.

Detective Decanter walked up behind us. "Pott, don't let me hear you call Kettle black again. Do you understand me?"

"Pott can't help it," I said. "He's a racist bastard."

"After you, *sir*," slurred Officer Pott as he held the interview room door open for me, slyly poking me sharply in the ribs while Decanter wasn't watching. I knew I shouldn't have insulted him since he tended to fly off the handle, but I couldn't help myself. The guy thought he was stainless steel, but he was just a dirty crock.

We sat down and Decanter came in a moment later. He pushed a button on the tape recorder. "Interview of Sam Kettle, Tuesday, March 7th, 10:20 a.m. Present are Detective Decanter and Officer Pott. So, Kettle, you finally lost it, yeah? You had the combination to the safe, and you just couldn't resist the opportunity to take the pearls, could you? Go ahead, explain yourself. Spill."

"I don't know what you're talking about."

"Oh, come off it, Kettle. Be just a *little* cooperative, can't you? We found the pearls in your office, right where you'd stashed them. Along with the combination to the Portmeirions' safe.

16

How'd you get that, by the way?"

"Lady Portmeirion gave me a paper with some numbers, along with the pearls. I didn't know it was the combination for her safe."

"Oh, so the lady *gave* you the pearls? Funny, she says they were stolen."

"I've been set up. She came to see me. Ask Lord Portmeirion. He can confirm it."

"Yeah, well, that might present a problem," scoffed Pott, "since you killed him and all."

A chill ran down my spine. "Killed? His Goblet is dead?"

"Crystal shards and red wine all over the floor. You really made a mess of it, Kettle. A very sloppy job. Your prints were all over the murder weapon that you left at the scene," said the detective.

"Ah. Let me guess. He was killed with the poker."

"Yeah," said the detective. "I thought you were smarter than that, Kettle."

"I didn't," Pott said.

"I *am* smarter than that," I exclaimed. "I didn't kill him. I've been set up. The cutler did it."

"The cutler, eh?"

"Yeah. I don't know her name. She's the one in charge of the cutlery. I think she and Lady Portmeirion are in cahoots. Talk to them."

"Okay, Kettle," nodded Detective Decanter. "I've always thought you were a little hotheaded, but I never pegged you as a killer. I'll check out your story. In the meantime, feel free to enjoy the comfort of our fine jail."

I'd been here before, and it wasn't all that comfortable.

Sometime later, Detective Decanter visited me in my cell. "We're letting you go for now, Kettle. But don't leave town. The investigation is ongoing, and you're still a possible suspect."

"Still a suspect? Didn't you arrest the lady and her cutler?"

"Actually, no," admitted the detective sheepishly. "They both seem to have skipped town."

"Damn. I knew it," I said. "The dish ran away with the spoon."

18

4

The Trouble with Time Travel

"The trouble with time travel is that it's so danged complicated," explained Professor Puffinhead. "But I think I've got all the kinks out of it now." He scratched his balding head and stifled a yawn. "Excuse me. I've been working without much sleep for the past week or so. I'm very excited to test my machine, you know."

Connor Underman stared dubiously at the complex machinery cluttering the lab in Berkeley, California. He looked even more suspiciously at the eight-foot-tall clear glass tube that he was supposed to step into. *But a hundred bucks is a hundred bucks*, he thought. *And seriously, what's the chance that the thing will actually work? The guy's obviously a crackpot.*

The professor turned a few knobs and pushed several buttons on the control board. "There. That should do it. Now, listen carefully, Mr. Underman. I'm going to send you just one hour into the future. I will be there to greet you. I want you to hold this control switch. If anything goes wrong—anything at all—just push the red button and you will be brought back to the current time."

Connor grabbed the switch and asked, "What do you think will go wrong?"

"Oh, nothing, nothing. It's for emergencies, that's all. Please step onto the platform." The professor pushed a button, and the glass cylinder slid upward.

Connor stepped onto the circular base, and the tube lowered around him. "What kind of emergencies?" he asked.

"Hmm? Um, nothing that I can think of, Mr. Underman. It's simply a precaution. Are you ready?" Not waiting for an answer, the professor pushed a few buttons.

"I'm not sure I—"

There was a flash of light, and Connor was suddenly floating in outer space. The Earth hung in front of him, an enormous blue ball with white clouds. He tried to scream, but the air flowed out of his lungs without making a sound. He couldn't breathe! And he was cold. Incredibly cold. *I'm going to die.* And then he remembered the control switch in his hand. He pushed the red button ...

... and was back in the glass tube. He gasped for air and dropped to the ground.

The professor raised the cylinder and ran toward him. "Mr. Underman! What happened? I pushed the button and you just collapsed. Did my machine not work?"

Connor caught his breath and stammered, "I wa-wa-was ... in outer space! I sa-sa-saw the earth! I almost died!"

Professor Puffinhead clapped his hand against his forehead. "Ah. I knew I had forgotten something. I'll have to modify the algorithm."

"What?"

"Don't you see, Mr. Underman? You traveled in time but not in space."

"If I didn't travel in space, why was I suddenly floating above the planet?"

"Ah, *you* didn't move, but the *earth* did. During that one hour, the earth continued to revolve around the sun. At thirty kilometers per second, it would have traveled, oh, about 68,000 miles or so in space. Thus, when you reappeared, the earth was long gone, you see."

"Holy crap! You could have killed me!"

"N-not intentionally," the professor stammered. "And remember, you're doing this for science. Oh, and for money, I suppose. Here's your hundred dollars. I do hope you will come back for another try once I make the necessary adjustments."

Connor took the money. "Not on your life, Doc."

"But consider what you could do when this machine finally works, Mr. Underman. You would have firsthand knowledge of the future! Wouldn't that be fantastic?"

Connor started toward the door, and he began to think about horse racing, football games, and stock markets. He turned back. "All right, Doc. I'm your guy. For science, right? Call me when you've got the kinks worked out—but not until then, okay?"

"Excellent! Thank you, Mr. Underman. You won't regret this decision." The professor walked off, talking to himself. "Now, let me think. I'll also need to adjust for the solar system's movement through the galaxy. And for the galaxy's rotation. And the galaxies are all moving apart from one another as well. Ah, time travel is so complicated ..."

Two weeks later, Connor returned to the laboratory to find the professor crouching next to one of the many electrical cabinets in the room, making adjustments with a screwdriver.

"There. That should do it. That's the last one." He closed the panel door and stood up.

Connor smiled nervously. "Are you absolutely sure you got the bugs worked out?"

"Oh, yes. I've adjusted for the orbital velocities of every celestial object I could think of. Very tricky, I must say, because every Newtonian frame of reference is equally valid, you see. So which one is the one that matters? I had to create a universal frame of reference that compensated for any type of motion and then translate the results back to an Earth-based focal point."

"I have no idea what you're talking about, Professor. But did you fix it?"

"Yes, yes. I made modifications for everything, as far as I know. I can say with a high degree of confidence that you will almost certainly reappear on Earth this time. Here's your control switch. I put it on a little strap that you can attach to your wrist. Isn't that nice? Well, are you ready?"

Connor checked his pocket. Yes, he had a pen and paper to note down the winners of the fifth race at Golden Gate Fields. If he returned quickly, he could place several bets online before the cutoff. He nodded to the professor. "I'm all set. Let's do this."

Connor stepped onto the platform. The tube came down.

"Okay, here we go," said the professor. "5 ... 4 ... 3 ... 2 ... 1 ..."

And Connor was suddenly flying very fast over some water. He looked around, but there was no land in sight. He quickly pushed the button ...

... and was back in the lab.

"You're back!" shouted the professor. "What happened this time?"

"I don't know. I was flying through the air above the ocean. I couldn't see any land. Nothing but water. I would've died out there if it weren't for the control switch."

The professor thought for a moment. "Nothing but water? Ah. The earth's rotation. Yes, I see."

"You told me you got all the bugs out!"

"Well, yes, I took care of celestial motion, but I neglected to adjust for the earth's rotation around its own axis. Silly of me. The earth rotates at about one thousand miles per hour, so in the hour that transpired, you would have reappeared a thousand miles west of here, at our current elevation of 170 feet above sea level. Yes, that would place you over the middle of the Pacific Ocean. Sorry about that. It's an easy fix, compared to the last one. Give me a day to work it out."

Connor walked out with another hundred bucks, wondering if this was worth risking his life.

The next day, Connor was back, presumably having answered the last question in the affirmative.

"Are you *really* sure you've got it right this time?" he asked the professor.

"Yes, Mr. Underman. As far as I can determine, you will reappear inside the glass tube."

"Do you absolutely guarantee it?"

"Ahem. Nothing can be unconditionally guaranteed, Mr. Underman, but I'm as sure as I can be. I would take the trip myself if I didn't need to operate the controls."

Connor wondered if the professor would have made the same claim the last two times he tried this. *Whatever.* He grabbed the control switch, strapped it to his wrist, and stepped onto the platform. The cylinder came down. 3 ... 2 ... 1 ...

... and suddenly Connor's body was flung sideways into the glass, which shattered on impact. With excruciating pain in his left arm, he blinked and saw the glass tube was still intact. Connor screamed and grabbed his wrist. The cylinder rose, and the professor rushed to his side.

"Am I in the future?" Connor asked.

"No. When I turned the machine on, you just started screaming."

"The glass cracked. My wrist hurts like hell."

The professor examined Connor's arm and determined that his wrist was broken. Then he scanned the glass cylinder. "The glass didn't crack ... unless it did so in the future. Ah. I think I understand. Angular momentum. You're a lucky man, Mr. Underman. You might have easily died in that attempt."

"Unlike the previous two, you mean? What happened to me this time?"

"Well, it's rather interesting, really. You see, we are all moving in a circular motion around the earth as it rotates. The only thing that prevents us from flying off into space is the earth's gravity. When you reappeared in the tube, the earth had been rotating for an hour. You were moving in a different direction when you left here, and you kept moving in that direction when you reached the future. I estimate that you would have hit the glass at something like 600 miles per hour. You should be dead. The only thing I can figure is that the control switch was the first part of you to hit the glass. It depressed the button and sent you back here before the rest of your body made impact."

"So why didn't this happen before?"

"It did, I believe, but there wasn't anything for you to crash into before. The first time, you were in space. Without any nearby objects for comparison, you wouldn't even have realized that you were moving. The second time, you said you were flying over the water, right? And you punched the button right away. You never lost much momentum, so you got back here okay. I should have realized that angular momentum was a problem when you said you were in motion over the water. I was too focused on the earth's rotational effect on your position. Sorry about that. It won't happen next time."

"There won't be any next time. I'm done with this."

"I see. That is your decision, of course. Here is my card. Please call me if you change your mind. In any case, let me take you to the hospital and pay for the treatment of your wrist. It's the least I can do."

Connor slipped the card into his jacket pocket, and they left the room. About fifty minutes later, the glass tube suddenly shattered into a million pieces that flew across the lab.

The following week, Connor received a phone call from the professor, asking if he'd be willing to give time travel one last try.

"Why me?" asked Connor.

"You already know how this works, for one thing. Plus, I don't want people to hear of my experiments until I publish my results. Academia is a frightfully competitive business, Mr. Underman. Until my paper is printed in a scholarly journal, the fewer people who hear of it, the better."

"Well, I don't know …"

"I'll pay you a thousand dollars for one last trial."

"When do you want me there?"

One hour later, Connor arrived at the lab with his left wrist in a cast. Professor Puffinhead greeted him at the door.

"I guess you figured out how to deal with the momentum problem?"

"Well, no, not exactly."

"What?? I'm not getting into that thing just to get squashed again, Professor."

"You won't be squashed. Listen. I tried to find a way to change the direction of your angular momentum so you arrive in the future standing still. It can't be done. Momentum is a conserved property, so changing its direction is only possible through the application of a sudden force, and the amount of force that this would require would kill you. But I figured out an easy workaround."

"What's that?"

"Instead of sending you one hour into the future, I will send you forward twenty-four hours. That way, the earth will have made a full revolution, and you'll arrive moving in the same direction as when you started."

"Okay, that makes sense. I guess."

"Very well. Here is a new control switch. I'm going to hang it around your neck this time. Are you ready for one more time trip?"

"A thousand bucks, right?"

"In cash. I have it right here."

"Then let's do this."

Connor stepped upon the platform, and a new glass cylinder smoothly lowered into place around him.

"Okay, Mr. Underman. For the video recording I'm making, the time is 4:00 p.m. on Tuesday, June 23, 2019. Here we go … 3 … 2 … 1 …"

Connor blinked, and the professor disappeared, along with the glass tube. The lab was empty, and there was glass all over the floor. *What the hell's up with that?* Connor wondered. *Anyway, the professor was supposed to be here to meet me.* He glanced at the clock on the wall. *4:01 p.m. The damn thing didn't work. No, wait. He said the machine would send me forward twenty-four hours, so the time wouldn't have changed. But is today still Tuesday, or is it Wednesday?*

Connor took out his smartphone and checked the date. Wednesday, June 24. *So it did work. I'm in Tomorrowland. I'll be damned.*

Connor walked out of the lab and had to duck underneath some tape that said "Crime scene – do not cross." *Weird*, he thought as he headed down Durant Avenue. At the newsstand, he bought a copy of the evening paper and immediately flipped to the back pages. There it was. Closing stock prices. Racing and sports results. *Now to get back and place some bets*, he thought.

As he walked back along Durant, Connor noticed the professor running toward him from across the street, shouting. Connor couldn't understand him at first, and then he heard …

"Mr. Underman, stop!"

Aw, hell, Connor thought. *The old fart's figured out what I'm doing.*

Well, he can't prevent me now.

Connor reached for the control switch.

"Whatever you do, don't push the—"

Let's return to yesterday. Here's how things looked from the professor's standpoint.

"Okay, Mr. Underman. For the video recording I'm making, the time is 4:00 p.m. on Tuesday, June 23, 2019. Here we go … 3 … 2 … 1 …"

The clock ticked forward. At precisely 4:01 p.m., Professor Puffinhead saw Connor disappear. A moment later, there was a loud explosion. Professor Puffinhead ducked as shards of glass flew across the room. When the worst was over, he raised his head to peer at the scene. The glass tube had been completely demolished, and Connor Underman's torn, motionless body lay on the floor.

He rushed to give aid, but there was nothing he could do. Connor was dead. Weeping, the professor dialed 9-1-1.

What could have gone wrong this time? the professor wondered.

It took fifteen minutes for the police to arrive. The professor opened the door to find two uniformed officers on the steps. An ambulance was just rounding the corner.

"Professor Peter Puffinhead?"

"Yes, that's me."

"Officers Randolph and Kowalski. We understand there's been an accident on the premises?"

"Yes. Please come in, officers."

They stepped inside and scanned the scene, noting the glass on the floor. They approached the body. Officer Randolph knelt to feel for a pulse, but he was certain he wouldn't find one. "Who is this man?"

"His name is Connor Underman. He's been working with me on a science experiment."

"I'm afraid he's dead, sir. What exactly happened here?"

The professor wiped his brow. "It was the experiment. I killed him."

This was clearly not the response that Randolph expected. The officer stood up and signaled to Kowalski, who was inspecting the source of the apparent explosion. "Excuse me, sir? Did you say that you killed him?"

"Um, sort of. Physics killed him, to be more precise. Angular momentum. I should have seen it coming though."

"Uh-huh. Well, I think the detective in charge will want to speak with you at length about this matter. Could you please come with us, sir?"

They handcuffed the professor and led him out just as the paramedics and the first of the forensic technicians began to arrive.

Detective Queeg held Professor Puffinhead overnight for questioning. It turns out that the police take an apparent confession of murder very seriously. Queeg and the rest of the homicide team knew that Puffinhead's time-travel explanation was a complete crock. Yet although he grilled Puffinhead for hours, the professor never wavered from his story.

"I think I know what happened," the professor said. "It's all about the conservation of momentum. We're all in circular motion as the earth revolves, moving at around 1,000 miles an hour. But the *speed* isn't the real problem for time travel—it's the *direction of motion*. The direction of our motion changes every second as we follow a circle around the earth. Let's say it's twelve hours later. You're now on the other side of the rotating earth, *and you're moving in the opposite direction from when you started.* There is a difference of 2,000 miles an hour in your velocity because you're now moving at 1,000 miles an hour *the other way.* If you were to suddenly go back in time twelve hours, you'd immediately hit any nearby object at 2,000 miles per hour."

"Okay, Professor," said Detective Queeg, "I'll take your word for that. But what's it got to do with Mr. Underman's death?"

"I thought I'd fixed this problem by sending Connor forward

in time by exactly twenty-four hours. That way, he'd be traveling in the same direction as when he started."

"Yeah, so?"

"Well, I didn't think about the return trip! What if Connor stayed in the future for a while? Every minute he's there changes the direction of his velocity. It wouldn't take long before the difference in velocity would make a return trip extremely dangerous. He'd have to wait a full twenty-four hours in the future before he could return safely."

Detective Queeg shook his head, not buying any of this.

"I failed to warn him about this," the professor sobbed, "mainly because I hadn't thought the problem through well enough. It's all my fault."

On Wednesday afternoon, the police decided that they had to release him, given the lack of evidence of ill intent. The professor was let go with a stern warning not to leave the Bay Area and to stay out of the lab, which was now a crime scene.

Professor Puffinhead stood up and put on his jacket. "What time is it?" he asked.

The detective looked at his watch. "4:05 p.m."

"Oh my God!" the professor shouted. "Why didn't I think? Maybe I can still stop it!" He rushed out of the room just as a representative from the coroner's office arrived.

"What was all that about?" she asked.

"Just some crazy guy. He says he sent the victim forward in time and the poor sod was killed by physics when he returned. Something about angular momentum and the fact that he stayed in the future too long. He's obviously looney toons."

"Time travel? My God. I know that seems daft but look at this." She tossed a newspaper on the detective's desk.

He picked it up and glanced at the headline. "It's today's paper. So what? What am I supposed to be looking at?"

"It's the newspaper that was underneath the victim's body. He had this on him when he died. When he died *yesterday*. Before that issue was published."

Professor Puffinhead left the police station and started running toward the lab. He was grossly out of shape, however, and had to slow down after a block and a half. Then he realized that he might be heading in the wrong direction. What if Underman had left the lab? Although the professor didn't know where the man went, he couldn't have gone far.

Where would I go? the professor mused as he ran. *Ah! To get evidence that I've seen the future! A newspaper!* He jogged as fast as he could toward Durant Avenue, hoping he didn't have a coronary on the way.

A few minutes later, the professor saw Connor Underman walking toward him on the other side of the street.

"Mr. Underman, stop!" the professor yelled.

Horrified, he watched as Connor reached for the control switch.

"Whatever you do, don't push the—"

Connor disappeared.

"—button."

The professor stopped, sat down on the curb, and cried.

Time travel's a bitch, he thought.

5

𝕭urma-𝕾habe

Raindrops dive-bombed the black-and-white patrol car on the side of the road, generating a hellish cacophony. Oblivious to the noise, Frank admired himself in the rearview mirror and noted how well the uniform fitted his slender but muscular frame. Traffic on the highway was light to virtually nonexistent, as usual for this time of night. A solitary car passed him slowly, probably suspicious that the police were using that newfangled radar gun to catch speeders. But Frank was doing no such thing. The Nevada police didn't even have the radar equipment yet.

Frank tilted the mirror down to get a better look at the uniform. His nameplate read "HTUOMYAW" in the glass. *Damn,* he thought as he stared at his reflection, *Officer Frank Waymouth, you are a handsome devil.* Frank combed his hair and placed the peaked cap on his head. Then he readjusted the mirror, checked for traffic, signaled, and pulled the Buick Century police cruiser carefully out onto the road.

Thirty years later, LIFE Magazine would name Nevada's Highway 50 "The Loneliest Road in America," but back in 1956, "godforsaken" might have been a more apt descriptor. At night, you could drive for hours without seeing the lights of another car—and you'd better carry some extra gas in the trunk in case you didn't make it to the next filling station. The solitude suited Frank, who was hoping for a quiet evening's drive as he set off in the direction of the California state line.

His lights illuminated the first of many small signposts along the side of the highway, placed there by a Minnesota shaving-cream company.

"NO MATTER," read the first sign.

"HOW YOU SLICE IT," said the second, a few hundred yards later.

"IT'S STILL YOUR FACE"

"BE HUMANE"

"USE"

"***BURMA-SHAVE***," proclaimed the last.

Frank drove on, knowing there'd be no more of these signs for at least a few miles.

The radio suddenly came to life. "Attention, all units. Two convicts have escaped from Ely Prison. They are dangerous and should be approached with caution. We believe they may have acquired civilian clothes. They may or may not be traveling together and are likely heading for Highway 50 or 93."

Damn, thought Frank. *There goes my peaceful evening.*

Roger Burnbaum rubbed his eyes and rolled the window down a crack, trying to prevent the monotonous sound of the windshield wipers from putting him to sleep. It let in some rain, but the breeze would help keep him awake. He tried the radio again, but he was too far afield to get a good signal. The only welcome distractions were the occasional Burma-Shave signs.

"WHEN DRIVING"

"IN THE RAIN"

"SLOW IT DOWN"

"OR FEEL THE PAIN"

"USE SOOTHING"

"***BURMA-SHAVE***"

His head nodded and quickly popped back up. *Damn. If this keeps up, I'll have to pull over for the night, even if it means missing the sales meeting in Reno. The boss will have a fit, but that'll still be better than running off the road in the middle of nowhere ... WHAT THE ...? God damn it!*

Roger slammed on the brakes and swerved to avoid hitting the guy standing on the side of the road with his thumb out. *Who the hell would be out trying to hitchhike in this rain, at this time of night?*

On the verge of driving away, he felt a sudden surge of pity for the man and brought the car to a stop, leaning over to open the passenger door just as the hitchhiker ran up and got in. He was drenched to the bone and had a couple days' stubble on his face, but he seemed reasonably clean.

"Much obliged, sir, I really appreciate it. It's a hell of a night out there. The name's Jim. Jim Smith. Pleased to meet you." He offered his hand.

Roger shook it. "Roger Burnbaum. Happy to help. I'm heading to Reno."

"That would be perfect for me, if you don't mind the company. Thank you kindly."

"There's a towel in the back seat. I keep one handy in weather like this. You can wipe yourself down. I'll turn up the heat."

"Much obliged, sir."

"Call me Roger."

"Okay, Roger." He flashed a smile.

"Truth is, Jim, I got a selfish reason for picking you up. You can help keep me awake. I almost dozed off before, and I can't afford the time to pull over."

"Well, now, Roger, if you want, I'd be happy to drive a spell."

Roger felt a brief shiver and wondered if he'd made the right choice by allowing this man into his car. "No, that's fine, Jim. I'll be all right with a little conversation."

They both stared out the window as some more signs appeared.

"DON'T STOP"
"FOR HITCHERS"
"AND BE THEIR"
"CHAUFFEUR"
"WE'D HATE TO LOSE"
"A CUSTOMER"
"***BURMA-SHAVE***"

Jim chuckled. "Well, well, well. I'm sure glad I wasn't standin' on the other side of them signs when you drove up."

Roger forced a laugh and said, "Aw, that wouldn't have made

any difference to me. Like you said, it's a hell of a night. What's your line of work, Jim?"

Jim finished using the towel and tossed it into the back seat. "Well, I guess I'm what you'd call a jack-of-all-trades. I do a little of this, a little of that. You know how it is."

"Yes. Yes, I do." He didn't.

"And yourself, Roger? What do you do?"

"I'm in sales. I'm on the road a lot. Have you been shopping for a new swimming pool, by any chance? We've got some nifty aboveground models. I got some brochures you can look at in the trunk."

"Ha, ha. No. Got no use for a pool. I live on the road."

"Do you, Jim? But you've got no bags with you."

"Yeah, I know. There's a story behind that. I'll tell it to you later, maybe. Meantimes, I was wonderin'—does this radio of yourn work?"

"It works fine, but it's hard as hell to get any reception way out here. You're welcome to try."

Jim turned the knob and got mostly static.

"Pfffzzz ... crackle ... sssss ... news on the hour ... pffzz ... two escaped convicts ... pffzz ... Ely, Nevad ... pffzt ... dangerous and ... szzztch ... do not ... schfffftpz ..."

Jim switched it off. "You're right, Roger. No reception way out here. Nothin' out here but us."

They drove on in silence for a few miles. Roger wasn't sleepy anymore.

Officer Frank Waymouth drove the cruiser cautiously down the highway, not wanting to have any unfortunate accidents in the pounding rain. *It's a perfect night for a jail escape*, he thought. *Terrible visibility and the dogs will have trouble picking up any scent in this weather.* He listened to the police radio, but so far there were no reports of any sightings.

"DRIVE CAREFULLY"

"AND DON'T LANE HOP"

"CAUSE THE NEXT BEND"
"MIGHT HIDE A COP"
"USE"
"BURMA-SHAVE"

Frank chuckled. He had to hand it to those Burma-Shave advertising guys. They really had a great sense of humor.

The radio broke the silence. "Attention, all units. We have a report of a naked body lying in the drainage ditch on the north side of Highway 50, about ten miles east of Eureka. Who can respond? Over."

A policeman closer to the location answered the call. "Car 71 here. I am en route. Ten minutes away. Over."

Damn, thought Frank. *This is getting serious. I need to step up my game. Time for a change of strategy.*

Frank stepped on the gas and resolved to pull over the next vehicle he saw.

Roger was gripping the wheel so hard that his fingers were turning white. He couldn't stop thinking about the little "insurance policy" he had stashed in the glove compartment. He might be able to reach over and grab it if the guy would just fall asleep, yet there seemed to be no chance of that for now. Jim was wide awake and appraised him curiously.

"You sure you don't want me to drive a piece?" Jim asked.

"No, I'm fine, thanks."

Roger wasn't sure whether he could take this guy one-on-one in a fair fight. More importantly, he didn't know if Jim had any kind of weapon on him.

Even if he's one of the escaped convicts they mentioned on the radio, he might not be armed, Roger figured. *Then again, he's not in prison garb. He must have gotten his street clothes somewhere. Who's to say he didn't pick up a knife as well? It's probably safest to keep driving until we reach some kind of civilization. But what then?*

"Penny for your thoughts," Jim said.

"Oh, just wondering how much further it is to Reno. Haven't

seen a signpost in a while."

"Yeah, except for Burma-Shave. They must have spent a ton of money planting those things all around the country. Look, here's another one."

"DON'T TRY TO PASS"

"THAT SPEEDING CAR"

"GET YOUR CLOSE SHAVES"

"FROM THE HALF-POUND JAR"

"OF"

"***BURMA-SHAVE***"

Jim chuckled. "Yeah, that's pretty darn good, don'tcha think, Roger? Hey, you happen to have any gum on you?"

Roger muttered, "Gum? No. I don't think so …"

Jim reached forward. "Maybe in your glove compartment?"

"NO!" Roger yelled. But it was too late.

"What the hell are you yellin' for? I only … Well, lookee here. What's this?" Jim reached into the glove box and pulled out a handgun. He turned it over, whistling. "Well, I'll be. If that don't beat all. What do you got one of these for?"

Jim put his finger in the trigger and smiled at Roger.

It was all Roger could do to stay on the road. As he slowed down, he noticed the flashing lights coming up fast behind him.

Jim glanced back. "Well, well, well. I guess you musta been speeding, my man. Let's just put this little beauty back in the glove box, shall we, and be careful what we say. The cops get very antsy about weapons. I won't mention the gun if you don't. I'd hate to have to shoot it out." Jim winked.

The car rolled to a stop and Roger turned it off, watching in the side mirror as the police officer got out of his vehicle and approached. Roger rolled the window down, saying a silent prayer.

The rain had slowed considerably. Frank got out of the cruiser and walked toward the driver's door. He bent down to peer inside.

"Good evening, gentlemen."

Frank noticed that the driver had a strange expression on his face. He seemed more nervous than a routine traffic stop should warrant.

"Would you mind stepping out of the car, sir?" Frank asked the driver. Then he pointed to the passenger. "And you, sir, are to remain inside the vehicle, please."

The driver got out of the car. *Strange*, thought Frank. *He hasn't even asked me why I pulled him over.*

"Would you please walk back here with me, sir? That's right. Now please put your hands on the trunk and lean forward for me. Just like that. Thank you."

While Frank patted him down, the driver muttered something. Frank leaned forward and asked, "What did you say, sir?"

"A gun," the man whispered. "The other guy has a gun. He hitched a ride. I think he's one of those convicts."

Frank quickly straightened up and unholstered his weapon. He said quietly, "You stay right here and don't move a muscle, you understand?"

Frank walked toward the passenger door with his gun drawn.

"Sir? I need you to get out of the vehicle very slowly, making no sudden moves. Am I clear? Okay, do it now."

The door opened, and the passenger got out saying, "Officer? What seems to be the problem?"

"Hands on your head. Now. Take five steps away from the car and turn around slowly. Keep your hands on your head. Now kneel down."

The man said, "Look, Officer. My name is Jim Smith. I don't understand …"

Frank shouted, "I said don't move!" and shot him in the forehead. The body formerly known as Jim fell backward into the drainage ditch.

Roger saw the whole thing and exclaimed, "You shot him! But he didn't reach for the gun! I think it's still in the car!"

And then Roger noticed the officer's gun, which was pointed directly at him.

"Please calm down, sir," the officer said. "Trust me, he was reaching for a weapon. Everything will be fine if you do as I say. Keep your hands on the vehicle."

"Was that man the escaped convict?" Roger asked.

"Him? No. Never saw him before in my life."

"Then why—"

"Quiet now, sir. Listen closely. I need you to get into the back seat of the car and strip down to your underwear. You can keep your socks on. Everything else comes off. Leave the clothes in the car. They're evidence. Now hand me your wallet and keys."

Roger handed over the items. "Please, I—"

"Shush now, Mister … Burnbaum, is it?" The officer was looking at the man's driver's license.

"Yes."

"Get in the car and do as I say. Please cooperate. It's perfectly fine, Mr. Burnbaum."

Roger got in while the policeman stood at the open door with the gun and watched him undress. When he was done, the officer said, "Now would you mind slipping your shoes back on and getting out for a moment? This will only take a sec. I appreciate your patience."

Roger was getting angry. He got out and noticed the nameplate on the officer's shirt.

"Look, Officer Waymouth, I—"

"My name ain't Waymouth," Frank said as he shot Roger point-blank in the right temple. Blood splattered Frank's face and uniform. Roger's body dropped heavily to the ground, and Frank kicked it into the ditch.

Frank dove into the back seat and rapidly changed into Roger's clothes, wiping his face clean with the towel. He exited and threw the towel and the police uniform into the ditch, keeping the gun. Then he patted down Jim's body, pocketed his wallet, and walked calmly back to the patrol car to turn off the flashers.

After closing the cruiser door, Frank sauntered back to Roger's car, jumped behind the wheel, and turned the key in the ignition. The whole process took less than three minutes from the time he first pulled the trigger.

I enjoyed being a cop tonight, Frank thought. *But there's no way I could keep driving the cruiser, now that they found the real cop's body out by Eureka.*

Frank admired himself in the rearview mirror and noted how Roger's clothes looked a little baggy on him. Still, they'd do well enough for now. *Damn,* he thought as he stared at his reflection, combing his hair. *Mr. Roger Burnbaum, you are a handsome devil.* The new Roger readjusted the mirror, checked for traffic, signaled, and pulled the Chrysler Imperial carefully out onto the road, keeping within the speed limit the entire way to Reno. *It generally pays to obey the little laws,* he thought. *Makes it easier to break the big ones.*

As Roger approached the Reno city limits, he noticed a set of signs.

"DO YOUR WHISKERS"
"MISBEHAVE"
"GRUNT AND GRUMBLE"
"RANT AND RAVE?"
"SHOOT THE BRUTES WITH"
"BURMA-SHAVE"

6

𝔇𝔬𝔡𝔬

The Dodo used to walk around,
And take the sun and air.
The sun yet warms his native ground —
The Dodo is not there!
The voice which used to squawk and squeak
Is now for ever dumb —
Yet may you see his bones and beak
All in the Mu-se-um

From *Bad Child's Book of Beasts* by Hilaire Belloc, 1896

ornelius Augustus Froop, King of the Dodoes, was lord over all he surveyed. Of course, at a height of three feet and with an inability to fly, he couldn't survey a hell of a lot. But it was enough for him. He lived in the forest on the island of Mauritius, east of Madagascar in the Indian Ocean. It was the middle of the rainy season, and food was plentiful. His wife was expecting to lay an egg any day now. Life was good.

Strutting along the edge of the forest near the cliff that overlooked the sea, King Froop noticed one of his subjects standing at the cliff's edge. He waddled over, proud of the extra weight he had put on during the past several weeks. It would come in handy when the dry season started and food supplies diminished.

"Salutations, loyal subject! And how are you this fine day?" hailed the king.

"Not well, my lord," replied the other dodo without even turning around. "There is trouble coming."

King Froop pointed his long beak skyward, indicating his displeasure. *I wish I had not approached him*, thought the king. *He is always so morose. If he weren't my wife's cousin, I never would have employed him as royal soothsayer.*

To avoid marital discord, the king wisely kept this opinion to himself, asking instead, "What kind of trouble, Soothsayer Silas? What sooth say you?"

"Look yonder upon the sea, my lord. Trouble approaches. It is the end of all."

King Froop extended his feathers for show and stared out at the water. He noticed an enormous creature riding the waves and fast approaching the shoreline.

"Is that a whale?" the king asked.

"It is not like any whale I've ever seen, your dodo-ship. Its head tapers to a point, and it has great white wings on its back that bulge in the wind."

"Why do you sooth that it be trouble?"

The soothsayer pointed his beak down and shook his body, demonstrating discomfort. "It brings death. I feel it. It is the end of us all."

King Froop pointed his royal proboscis at the sky. "Methinks you need a bath and a good meal, Silas. I'm sure whatever it is will leave us in peace."

"No. It is our enemy."

The king was not used to others disagreeing with him. He turned abruptly and waddled back into the forest, thinking that he should have made Silas the royal crab-catcher instead of royal soothsayer—and wondering what an "enemy" was.

Admiral Wybrand Van Warwyck examined the island with his telescope as the Dutch ship approached. He had resolved to land

and name it "Mauritius" after Prince Maurice of Nassau. The year was 1598.

They anchored off the southeastern coast and took several small boats ashore. The chosen officers and crewmembers disembarked and stood in a circle while Admiral Van Warwyck planted a flag and claimed the island for the Dutch Republic. Although the Portuguese were the first to visit there, they never settled and the Portuguese government was uninterested in laying claim.

The admiral noticed several large birds moving haphazardly around the beach, hunting for crabs. They sported brownish plumage and yellow feet, but their most distinctive feature was a large green, yellow, and black beak. Van Warwyck wondered what the bird would taste like. He wouldn't have to guess for long. The creatures displayed no fear of humans and walked straight up to them. If startled, the dodoes could run away very quickly, but they never exhibited a capacity or an inclination to fly.

The birds didn't know what they were in for.

Van Warwyck later named the flightless feathered thing *walghvoghel*, meaning "tasteless bird" or "boring bird." Some years afterward it became known as the dodo, possibly based upon the Portuguese word "doudo" meaning "crazy."

The dodo made a sound similar to that of a pigeon, to which it was related. It went "doo-doo."

From the shade of some nearby trees, Soothsayer Silas watched the landing of the humans. Being of an unusually untrusting mindset, he declined to walk up to the strange, lumbering creatures for a better view, unlike many of his fellow dodoes—which was why he was able to escape and bring the news back to the king.

"King Froop! King Froop!" Silas exclaimed, out of breath.

"Calm yourself, Soothsayer Silas. What is the matter?"

"The creatures! They came ashore from the 'not-a-whale.' It must've spit them out. I told you they were the enemy. They attacked our people."

Beak up, the king tried to remain calm. "Slow down, Silas. Not so fast. What is this word you speak—'enemy'—and what do you mean by 'attacked'? I don't understand."

"I ... I mean ... the creatures that travel with the 'not-a-whale' mean us harm! I think they intend to eat us."

"Doo-doo, doo-doo," the king laughed. "How can they do us harm? Nothing eats us. We eat crabs. And fruit. And nuts. And seeds. But none of them eat us. How could they? Nothing on this island can do us harm. You're making no sense."

"Nothing could harm us before, that is true. Not until today."

"That is doo-doo," said the king definitively. "What has happened before must continue to happen. This is the way of the world. No one has ever eaten us. Therefore no one will ever eat us. We dodoes are the dominant form of life on Earth, and we shall always be the dominant form of life on Earth. That just stands to reason. You are being foolish, Silas. Can't you at least try to be agreeable? Get out of my sight. You are dismissed."

Silas walked away with his bill down, shivering.

Some days later, Silas noticed that several members of the court had disappeared. The king shrugged it off, reasoning that they must have joined another flock. "What else could possibly have happened?" he asked.

Continuing to watch the new creatures from the trees, Silas never approached them.

Then he realized that the new creatures weren't even the worst part.

The creatures had brought other creatures.

And the other creatures brought death. They brought worse than death. They brought extinction.

King Froop's wife Imelda was inconsolable.

She knew she had left the egg safe in the nest, and it was much too early for it to have hatched. The crabs would never find their way up here, and even if they had, they would have left the broken shell as evidence of their presence.

The egg was simply gone.

How could it have moved? Could another dodo have done it? No, that was impossible. Unthinkable, she thought, the situation making her angry. She raised her beak to the sky.

And that's when she saw the thing in the tree. A thing she had never seen before.

It was looking down at her, holding the egg in its furry hands.

And then it broke the egg open and licked out the contents.

"Doo-doo!" Imelda cried.

Extinction doesn't happen overnight. Well, maybe it does when you're down to the last survivor and it dies in its sleep. Or when a large-enough meteor strikes the earth. But as a general rule, extinction takes centuries.

For the dodo, it took about seventy years. The humans caused it, of course, but not quite in the way you might think.

There were never more than fifty or so people living on Mauritius in the seventeenth century. Truth be told, many of them didn't care for the taste of dodo. Humans did not hunt the dodo to extinction. There were two other problems.

First, there were the trees—or rather, the lack of them.

Lumber was a valuable commodity back then, as it still is today. Unfortunately, Greenpeace was not yet sailing the waterways and there were no environmentalists around to stop the Europeans from bringing down an entire ecosystem. So that is what they did.

Little by little, year by year, the forest on Mauritius disappeared, forcing the dodoes to move farther and farther into the island's interior where food was not as plentiful.

Second, as already mentioned, the European sailors did not travel alone. They had non-human companions, some by choice and some not.

There were rats. They stowed away on the ships, and some of them got to shore.

There were cats. The sailors had brought these on board to help control the rats.

There were live pigs, occasionally slaughtered for meat.

There were a few dogs.

All of these were bad, at least from the dodoes' standpoint; but worst of all were the macaques, also known as old-world monkeys.

Macaques adapted well to living with humans and were popular exotic pets in Europe. The sailors brought them back from India and other locations in Asia, selling them at a nice profit at home. The macaques were agile. They were fast. And they were oh, so very clever.

And now they were on Mauritius.

They loved to eat crabs. And dodo eggs.

Several years passed on the island, and life for the dodo seemed little changed except there were fewer crabs, fewer trees, fewer edible plants, and fewer egg hatchings. Every now and then a dodo would have an unfortunate encounter with a dog or a pig or a human. Still, King Froop looked down from the cliff at several "not-a-whales" swimming placidly in the water, and he judged that life was good. If he'd thought hard about it, dodo life clearly wasn't as good as it used to be, but the king had a pigeon brain and couldn't recall back that far.

Soothsayer Silas did remember the past. More importantly, he could envision the future. He saw where this was all heading and felt terrible about it, but he couldn't convince anyone that the danger was imminent.

Because it wasn't *exactly* imminent. It was gradual. Creeping. Insidious.

"What do you mean the trees are gone, Silas?" asked King Froop. "Trees do not disappear. They stand forever. There are plenty of trees. Look around."

"There are trees here, yes, but not where we used to live. Next year, these trees will be gone, and we will have to move again."

"Nonsense."

"Look at this graph I made with my beak in the dirt. It plots the number of treed acres along with egg hatchings and the total dodo population versus time. Do you see the lines all sloping downward? This means something. Something very bad."

King Froop stomped upon the dirt and rubbed out the lines with his bill. "Doo-doo! Lies! Deceit! Science!" (The latter being the very worst kind of falsehood, according to the king.) "I am tired of your counsel, Silas. You are not a team player! You are unhelpful, disagreeable, and unsupportive! I've had it! You will sooth no more. You are dismissed and banished from my sight. Off with you!"

Silas pointed his beak toward the ground and shivered. Then he waddled off into the forest.

According to researchers who make it their business to know such things, the average lifespan of the dodo is presumed to have been about twenty years. From the day the first "not-a-whale" arrived, it took four generations for the dodoes to disappear from Mauritius and a few of the surrounding islands. Each generation thought it lived in the best of all possible worlds, which was nice.

King Froop lived a long life and died a happy death, believing that he had been the greatest dodo king who ever reigned. Queen Imelda laid another egg, which she guarded around the clock and which hatched without incident. The hatchling was named Prince Blotto. He eventually became king, and although he did things differently from his father, he didn't do much.

As for ex-soothsayer Silas, he expired peacefully while drawing graphs in the sand. A hundred years later, his bones were recovered and shipped to the Oxford University Museum of Natural History. The curator reassembled the skeleton and positioned it with its beak pointed toward the ground.

7

Little Red Rosie Hood

Once upon a time, there was a young girl named Rosie Hood who lived in the middle of a deep forest. Because she had red hair, everyone called her "Little Red." Her father, whose first name was Robin, had a flourishing business involving the forcible removal of cash and pawnable objects from wealthy "customers" whom he met on the road. Being civically minded, he donated a significant portion of his profits to various charitable organizations for the financially challenged. Still, he kept most of his earnings since one had to make a living, after all. Rosie's mother was an excellent parent and housekeeper, there not being many openings for female CEOs in those days. No one knew her first name because, for as long as people could remember, everybody just called her Mother Hood.

One day, Mother Hood prepared a picnic basket for Little Red to take to her grandmother who lived in Manahawkin. Nowadays one might be quick to criticize this woman for sending a nine-year-old child on a fifteen-mile hike through dark, dangerous woods. But once upon a time, this was perfectly normal behavior. There were no 80-mph vehicles or drug cartels to worry about. Just the odd bear, wolf, troll, or witch. So it was all good.

As it happened, Little Red was only two hours into her trip when she chanced upon a hungry timber wolf. The beast was very clever and decided he would interrogate his lunch before devouring her.

"Good morning, little girl," said the wolf.

Back then, as everybody knows, animals could talk. Possibly they still can, but one day long ago they simply chose to stop. Zoologists speculate that animals came to fear talking after seeing what a mess people made of their lives when they tried to use words to communicate.

"Good morning, Mr. Wolf. Howl's it going?" replied Little Red Rosie Hood. (It should be explained that Rosie was a punster. This should not be held against her, so please ex*pung*e any com*punc*tion to *pun*ish her.)

"It's going fine, thank you. And where are you heading this sunny, fair day, unaccompanied and all alone, just waiting for some enterprising young animal to pounce upon you and eat you whole?" the wolf salivated.

"I'm going to visit my grandmother in Manahawkin."

"Ah, what a spicy bite for me! I mean, what a *nice delight* for she! For *her*, I mean. To see you."

Little Red looked curiously at the wolf. "Um … yes. I'm bringing her this basket of goodies."

"Indeed. I'm sure you'll both be appetizing. I mean, I'm sure you'll both find them appetizing. The goodies, I mean. In the basket."

"Are you feeling alright, Mr. Wolf? Your nose is twitching, and there's a little drool coming out the side of your mouth."

"I'm fine," said the wolf, wiping his mouth. *Don't eat her now,* he thought. *Find the grandmother and have them both.* "And where does your grandmother live, my dear?"

"In a house. Close to the sea but not *that* close. It has other houses around it. You know the one I mean?"

"Oh, yes," said the wolf. "The house with other houses nearby. I know the one. Thanks."

"Oh! Oh! I have a wolf joke for you! Why did the wolf cross the road?"

"I give up. Why?"

"It was chasing the chicken. Get it? Haha. The chicken that crossed the road."

"Very droll. Oh, look! Were you aware that the path over there is a shortcut to your grandmother's house?"

"Is it? I didn't know that. Thanks, Mr. Wolf. Gee, it was nice talking with you. I guess you'll be off packing now, huh? Get it? Wolf pack? Off packing?"

50

Eat her and have done with it, said a voice inside the wolf's head.

"Very amusing," said the wolf, who turned and trotted off to Grandmother's house, ignoring the voice in his head.

Little Red started down the path the wolf had indicated.

It wasn't a shortcut, but you'd probably already guessed that.

The wolf followed Little Red's unambiguous directions and found Grandmother's house in a senior development just off Route 72. Unfortunately for him, Grandmother was not at home. He decided to wait for Little Red's arrival and shrewdly disguised himself by wearing Grandma's robe and getting into her bed.

A few minutes later there was a delicate rapping at the door.

"Grandmother?" a voice called. "Are you there? It's Little Red Rosie."

"Yes, dear," said the wolf. "The door's open. Come on in and be lunch. I mean, *have* lunch. With me, I mean."

Little Red walked in and placed the basket of goodies on the kitchen table. Then she stepped into the bedroom.

"Oh, Grandmother! Still in bed! Are you ill?"

"No, my dear, just a little tired, that's all. Come closer, won't you, Little Red?"

"Oh! Grandmother! What large hands you have!"

"The better to hug you with, my dear!"

"Not with those big fingernails, you won't! When's the last time you had a trim? Don't worry, I'll do it for you."

Little Red got the nail clippers but quickly realized they weren't up to the task. She went into the garage and retrieved a pair of heavy-duty bolt cutters. In a jiffy, she had clipped off the wolf's sharp claws.

"And we should do your toenails while we're at it," Rosie said.

"No, no, my dear, that's alright," said the wolf. But in a flash, it was done.

"What big ears you have, Grandmother!"

"The better to hear you with, my child."

"But you've lost your hearing aids! Don't worry, I'll get them."

51

Little Red found some spare hearing aids, but they wouldn't stay in the wolf's ears, which were too large. So Little Red grabbed a tube of superglue and cemented them in place.

"What a big nose you have, Grandmother!"

"What?"

"I SAID, WHAT A BIG NOSE YOU HAVE!"

"The better to smell you with, my dear," said the wolf.

"I SEE IT HASN'T BEEN POWDERED IN A WHILE. I'LL TAKE CARE OF THAT."

"No," whimpered the wolf. "Please."

Rosie found a box of baking powder and emptied it onto the wolf's face.

"Achoo!" sneezed the wolf. "I can't smell anything now!"

"WHAT BIG EYES YOU HAVE, GRANDMOTHER!"

"The better to see you with, my dear."

"I NOTICE YOU'RE NOT WEARING YOUR GLASSES …"

"No! Not the eyes! Have mercy!"

Grandmother's spare eyeglasses wouldn't fit, so Little Red improvised by winding an entire roll of plastic wrap around the wolf's head.

"I can't use my claws, I can't hear, I can't smell, and now I can't see," complained the wolf. "And you still haven't asked me about my large, terrible mouth. I can't eat you unless you ask. There are fairytale rules, you know. Cooperate. Do it for the story. Now, will you please comment on my big mouth so we can get this over with?"

"OH, I'D NEVER TELL MY GRANDMOTHER THAT SHE HAD A BIG MOUTH. IT WOULD BE RUDE."

"Perfect. Great. Now what do we do?"

"I COULD DRAW YOUR PICTURE. OR WE COULD WATCH A KOREAN SOAP OPERA ON TV."

I knew I should have stayed in the den today, the wolf thought.

"IF YOU LET ME DRAW YOUR PICTURE, I'LL SAY SOMETHING ABOUT YOUR BIG MOUTH."

"Fine. Fine. Draw my picture then."

Rosie took out her sketchpad and a pen, which she always carried with her, and began to draw.

Several hours later, the wolf was getting antsy. On the plus side, his hearing had partially returned so at least Little Red no longer had to yell.

"When will it be done?" he growled.

"You can't rush art," Little Red admonished. "That's what I always tell my father anyway. I'm doing the illustrations for his new book called *Robbin' Sherwood Till It Hurts*."

Forty minutes later, there was a noise at the door. "Hellooo? Is anybody there?"

"I'm back here, Grandma, with this silly wolf!"

"Hey, wait," said the wolf. "You knew I wasn't your grandmother?"

"Of course I knew. You don't look anything like her. You're a wolf, for goodness' sake. How dumb do you believe I am?"

"She's very intelligent for her age," said Grandma, who was standing at the bedroom door with a shotgun. "You might want to be leaving now, Mr. Wolf. Don't even think about bothering Little Red on her return. I'm calling her a limo. Out."

"My grandmother has a shotgun pointed at your head," added Little Red. "Just in case you couldn't see it."

The wolf knew when he was beaten and he slunk out of the house, mumbling about how the forest had deteriorated and how its characters just weren't as accommodating as they used to be.

"Well, that was interesting," said Grandma to Little Red. "Honey, you're a limo. Dear me, I'll have to wash these sheets now."

"I'll help, Grandma. And I'll make us some tea." Little Red pawed through the picnic basket. "I have barley tea, green tea, black tea, oolong, chaga mushroom tea, chai, chamomile, chrysanthemum, dandelion, hibiscus, macha, …" she said, pausing to take a breath, "nettle tea, peppermint tea, pu-erh tea, raspberry leaf, pau d'arco, rose tea, rooibos, senna tea, sencha tea, spearmint, yerba mate, white tea, and butterfly pea flower tea."

"Do you have Lipton's?" asked Grandmother.

"Yes, of course. Two Lipton teas coming up."

8

Fatuous Feline

The horizon shimmered in the hundred-degree desert heat as Officer William "Bull" Puppy stepped from his patrol car into the dry furnace otherwise known as Tuba City, Arizona, and scanned the scene. Apart from the road and the rest of the investigation team, there was nothing there but dirt, cactus, and burrow weed. Puppy walked toward the group of white-jumpsuited technicians who were cordoning off the area around the body.

A photographer took pictures of the crime scene while the coroner kneeled over the deceased. The coroner glanced up as Puppy approached. "Hot enough for you, Bull?"

"If you can't stand the heat, you shouldn't be living here, Tom. Wadda we got?"

Tom looked back down at the body, which was lying facedown in the sand. "Caucasian female, approximately forty-five years old. She has a depressed skull fracture on the parietal bone, which almost certainly was the cause of death. I'll confirm this in the lab. There are several other contusions on her skull and shoulders."

"So she was beaten to death?"

"No. The other contusions are older. I believe she was killed by a single blow to the back of the head by a blunt object."

Bull nodded and wiped the sweat off his brow with his sleeve. "What kind of object, do you think?"

"Again, I'll confirm this in the lab, but I believe the murder

55

weapon is right over there in that creosote bush." Tom pointed to his left.

Bull crouched down and examined the bloodstained cuboid. "A brick ... Jesus. He hit her in the head with a brick?"

"We don't yet know that it was a man, and I suspect the brick may have been thrown at her from the road. When I arrived, there were no footprints in this area, apart from her own."

"No footprints? Who found her then?"

"Apparently, some guy noticed her body as he drove by. He telephoned 911 from his car and didn't give his name. The dude drove off without even bothering to get out and see if she was alive."

"I assume we got the phone number though? I'll track down the bastard. He might even be the perp."

"Not going to happen, Bull. It was a burner phone. Untraceable."

Officer Puppy cursed softly. He gauged the distance to the highway and whistled. "If the killer threw that brick from the road, he had quite an arm and incredible accuracy."

Tom decided to let the gender assumption slide this time. "Yeah, I know. But that's all I can figure. The ground around her wasn't disturbed at all."

"Could he have hit her near the road, and maybe she walked out here before collapsing?"

"And then he threw the murder weapon into the bushes right next to her body? Why would he do that? In any case, I doubt she could have stumbled out here after receiving that fatal blow to the head. Her footprints indicate she walked smoothly to this point, where she fell."

Bull scratched his head. "What was she doing way out here? There's nothing around for several miles. How'd she get here?"

"Dunno. Maybe she walked. Or perhaps she drove out here with her killer."

Bull grimaced and looked toward the mountains. "Any identification on her?"

"Nothing yet. There could be something underneath the body. I was just about to turn her over when you arrived."

"Well, go ahead then, Tom. It ain't gettin' any cooler out here."

Tom signaled to two technicians who reached down and

carefully flipped the body onto its back, revealing a small pocketbook lying beneath. More photos were taken. When that was done, Tom picked up the purse and rooted inside.

"Driver's license identifies her as Katherine Herriman. She lived in Tonalea, just down the road. Oh, and here's her cell phone."

Officer Puppy pulled on some latex gloves, gently took the phone, and pushed a few buttons. "It's not locked. The last number she called was to a woman named Lill Ainjil. The phone's got an address for her. I'll go and check it out." He placed the evidence into a plastic baggie and sealed it, then slipped it into his pocket. "I may need this for questioning," he said. "You got anything else before I take off?"

"Nope. I'll call you after I complete the postmortem."

"Sounds good. Thanks, Tom. And, hey, use more sunscreen. The back of your neck is pretty red."

"Yeah, okay. See ya, Bull."

Officer Puppy turned off Caliche Road into the pebbled driveway and double-checked the house number before getting out of his car. The house was tiny and looked like it could easily be blown away in a strong wind. The garden was tastefully adorned with broken toys, empty beer cans, and tumbleweeds. He rang the doorbell. Not hearing any sound inside, he banged on the door.

After a moment, a petite woman of indeterminate age answered the knock in a grey housecoat and slippers and took a drag on her cigarette. "Yeah? Waddaya want?" She exhaled smoke in Officer Puppy's general direction.

"Good morning," replied Bull. "I'm Officer Puppy from the Tuba City police. Would you be Ms. Ainjil?"

The woman's eyebrows lifted until they almost reached her scalp. "Who? You got the wrong address, hon."

"I'm looking for someone who goes by the name of Lill Ainjil. Short for Lilly, perhaps? Does she live here?"

"Never heard of her, officer. You got your wires crossed. It's just my husband and me and our three boys." She looked back into the house and yelled, "FRIEDMAN! GET DOWN OFF THERE AND UNTIE YOUR BROTHER RIGHT NOW! AND THURGOOD, DON'T THINK I DON'T SEE THAT FLAMETHROWER! PUT IT AWAY!"

She turned back toward Officer Puppy and took another draw on the cigarette. Her eyes narrowed.

"Would you mind giving me your name, ma'am?"

"No. I'm using it. Anyway, why would you want my name? Ain't you got one of your own?"

Puppy had to think about this. "Um … I don't want to adopt your name. I just want to know who I'm speaking with."

"Oh. Why didn'tcha say so? It's Mauss. Matilda Mauss. We're the Mauss family. Lived here for fifteen years or so. Never heard tell of no Lilly Ainjil. We done now?" Ms. Mauss swung her head back. "BERLIN! I TOLD YOU NOT TO FEED THAT RAT POISON TO THE DOG! PUT IT DOWN!" She returned her gaze to Officer Puppy. "I asked if we wuz done."

Looking confused, Officer Puppy nodded and started to leave. Then he turned back. "Hold on. Do you happen to recognize this phone number, ma'am?" He pulled Katherine Herriman's phone out of his pocket, pushed a few buttons without opening the plastic, and held the phone up to Matilda's face.

Matilda squinted at the small screen. "That's my husband's cell number. But he sure ain't no 'Lill Ainjil,' that's fer sure. Whose phone is that anyway? What's this all about?"

"I'm afraid I can't say, ma'am. Is your husband home? I'd like to speak with him."

She took a final draw on the cigarette and threw the stub into the yard. "He ain't here. He's gone to the brick factory."

"Thank you, ma'am. And what is your husband's name?"

"Ignutz. Ignutz Mauss." She swung around. "HEY! PUT THOSE GOLDFISH BACK IN THE BOWL THIS INSTANT AND TURN OFF THAT DAMN BUZZ SAW!" She slammed the door behind her without even wishing Officer Puppy a good day.

Colin Kerry's Brickyard was just a few miles farther up Highway 160. A portable signboard out front read, "Best bricks in Coconino County! All sizes and colors but only one shape. Buy twelve and get the thirteenth free!"

Puppy parked his car and walked into the main showroom. He approached the woman behind the counter, who glanced up from the Sunday comics and donned her best fake smile. "Good morning, offissa, are you interested in some designer bricks? We're running a special on red clay this month."

Bull shook his head no, and her smile shrugged and went outside for a smoke. The woman remained, sans smile, waiting for an explanation.

"Police business, ma'am. I'm looking for a man named Ignutz Mauss. Is he an employee here, by any chance?"

"Ignutz?" the woman clucked, "Ignutz ain't no employee. He's one of our best customers—or he would be, if he ever paid his bills on time. I think he's in back, on the practice range."

"Practice range?"

"Yeah, we built it just for him. Behind this building. Go back outside and walk around. You can't miss it. Just make sure you let him know you're coming before you turn the corner."

Officer Puppy tilted his head quizzically and thanked the woman. He sauntered out and nodded to the smoking smile, which studiously ignored him. As he approached the back of the building, he heard a heavy clunking sound that repeated every few seconds, followed by randomly alternating exclamations of "Dat's the ticket!" and "Aw, krap!"

A handwritten sign on the wall stated, "Anownce useff orr suffa da conchequenches!"

"Hello?" Puppy shouted. The clunking stopped.

"C'mon thru," a voice responded.

Puppy turned the corner to see a group of wooden posts at varying distances, with circular targets painted on their tops. The ground around them was littered with bricks. Standing about ten yards away and facing him was a man holding a brick, with a large number of bricks stacked neatly at his side.

"Um, would you be Ignutz Mauss, by any chance?"

"Who wants to know, and *why's* he want to know?"

"I'm Officer William Puppy with the Tuba City police. I have a few questions for Mr. Mauss. Is that you?"

Ignutz (for indeed it was he) scratched his unshaven chin and said cagily, "Ah mebbe. An' ah meh not be. Axe yer questions and we'll see."

"Do you know a Ms. Katherine Herriman?"

"Kat? Dat crazy woman? Course ah knows her. Ah wished ah didn't."

"You wish you didn't? Why is that, Mr. Mauss?"

"Cause she's always chasin' after me, is why. Calls me her lil' ainjil. Drives me crazy. Ah try to convince her to keep her distance but it's never any use. She seems to *like* gettin' hit in the head with bri—" He stopped short and corrected himself. "Ah mean, she seems to like bein' politely axed to go away. Very politely and properly, without any bricks at all. Anyways, why are you axin' about her?"

"Ms. Herriman was killed this morning after being struck by a brick in the back of her head."

Ignutz laughed. "Nah. Nah. Dat can't be. Ah don't believe it. A brick to the back of her head wouldn't kill her. Ah should know. Ah throwed enuf of dem, ah can tell you."

"You admit that you threw bricks at her?"

"Sure. Plenty. But it ain't never hurt her none. She seems to like me even more after ah does it. Like ah said, she's crazy. Crazy Kat, ah call her."

"Mr. Mauss, you're going to need to come along with me. You're under arrest for first-degree murder. Your brick hit its mark a little too well this time."

"Aw, krap!" exclaimed Ignutz.

Officer Puppy handcuffed Ignutz and marched him to the squad car. Once he was inside, Bull's phone began to ring.

"Officer Puppy here."

"Bull? It's Tom. You … you won't believe this."

"What's up, Tom?"

"Katherine Herriman. She's … not … technically … dead."

"What??"

"When I got back to the lab, she was sitting up on the gurney and rubbing the back of her head. I can't explain it. I thought for sure she was a goner. I'd swear that when I examined her in the desert, she had no pulse. It's the darndest thing. Anyway, she knows who threw the brick, and she doesn't want to press charges against him."

"I've got the guy right here in the back of my squad car. She doesn't have to press charges. He's going to jail for this, for sure."

"You've got him? ... Wait a sec ... What's that, Ms. Herriman? ... Um, Bull, Ms. Herriman is with me and asks to talk to the man. Can you put your phone on speaker?"

Bull did, and a high-pitched voice rang out. "Ignutz? Is that you, my love? My Lil' Ainjil? I got your gift brick. Thank you sooo much."

"Aw, krap!" muttered Ignutz.

Shoot, thought Bull. *She's not going to be very helpful at the trial.*

9

The Queen's Gambit

Everyone in the kingdom of Blanc-de-Blanc knew that the real power resided not so much with the king, but with the queen. Well, everyone knew this except for the king, who continued to give orders as if he were actually in control. But no one paid much attention to him, and the king was too tired to press the point.

King Ivory deBlanc the Virtuous had married Princess Blanche duPlicitous the Dubitable when he was seventy years old. His bride was twenty-five at the time and hungry for power. That was ten years ago, and Queen Blanche's lust for dominion had grown even stronger as the king's appetite for power (and for pretty much everything else) diminished, along with his physical stature. Now at eighty, King Ivory no longer moved very far or very fast, whereas the queen could sweep swiftly through the kingdom in any direction. She seemed to know everything that transpired in the realm before it even happened, aided by a small network of exceptionally capable spies.

Life in the kingdom had been peaceful for many years. The dragons had all been vanquished, the witches were driven out, and the fields were fruitful. Even the rats had been ousted by some traveling magician with a flute who played a tune that drove them all into the river to drown. (That was a very lucky occurrence indeed, because when the Black Plague ravaged the rest of the land, the kingdom of Blanc-de-Blanc was wholly unaffected, rats being the primary carriers of the disease.)

The only problem in the land was the increasing restlessness of the queen, who had already gained as much power as she could within the kingdom.

So she began to look outside it.

Not very far away from the land of Blanc-de-Blanc was the neighboring kingdom of Charbon-Noir, ruled by King Ebony LeNoir and Queen Raven. Their land was virtually identical to Blanc-de-Blanc in every way. It was the same size with the same resources and soil fertility. It had a roughly equal population of subjects, with an exactly equal total absence of dragons, witches, and rats. The people were equally happy.

Yet despite all of this good fortune and happiness, diplomatic relations between Blanc-de-Blanc and Charbon-Noir had been steadily deteriorating for several years, to the point that both sides had closed their respective embassies and had been strengthening their defenses against a possible sneak attack from their neighbor. Some whispered that the worsening situation was the work of Queen Blanche, but no proof of this was ever found. Nor were any traces of the people who had been doing the whispering, so the whispers soon stopped. In any case, no one could come up with a logical explanation for why the queen would want to nudge the two kingdoms closer to war.

Wanted or not, however, war was fast approaching.

The royal charter of Blanc-de-Blanc was the sacred document which defined the kingdom's most important laws. It was written by King Richard deBlanc the Wise so long ago that they hadn't invented the concept of a calendar yet. Under the terms of the charter, the king and queen of the land each got to appoint a rook who served as their primary advisors in military and political matters, a bishop who advised them on spiritual matters, and a senior knight who carried out special tasks. The system worked fine as long as the king and queen were generally in agreement. But if there were differences of opinion between the two heads of state, the king's men (or women) tended to side with the king's point of view while the queen's appointees tended to side with her. As already described, at the time of this story everyone in Blanc-de-Blanc deferred to the queen. This pleased the queen's appointees, while the king's men were somewhat less influential and often had to stifle their dissatisfaction at court.

King Ivory's bishop was known as Bishop Alabaster. On this particular day he was working in his garden when a messenger arrived with an urgent letter from Sir Silverknob, the king's trustworthy senior knight. In his note, Sir Silverknob asked that the bishop come quickly in order to perform last rites for a fallen citizen. No details were provided and the missive appeared to have been scribbled in haste. The bishop gathered a few items and mounted his steed. The messenger sped off, and the bishop followed.

After riding for several hours, the king's bishop approached a group of men clustered around an object lying in the field. As he drew closer, the bishop saw that the object in question was a man. *No, not a man*, the bishop soon realized. *A boy.* He crossed himself and murmured, "Lord, save us all."

Sir Silverknob was standing over the body and looking grim, his hands behind his back. He glanced up at the incoming clergyman.

"Ah, Your Eminence. Thank you for coming so quickly, but I'm afraid it's still too late. The poor boy expired five minutes ago. Our surgeons could do nothing for him."

"Who was the unfortunate lad?" the clergyman asked.

"One of the queen's pages. I don't know why he was traveling out here, so close to our kingdom's border."

"I see much blood, but where is the wound?"

"It's on the other side of the corpse. The surgeons insisted he would fare better by resting on his stomach. It didn't help, obviously. I was just about to have my men flip the body back over."

"Yes, well, please finish your work, and then I shall pray."

The knight gestured to his men and said, "Turn the page."

As they rolled the body over, the source of the blood became apparent. There was a large gash in the boy's left side.

"The wound was caused by a very sharp dagger. It appears he was struck in passing," observed the knight.

"He died *en passant*?" exclaimed the bishop. "Who would do such a terrible thing?"

The knight did not respond as he checked the boy's clothing. Finally, he said, "The page was carrying a message. Here is the pouch, but the seal is broken and it's empty."

"Was it just a theft then? Was the boy killed for the contents of his purse?"

The knight frowned and spoke quietly so that his men would not hear. "This was no simple robbery. That poor boy had been someone's pawn, and his death is likely to be only the first casualty in a bloody war. You had better pray long and well, Your Eminence."

News of the page's demise spread quickly, and the queen convened a war council for that afternoon. In attendance were the king and queen and their royal court, consisting of the two archdukes, two bishops, and two senior knights. In the opinion of Sir Silverknob, the meeting had started badly and was getting progressively worse. Sir Silverknob's boss, Archduke Ghastly, currently had the floor.

"This incursion must be swiftly redressed," sputtered the archduke. "We cannot allow King Ebony to assassinate one of our pages and get away with it scot-free. We must immediately take one of his men in a similar fashion. Show him what's what, eh?"

"Do calm yourself, my dear archduke," the king replied. "Your face is growing red, and we do not wish you to die of apoplexy. Please sit down. Page, fetch our archduke a glass of water. Now, why do we think this killing is the work of Charbon-Noir?"

Sir Silverknob wished to respond that it was premature to

accuse the neighboring kingdom of this deed, but he remained silent, knowing that his opinion would not be welcomed by Archduke Ghastly. Luckily, his counterpart, Sir Snowball, saved him the trouble.

"In point of fact, Your Highness, we know nothing of the sort right now. The attack happened in Blanc-de-Blanc territory, and there is no evidence that any of King Ebony's men crossed the border to do this deed."

The queen leaned forward and asked, "But is there any evidence that they did *not* do so, Sir Snowball?"

"My lady, no. But it is impossible to prove a negative."

The queen's face grew red. *That is never a good sign of a happy outcome*, thought Sir Silverknob.

"It is *not* impossible," said the queen. "For example, if you were to prove that one of our own subjects was the culprit, then it would clearly rule out King Ebony's people—unless he bribed someone on our side to do it, of course. I wouldn't put that past him for a moment. In any case, do you *suspect* anyone in Blanc-de-Blanc, Sir Snowball?"

"We have no suspects at present, my lady."

"Then it would not be an *unreasonable* assumption on our part to say that King Ebony is the primary suspect?"

The queen smiled a tenuous smile, the meaning of which no one in the court failed to understand, least of all Sir Snowball. No one would *dare* to suggest that the queen was unreasonable, as many an exiled knight, bishop, or archduke could readily attest, were they still around to do so.

Snowball began to melt under the queen's gaze, and he quickly backtracked. "No, My Queen, you are perfectly correct. King Ebony must be the prime suspect until proven otherwise."

"Quite right, quite right," added Bishop Raven unnecessarily.

Sir Silverknob forced himself to look away from Bishop Raven's smug expression. *What a fawning, treacherous lapdog that man is*, he thought.

The queen sat back, satisfied.

Sir Snowball wisely resumed his chair, wiped his forehead, and resolved to say nothing more in this meeting if he could avoid it. Sir Silverknob shot him a commiserating glance, inwardly rejoicing that he had remained silent on the matter.

"Was there any physical evidence at all?" the queen asked.

"Was the page carrying anything, for example?"

"We found a mail satchel, my lady, but it was empty," Sir Silverknob replied.

The queen nodded thoughtfully and brought the meeting to a close. "Since we have no *firm* evidence that King Ebony is behind this, we will *defer* our decision to wage war against Charbon-Noir. In the meantime, we charge Sir Silverknob with the task of *obtaining* such evidence. Archduke Ghastly, you shall triple the border guard. *When* you find any of King Ebony's spies or soldiers on our land, you are to capture them *alive* and bring them back to our dungeons for questioning. Is that clear?"

Choruses of "Aye, My Queen" and "Yes, my lady" sounded around the table.

"Well said, O Exalted One," added Bishop Raven. Sir Silverknob wisely stifled a groan while the bishop continued, "Now, might I request a personal audience with Your Highness on an unrelated matter of some urgency?"

"Granted, Bishop Raven. Attend to us in our chambers in ten minutes," replied the queen. "This meeting is adjourned."

"We think—" the king started to say, stopping abruptly when the queen kicked him underneath the table.

Everyone pretended not to notice.

Sirs Silverknob and Snowball quaffed their third tankard of ale and ordered one more from the serving wench. The alehouse was packed, and it smelled of beer, sweat, and vomit. A fistfight was taking place in the corner with observers betting on the outcome, and several patrons had passed out on the floor. In other words, it was a normal night at The Checkered Mate.

"I don't understand why you suggested we meet here to discuss this confidential matter," shouted Snowball into Silverknob's right ear. "It's filled with people."

"Exactly my reason, Sir Snowball," responded Silverknob loudly. "No one will care to listen to us here, and they would be unable to hear our conversation if they tried. Trust me, if we had instead met in a deserted alleyway, it would have aroused suspicion; we'd have had ears turned toward us in all directions. This pub is much safer."

"All right. So what have you discovered?"

"Nothing that the queen wishes to hear. I don't believe the culprit was from Charbon-Noir. One of the queen's handmaidens saw the murdered page leaving the queen's chambers on the afternoon he was killed. I think the queen dispatched him to Charbon-Noir with a message, and he was executed before he could deliver it."

"But if the queen sent a message, why didn't she mention it during the council meeting?"

"Why, indeed?"

"And why would Charbon-Noir's spies kill a messenger who was on his way to them?"

"They wouldn't. It must have been someone from our own kingdom."

"Ah. The queen won't like that. How are you going to break the news to her?"

"I don't plan to. I think she already knows it."

Before dawn the next morning, Sir Silverknob was awakened by a messenger who said that his presence was requested at the border immediately. The knight dressed quickly and ran to mount his horse, not needing to be informed that the situation was urgent. His instincts told him that every second counted now. He could almost hear the clock ticking in his head.

Upon his arrival at the newly established border encampment, the knight proceeded directly to Archduke Ghastly's tent where a heated discussion was in progress. The archduke noticed the knight and waved him in.

"We are in the heat of it now, Sir Silverknob. The battle is on. We are at war."

"How did this happen, Archduke?"

"Last night, we killed a Charbon-Noir spy. Their response was swift and terrible. We have lost our bishop!"

"Ah, no. Which one? Not Bishop Alabaster?"

"No, the other one. Bishop Raven is dead."

"I see," said the knight, ashamed by the rush of relief this news brought. "And the spy we killed—he was in our territory, I assume?"

"Well, yes. Practically."

"Practically? You mean he was standing on Charbon-Noir land when he died?"

"Look, he was only a few short steps from the borderline. I'm sure he would have crossed over it. Our sentry simply got a little excited and took him out a few seconds before the spy could do so. Everyone has been on edge since the page died. It was an understandable lapse, given the circumstances, don't you think?"

Sir Silverknob involuntarily clenched his fists. "No, sir, I don't think that at all. How was the bishop killed?"

"A stealth attack. He was found dead in his apartment this morning after he failed to show up for vespers. We're still searching for the Charbon-Noir assassin who did this."

"The bishop was killed in his apartment? Not on the front line? What makes you believe he was murdered by an agent of Charbon-Noir?"

"It stands to reason, doesn't it? We are at war!"

A war you just started, the knight thought. *They may not even know of their pawn's death yet. They certainly wouldn't have had time to respond by sending an assassin to the city. And why kill our bishop? None of this makes sense.*

"I need you to lead an attack on their left flank, Sir Silverknob."

"Yes, sir. I will ready the men." *But not immediately*, the knight thought. *I need to check something first. Maybe the situation can still be salvaged before all hell breaks loose.*

The knight saluted and left the tent. Because war was imminent, he began to move furtively such that any nearby enemy archers would have trouble hitting him. It was the first thing they had taught him in knight school.

Two steps forward, one sideways. One step forward, two sideways. Two steps forward, one sideways …

Sir Silverknob slowed his horse as he approached the abbey. He jumped down and rushed inside to find Bishop Alabaster, who readily granted permission for a search of Bishop Raven's apartment. The two of them hurried to the dead bishop's lodgings.

"What are you looking for?" asked Bishop Alabaster.

"A piece of paper that will hopefully shed light on the mess we are in."

"You may be out of luck. The late bishop's rooms were ransacked during last night's attack."

They arrived at the apartment to find it as Bishop Alabaster had described. Clothing, books, and all manner of objects lay strewn across the floor.

Disheartened, the knight said, "Time is short. There's no point in searching through this mess. It looks like it was a thorough job. If the paper was here, the assassin already has it, so let's assume it wasn't here. If you wished to hide an important document somewhere outside your apartment, where would you go? Don't think in straight lines. Think diagonally."

The bishop, who was rather good at diagonal thinking, considered the problem for a moment then lifted his head. "The cathedral! And I know just the place. A room where no one but Bishop Raven ventured. Follow me!"

They rushed to the church, and the bishop pulled a key ring from his robe and unlocked a heavy wooden door at the back of the cathedral. They hurried down a circular stone stairwell to the crypt.

Forty steps later, it was cold, damp, and pitch-black, and they slowed down to avoid breaking their necks. The bishop felt his way down by leaning against the clammy wall and carefully moving his feet forward until he felt the next step. The knight followed.

"It might have been a good idea to bring a torch," suggested the knight.

"I know. I got a little overexcited and rushed forward without thinking. But there is one at the bottom of the steps, along with a flint we can use to set it aflame. Just a few more steps, I believe."

When they reached the bottom, the bishop felt along the wall until he located the torch. After a few false starts, he managed to light it. The knight looked around. The chamber was a cube of about thirty-two feet on each side. Its floor consisted of alternating black and white squares, each one approximately four feet on a side. There were eight rows and eight columns of these squares. Lining the other three sides of the hall were twenty-four doors, each one painted either black or white, corresponding to the square upon which it was located.

"This is the crypt. By tradition, the king's bishop, which honor I hold, is allowed to step only upon the white squares and enter the vaults with white doors. Bishop Raven was the queen's bishop, and he could step only upon the black squares. I suspect the paper you seek lies behind one of those black doors. Under the circumstances, I believe we can dispense with the ritual requirements. Let's grab another torch from the wall and split up. I'll take the first black door on this side while you take the one on the opposite wall. We will work toward the middle until one of us finds something."

Sir Silverknob opened the first black door on the right. This was a crypt, all right. The passage led to a vault lined with stone coffins containing the remains of long-dead royalty and senior clergymen. Hoping Bishop Raven hadn't hidden the paper inside one of the caskets, the knight resolved to check all the rooms first before attempting to remove any of the heavy stone lids. No doubt he'd need help to do that, in any case.

As he inspected each chamber, he found nothing but coffins and more coffins. One room also contained an urn filled with the ashes of a Queen Segreta, who apparently reigned three hundred years ago, according to the label on the jar. Apart from that, the crypts were barren. There was no furniture or objects that could be used to hide anything. The knight girded himself for the distasteful prospect of opening the sarcophagi one by one.

Having found nothing, the knight and the bishop met in the twelfth black vault, and Sir Silverknob mentioned the urn.

"An urn?" exclaimed the bishop. "There should be no ashes here. Cremation of royalty has never been permitted. What did you say the queen's name was?"

"Queen Segreta."

"I've never heard of her," said the bishop, "but 'segreta' means 'secret' in Italian."

They rushed back and pulled the cover off the urn, and the bishop dubiously sniffed the contents. "I think this is simply wood ash," he said.

The knight lifted the urn and dumped the contents onto the floor. Among the ashes lay a letter. He picked it up, and noting that the seal had already been broken, he opened it and silently read the contents.

"As I suspected," said the knight. "We need to see the king and stop a war."

"Don't you mean we need to see the queen?" asked the bishop.

"No. This decision lies with the king, and the king alone."

Sir Silverknob gained a private audience with the king, who decided to handle the matter at the war council that was just about to begin. They proceeded to the chamber.

Upon entering the hall, Sir Silverknob was immediately set upon by Archduke Ghastly. "Silverknob!" he sputtered. "I gave you a direct order to lead an attack! You have disobeyed me!"

"Not so, Archduke. The men are ready, as you requested. I only await the king's or queen's word to launch an attack. Surely it is they who must give such an order?"

Overhearing their conversation, Queen Blanche spoke. "Sir Silverknob is quite right, Archduke Ghastly! Was it your intention to usurp our authority?"

"No, of course not, My Queen, I only—"

"Sit down and remain quiet, little man."

The archduke took his seat with a scathing glance at the knight.

The queen began. "We have convened this council because we have decided to wage war on Charbon-Noir. The attacks on our page and bishop are an affront which cannot go unanswered and—"

Sir Silverknob stood. "Excuse me, Your Highness, but before you continue, may I make a report?"

The queen's face reddened. "You dare to interrupt us when we are speaking? What is the meaning of this?"

"You may speak, Sir Silverknob," the king said.

The queen kicked him under the table, and to the entire room's surprise, the king kicked back. Then he stood up. "I command you to give your report, Sir Silverknob." He turned to the queen and said in an icy tone, "And you shall remain silent, woman."

For once, the queen didn't know how to respond.

Sir Silverknob began. "As you are aware, Your Highness, I was charged to investigate the murder of the queen's page. I have determined that his death was caused by someone from our own kingdom of Blanc-de-Blanc, not by spies of Charbon-Noir."

"Nonsense!" shouted the queen.

"BE SILENT, OR WE SHALL HAVE YOU CHAINED AND MUZZLED," bellowed the king to universal surprise. In a much quieter voice, he said, "Please continue, Sir Silverknob. Let no one in this chamber interrupt, on pain of imprisonment." He scanned the room, and no one doubted that the old king had suddenly regained his authority.

The knight continued. "The page was carrying a private message from our queen to King Ebony of Charbon-Noir. For this, he was killed. I do not yet know who wielded the knife, but I intend to find out. However, I do know who ordered the attack and the theft of the letter. It was Bishop Raven."

"Lies!" shouted the queen, rising to her feet. The king signaled to his guard, who approached the queen. She retook her seat.

"Earlier this morning, Bishop Alabaster and I found the letter hidden in a vault that only Bishop Raven was allowed to enter. I believe that Bishop Raven had the letter stolen so that he could blackmail the queen with it. I believe that he attempted to do so and was subsequently killed at the queen's order."

"Mmmm," the king said. "We always thought that Raven was a bad bishop, but this is a very serious charge against the queen, Sir Silverknob. Where is your evidence?"

"Here is the letter, My King. It is written in the queen's own hand and proposes that our kingdom be merged with Charbon-

Noir, under the guise of war. It suggests that Your Highness and the Charbon-Noir queen might somehow be killed during the war, following which King Ebony and Queen Blanche would jointly rule the combined land."

The king addressed his court. "We have already read this letter, and we confirm that it is written in the queen's hand. Sir Silverknob, you may pass it around and allow everyone to affirm this for themselves. Guards, arrest Queen Blanche for treason and imprison her in the dungeon, pending trial. Then search her apartments for further evidence."

As the queen was led out of the room, she shouted, "All this because my stupid page failed to deliver a letter? I'm worth nine of him! I should have delivered it myself."

When she was gone, the king again addressed his court. "We are not finished, my dear sirs. Please be seated. Now, Sir Silverknob, have you uncovered any evidence that King Ebony was complicit in the queen's plan?"

The knight stood. "No, my lord. Clearly, this particular letter never reached him, but I have no way of knowing whether the queen sent any other missives."

"Very well," responded the king. "Here is what we shall do. Archduke Ghastly, please draft a letter from ourselves to King Ebony, apologizing for the accidental killing of his sentry and informing him of the arrest of our queen for high treason. We shall wait to sign the letter until after our men have searched the queen's apartment. If no evidence of King Ebony's complicity is found, we shall immediately send this message and sue for peace. But if it turns out that the neighboring king was involved, we shall have to reconsider whether war must be waged. That is all."

Since no evidence of King Ebony's knowledge of the queen's gambit was ever uncovered, war was avoided, and a tenuous stalemate continued to exist between the two nations. Archduke Ghastly retired at King Ivory's command, and Sir Silverknob was promoted and assumed his role. The queen was tried, convicted, and imprisoned in the tower until her eventual death.

King Ivory ruled for another twenty years. He never remarried.

10

Piglet, Prince of Denmark, WI

Prince Piglet strutted up and down in his spacious pen to keep warm. It was a blustery fall night in Denmark, Wisconsin, and all the animals on Macbeth Family Farm knew winter was coming, even though none of them owned a wall calendar or an iPhone.

Normally, Piglet would be fast asleep in his bed of straw by this time, but tonight he was restless. Something was rotten in the village of Denmark, and it wasn't just the half-eaten apples that Farmer Odious Macbeth had thrown into the trough. *It has something to do with the wind*, Piglet thought. *It's whispering.* Though he couldn't make out the words, he could tell the news was bad, and as the son of the recently deceased king of the farm animals, Prince Piglet had a duty to protect the community from whatever evil was coming their way.

The moon disappeared behind some clouds, making it difficult to see. Piglet was about to give up and go back to bed when he heard the faint sound of a tolling bell coming from the clock in the village mall, several miles away. Piglet counted ... *ten ... eleven ... twelve. Midnight. The witching hour.*

"Spooky, isn't it?" said a voice in his right ear.

Seeing no one, Piglet jumped. Then he recognized the voice. "Charlotta! You scared the bejesus out of me. Don't sneak up on me like that!"

"I'm sorry, sire," replied the tiny black widow spider, "but I can't make much noise, even if I wanted to. I need to be inside your ear before you can hear me at all."

"Yes, yes, well ... but why are you up this late, my friend? Missing your ex-husband, perhaps? It is very strange that he disappeared so soon after your wedding."

"Yes," replied the spider wistfully, "I do miss him. Frank was very ... nourishing."

"I am sorry for your loss." Piglet shivered. "It is indeed spooky this eventide. Ghosts and daemons roam on nights such as these."

"Surely you don't believe in such things, My Prince?"

"There are more things in Heaven and Earth than are dreamt of in your philosophy, Charlotta."

"My philosophy is 'eat or be eaten.' That is the cruel reality of life, sire."

"Hold!" commanded Piglet. "But lo! What is yon specter which doth approach?"

Charlotta crawled out of Piglet's ear to take a look, then scampered back in. "It appears to be an apparition, sire! Methinks it resembles your departed father."

This vision before me does indeed look like my father, thought Piglet, *except I can see straight through his body to the farmhouse beyond. And to my recollection, Father never floated in midair before.*

"My King! Father! Royal swine!" Piglet called. "Answer me! It is I, your son, Piglet! Why does your soul walk these trails in the dead of night? Why are you not feasting in Pighalla?"

"Mark me," commanded the ghost.

"I do, Father. Speak!"

"My soul has no peace. I cannot rest until I am avenged, my son. It falls to you to do this, as I am unarmed now." To demonstrate the point, the ghost's appendages turned into mist while the rest of his body continued to hang in the aether.

"Avenged? Wherefore avenged, noble torso?"

"They lied to you, Piglet. My death was not an accident. I was murdered. Dismembered. Eaten."

"Heaven help us!" cried Piglet.

Charlotta whispered, "Wow, that's heavy, Pig, but being eaten is a good way to go. Did I ever explain my philosophy of life?"

Ignoring her, Piglet asked the ghost, "Who did this foul deed, Father? Who would dare?"

The shade looked down. "Farmer Odious Macbeth dispatched

me. He and his goodwife, Gertrude."

Piglet was aghast. "The *humans* killed you? How can that be? They are our servants. They care for us. They feed us. They cure our sicknesses. Why would *they* do such a thing?"

"I have learned that this is what they do, my son. They will do the same to you one day."

"Do they eat all the animals on the farm then?"

"No. They have other uses for many of them. They steal their milk and their eggs. They make some of them work, as you already know. But pigs are always eaten."

"Oh! Villainy! Treachery!"

"Avenge me, Piglet!"

"I shall, Father. I swear it."

"Adieu then. Adieu. Remember me. Remember me."

The remainder of the ghost slowly dissolved into the air.

"Well, ain't that a kick in the ass?" said Charlotta.

The following morning, Piglet considered his options.

"To be, or not to be?" he wondered aloud.

Not realizing the question was rhetorical, Charlotta said, "I rather think it's generally better to be, all things considered. Although to be honest, I haven't personally tried the latter. My ex-husband has, but unfortunately we are no longer on speaking terms so I can't ask him about it. Anyway, have you come up with a plan for your revenge?"

Piglet nodded, which was somewhat ineffective since Charlotta could not see it from her vantage point. "Tell the rest of the farm animals that we shall have a barn meeting tonight. We must enlist their support for our war on the humans. No dogs or cats, of course. They are the humans' spies and can't be trusted."

"Right you are, sire. And I shall make some placards." Charlotta scampered down Piglet's foreleg and ran to make preparations.

That spider loves to make placards, Piglet thought.

79

Twelve hours later, the animals were assembled in the barn, curious to hear what Prince Piglet had to say. They wondered if he was finally ready to accept the office of farm king, now that the official grieving period for his father had passed, but they were somewhat confused by the placards hanging in the barn.

"ALL ANIMALS ARE EQUAL, AND EVEN THE WORST OF THEM ARE MORE EQUAL THAN HUMANS."

"4 LEGS GOOD, 2 LEGS BAD. EXCEPT FOR YOU CHICKENS. YOU'RE ALRIGHT."

"8 LEGS ARE ACTUALLY THE BEST. NO OFFENSE, JUST SAYIN'."

The prince approached the royal podium, otherwise known as an old bucket turned upside down, and the room became quiet. When he judged the moment was right, Prince Piglet began to orate.

"Friends, Denmarkers, Comrades, lend me your ears! (No, Porky, put the corn down. Don't take me so literally.) I have terrible news to share. Last night, I encountered the ghost of my father. Charlotta was there and can vouch for the truth of this."

They waited several minutes for Charlotta to write "true" in her web. Upon its completion, the animals expressed their shock, awe, and dismay that the king's ghost had made an unscheduled visit. There were protocols for such things, after all. The meeting continued.

"Our beloved king told me he did not die by accident. He was slaughtered and eaten. *By the humans!*"

The room erupted into chaos. There were brays, whinnies, howls, caws, clucks, bleats, and squeaks. Piglet waited patiently for the noise to abate.

"The king asked me to avenge his death. This I shall do—by myself if necessary—but it would be better if I had your help. I intend to call a vote on the question of whether war should be waged against the farmer and his wife. I open the floor for questions."

"Do the humans eat mules?" a mule asked.

"Um, not to my knowledge," replied the prince.

"Or horses?"

"No."

"Or insects?"

"Definitely not in Wisconsin."

"Or goats?"

"Not that I've heard."

"Alpacas?"

"I can't imagine."

"Cows?"

"Um, I'll have to get back to you on that one. Not as a rule, I believe."

"Or chickens?"

"Possibly. I'm not sure, to be honest. But I do know they steal your eggs."

"It's not theft—it's a fair exchange," said the chicken. "They give us food and shelter, and we give them eggs. It's capitalism at work."

"I thought we didn't like capitalism," commented an alpaca.

"Well, it's socialism then. Same thing," sneered the chicken.

"But they eat pigs!" shouted a pig. "We must stand together, comrades!"

The pigs unanimously assented to this suggestion. The other animals were silent.

"Time for a vote on the motion," said Prince Piglet. "As usual, we will allow one vote per species. Mr. Mouse, please call the roll."

"Horses? Do you say yea or nay on the question of war against the humans?"

The horses conferred amongst themselves. "Neigh," said their spokeshorse.

"Pigs?"

"Yea!"

"Sheep?"

"Bah! ... I mean, nay."

"Alpacas?"

"Nay."

The voting continued. Only the pigs and the spiders voted in favor. The cows and chickens abstained, pending further evidence.

"I'm afraid the motion has failed, My Prince," Mr. Mouse reported.

Well then, I'll get no help from them, Piglet thought. *I'm on my own. To swine own self be true.*

To the audience, the prince said, "Be it on your heads, you unharmonious rabble. I order you to keep the proceedings of this night secret, on pain of death—or a bath, whichever you fear most. The humans must not find out that we know of their pigicidal tendencies. This meeting is adjourned." Piglet left the podium and walked outside, deep in thought.

Meanwhile, four uninvited eyes jumped down gracefully from their perch on the outside windowsill and trotted back unseen to the farmhouse.

The cock crowed as the sun rose on the horizon. Piglet had not slept that night.

Charlotta clambered up his side and spoke in his ear. "Do you have an alternate plan, my lord?"

"I do. First, I must find out what the farmers know. I will try to get information from my old friends Slurpees and Zoophilia."

"But ... they are dogs, My Prince."

"I know you don't like them, but there is no need for slurs."

"I merely state a fact. They are both of the canine persuasion, and as such, they are loyal to the humans. Their father Felonious is chief counselor to Farmer Macbeth, for God's sake!"

"You think I am unaware of this? Felonious will not be a problem. He is twelve years old. A doddering old fool. And, of course, I must be devious if I am to achieve my revenge. The dogs will not learn of my plans. I will put them off any suspicion by feigning madness."

"Aha!" exclaimed the spider. "And I know just how I can help you to fool them. When I'm finished, they'll be sure you're a raving lunatic."

"What will you do?"

"I'll post a message on the web," answered the spider

gleefully.

"Thank you. I think," said Piglet as Charlotta scampered back to the barn.

Later that afternoon, Piglet noticed Zoophilia romping about in the field, and he called to her. She leaped over the fence in a single bound and landed next to Piglet.

"How fares my lord pig today?"

"Ah, hello, my dear Zoophilia. We haven't spoken much since my father passed away. How are you and your esteemed family?"

"We're good," she replied. "My dad's been busy tending sheep. It tires him, but he'll be receiving some help soon. The farmer recently sent my brother Slurpees off to sheep-herding school."

"That is well. Your father is getting too old to do such work. Farmer Macbeth is cruel to use him thus."

"Do you remember when we were young, dear pig? The games we three would play? Little pig, little pig, let us in …"

Piglet smiled. "Not by the hair of my chinny-chin-chin. Yes, I remember." Then his face clouded again. "But those bright days are long gone. Now there is only darkness."

"You never answered my first question," said Zoophilia. "How fares the prince?"

"I am much troubled in my mind. I was wondering what you could tell me about my father's death. Farmer Macbeth said it was an accident. What kind of accident exactly?"

Zoophilia regarded her old friend with a sad expression. "I … I really can't say." She stared off into the field.

"You can't say, or you won't? Who are you protecting, Zoophilia? Look me in the eye and tell me you know nothing about it!"

Zoophilia continued to stare at the horizon. "Oh, Piglet, why can't you just enjoy your life? Your father is gone, and nothing can bring him back."

"I saw his ghost two nights ago," said Piglet. "He spoke to

me."

Zoophilia regarded him with concern. "You saw …? No. It was a hallucination, Piglet. You are unwell. Perhaps I should ask the farmers to send for the vet."

"I … AM … NOT … CRAZY!" exclaimed Piglet, throwing himself down and rolling in the mud. Zoophilia stepped back to avoid being splattered and noticed the brand-new spider web on the barn door. It contained a message.

"MAD PIG!" read the cobweb.

Zoophilia regarded the wallowing pig and ran barking back to the farmhouse. Piglet stopped mudding and waved a thankful hoof toward Charlotta's web.

Farmer Odious Macbeth finished locking the sheep in their pen for the night and looked down at Felonious. "That'll do, dog," he said. "That'll do." Felonious barked a quick acknowledgment and walked slowly back to the house. He appeared to have a slight limp.

He's been a good dog these many years, the farmer thought. *It will be a real shame to put him down. I'll have to do it soon though. As soon as his son is fully trained.* He quickly caught up with the aging border collie.

"I'm worried about Piglet," the man began.

"Ah, Piglet, yes," sighed Felonious. "Zoophilia told me about her meeting with him this afternoon. He is apparently quite troubled. Even mad, some say. The death of his father has deranged the poor lad."

That's not what the cats told me last night, Macbeth thought. *That secret barnyard meeting was the last straw. The pig must die, but I need to be cautious. I can't risk turning the other animals against me. Piglet is royalty, and it's been too soon since his father's death. Plus, I need to find out whose help he has enlisted. For that I need spies.*

"Zoophilia is very close to Piglet, isn't she?" the farmer asked.

"Oh, indeed. She and Slurpees grew up with the prince. They are all great friends."

"I understand that Piglet is spreading a rumor that I was responsible for his father's death."

Felonious stopped and tilted his head. "But ... you *were* responsible for his death. I watched you slaughter him, Master."

Saints preserve us from dumb animals, Macbeth thought. "Yes, but the rest of the animals aren't supposed to *know* that, Felonious. We must keep order, after all."

"Ah, yes, order. Yes."

"I'd like you and your daughter to keep an eye on dear Piglet for me, my friend. I must discover whether he is truly mad or just faking it. If he is mad, we shall have to get the vet out to examine him. I must also know with whom he speaks, and how frequently. May I count on you?"

"Of course, of course. I am here to serve, as always."

They walked on, Macbeth sincerely hoping that Slurpees would prove to be as stupid and pliable as his father.

Piglet slept fitfully that night, which was a vast improvement over no sleep at all. He was awoken by the cockcrow to find two cats watching him with steady eyes.

"Good morning, Prince Piglet, my good friend. You must remember me. I am Rosencatz," the first cat said.

"And I am Geldertom," the second cat added.

"I don't understand why you two need to introduce yourselves every time we meet," the prince responded groggily. "I've known you for all your eighteen lives, Rosencatz and Geldertom."

Another voice in Piglet's right ear whispered, "Don't trust them, My Prince. They are spies."

"Do you think I don't know that?" Piglet answered.

Charlotta was silent, but Rosencatz said, "No, Prince, we are aware that you know our names. We just enjoy saying them."

"And to what do I owe this visit?"

"We wanted to see if you were all right," said Geldertom.

"I wanted to warn you about them," said Charlotta

simultaneously.

"I wasn't talking to you," replied the prince.

The cats looked at one another. "We wanted to see if you were all right," said Rosencatz.

"Someone told us you had gone mad," added Geldertom. "If it's okay for me to speak now, that is."

Charlotta said, "Don't talk to me. They can't hear me, and they don't know I'm in your ear."

"Okay," Piglet acknowledged.

"So are you …" started Rosencatz.

"Mad?" finished Geldertom.

Prince Piglet stood up. "Why would I be mad? What have you done that would make me angry?"

"Not *angry* mad …" said Geldertom.

"*Crazy* mad," added Rosencatz.

The two cats got up and paced back and forth in front of Piglet while providing further clarification.

"Absurd," said Rosencatz as he paced to the left.

"Delirious," said Geldertom as he paced right.

"Demented," said Rosencatz as he walked to the right.

"Kooky," said Geldertom as he walked left.

To save paper, we shall consolidate their next comments instead of giving them a full line apiece. The bold text was spoken by **Rosencatz** and the rest was uttered by Geldertom.

"Nutty," "Psychotic," **"Aberrant,"** "Bananas," **"Batty,"** "Crazed," **"Cuckoo,"** "Deranged," **"Illogical,"** "Imprudent," **"Irrational,"** "Loony-toons," **"Lunatic,"** "*Non compos mentis*," **"Nonsensical,"** "Of unsound mind," **"Off one's rocker,"** "Out of one's mind," **"Preposterous,"** "Rabid," **"Raving,"** "Senseless," **"Unbalanced,"** "Unhinged," **"Unsound,"** "Unstable," **"Wacky—"**

"GOOD GOD, MAKE THEM STOP!" Charlotta yelled into Piglet's ear.

"ENOUGH!" cried Piglet.

"Insane," finished Geldertom.

"Was that clear?" asked Rosencatz.

Piglet sighed. "Non compos mentis? Really?"

"It's a thing," said Geldertom.

"To answer your question, I am not mad," stated the prince definitively. "Am I, Father?"

The cats looked at one another, then back at Piglet. "Did you just say something about your father?" Rosencatz inquired.

"I asked him to confirm that I was not mad. He agreed with me. Didn't you hear him?"

"Your father is dead," said Geldertom.

"Deceased," "Lifeless," **"Expired,"** "Cadaverous," **"Departed,"** "Pushing up the daisies—"

"Stop!" commanded Piglet. "I know he's dead, just as surely as I know that his ghost stands right behind you."

Both cats jumped straight up into the air. Unfortunately, their directions were not parallel, and they crashed into each other mid-flight, landing together in a jumbled ball of fur. They disentangled themselves.

"Don't *do* that!" yelled Geldertom.

"There's nothing even *there*!" added Rosencatz.

"Of course, he's there! He just told me not to trust you."

"But you *can* trust us, my dear pig ..." said Rosencatz.

"With your very life," finished Geldertom.

"Or your catnip," added Rosencatz. "Do you happen to have any catnip that we can keep safe for you, My Prince?" Both cats sat back and looked up hopefully.

Charlotta whispered, "Let us finish this, sire. Send them back to the house thinking thou be mad."

"What's that, Father? You say I should dance for them? Well, then, cats. Watch me dance."

Piglet jumped around and contorted himself, squealing most awfully. The cats had to leap out of the way several times to avoid being trod upon. When the prince finished, he said, "Go now, my friends, and tell the farmers that my father sends his highest regards and wishes them wealth, happiness, and a long, long life. Be off with you!"

Piglet charged the cats, and they retreated, dashing back to the farmhouse.

Felonious summoned his daughter to his side.

"My dear Zoophilia," the old dog began, "I should like to see the evidence of the young prince's madness for myself. Let us go to the barn. I shall hide in the hay while you speak with Piglet. If he be mad, I shall convince the master to send for the veterinarian."

Zoophilia agreed to do as her father bade, and they proceeded to the barn. When Felonious had hidden himself in the hay, she called for Piglet, who was taking the sun outside.

Piglet entered, but he was not alone.

"Be watchful, my lord. Spies are everywhere," advised Charlotta.

"How fares my lord pig today?" asked Zoophilia.

"Hopefully worse than one would think yet better than can be expected."

"My lord?"

"I am murderously well, my lady."

"That's ... good, I suppose. There have been no further sightings of your father?"

"My father is dead," said Piglet.

"Yes. That is true," agreed Zoophilia, much relieved.

"And you know how he died, Zoophilia. Tell me."

"I do not know, My Prince! I was not there. I swear it, upon my honor!"

"The lady doth protest too much, methinks," Charlotta chimed in.

Piglet shouted, "Honor indeed! Dogs are treacherous! The humans' playthings! Swear it on your everlasting soul instead!"

"I ... I don't know what to say, my lord."

"Say only the truth! Is that beyond thee?"

"I ... I ... don't—"

"MY FATHER WAS EATEN AND YOU KNOW THIS! YOU LIE FOR THE FARMERS! FALSE FRIEND!"

Piglet approached Zoophilia menacingly with fire in his eyes.

Zoophilia backed up. "You're scaring me, Piglet! I ... I need to pee."

Piglet began pacing back and forth in front of Zoophilia, chanting crazily. "To pee, or not to pee, that is the question: Whether 'tis nobler in the mind to suffer the silent pains of holding one's bladder, or to let fly a sea of troubles and, by releasing them, relieve oneself. To pee, to stream—to stream, perchance to fart—ay, there's the tub."

"Stop, Piglet! You're acting crazy! Oh, I really need to go now!"

"Well, do not do't in the barn, bitch. Off with you! Get thee to a shrubbery!"

Whimpering, Zoophilia ran out of the barn.

Piglet noticed some movement in the hay. "What, ho! A spy! Could it be my enemy, the farmer? Destroyer of pigs? Eater of souls? Take this then, villain, and die!"

The angry prince lowered his head and charged the hay at full speed. Charlotta wisely jumped out from his ear just before impact. The top of Piglet's skull connected with the cowering body of Felonious.

"O, I am slain!—" he cried and tried to stand, but the old dog collapsed and died on the spot.

"Felonious?" Piglet started, nudging the body. It did not move.

Charlotta crawled back up into the pig's ear. "What hast thou done, Piglet?"

Piglet recovered. "I thought it was the farmer, but I do not regret his death. Felonious was a spy. Not only that, he knew of Macbeth's crime and said nothing. I mourn him not."

"He wasn't a bad animal, Piglet."

"The evil that dogs do lives after them; the good is oft interred with their bones. So shall it be with Felonious."

Charlotte dropped out of the pig's ear as the prince turned and left the barn. Once outside, Piglet glanced up to see Rosencatz and Geldertom jumping down from the barn windowsill.

The next day, Slurpees returned from sheep-herding school upon hearing of his father's death, and angrily sought out Farmer Macbeth for an explanation. He bounded up the porch steps and entered the house, finding Macbeth and his wife in the kitchen with the two cats.

"O, thou vile master," growled Slurpees, "where is my father? Present him to me."

Having never seen Slurpees in such a state, Odious Macbeth stepped back a few paces in fear. "Alas, your father is dead, Slurpees, but not by my hand, I assure you!"

"Dead? How came he dead? Speak, man."

"It was your friend Piglet. He killed your father in his madness."

"Piglet? No. He couldn't have. I would believe *you* capable of such evil, you scoundrel, but not he. Tell me the truth!" Slurpees began frothing at the mouth and took two steps toward the farmer.

"The cats saw it! Tell him, cats!" Macbeth screamed.

Rosencatz and Geldertom reluctantly stepped forward.

"I am Rosencatz," said Rosencatz.

"And I am Geldertom," said Geldertom.

"I know who you are! What did you see?"

"We sat in the barn window ..." began Geldertom.

"And we saw the whole thing," finished Rosencatz.

"Piglet and Zoophilia were arguing," explained Thing Uno.

"It had something to do with pee," added Thing Dos helpfully.

"Zoophilia ran out of the barn crying," said Thing Uno with a smug expression.

"But your father had been hiding in the hay. He made a noise ..."

"And Piglet heard it."

"Piglet rushed him without thinking."

"It was a resounding head-butt."

"Your father said 'O, I am slain!—'"

"And he collapsed."

"Dead."

The two cats got up and paced back and forth in front of Slurpees while providing further clarification. They didn't want to be misunderstood on this critical point of fact.

"Deceased," said Rosencatz as he paced to the left.

"Inanimate," said Geldertom as he paced right.

"Departed," said Rosencatz as he walked to the right.

"Bereft of life," said Geldertom as he walked left.

"Defunct," "Expired," **"Gone to meet his maker,"** "Offed," **"Pushing up—"**

Slurpees lunged and caught Rosencatz between his jaws, biting down. Geldertom was too shocked by the dog's sudden movement to react, and before he knew it, a heavy paw had knocked him hard against the wall. He saw the dog's jaws approach, and then all went black.

Odious and Gertrude watched in horror as the dog raised its head and stared at them, blood dripping from its jaws. "And where is my sister?" he growled.

Gertrude swallowed. "She was found this morning in the pond, Slurpees. I am truly sorry for your loss."

"What? Zoophilia went swimming after Father died?"

"No. Your sister is drown'd, drown'd," said Gertrude. She clenched her eyes shut and raised her arms to defend herself against a blow, but none came. When she dared to open her eyes a minute later, the room was empty except for the corpses of two cats.

Farmer Odious Macbeth knew that Slurpees was dangerous, but he needed him to help destroy Piglet. He couldn't personally kill the pig in view of the other animals, and the prince's sudden disappearance would raise questions, particularly since Piglet had told them that the farmers had murdered the pig-king. If the animals began to fear for their lives, they could revolt. In his current state, Slurpees was Macbeth's best instrument to defeat the treacherous swine. He chased after the dog.

"Slurpees! Heel! I mean, please return! I have a plan!"

Slurpees stopped and looked back suspiciously at Farmer Macbeth.

"You can have your revenge on the bastard pig that killed

your father," said Macbeth.

Slurpees appeared curious, tilting his head.

"I have poison," the farmer said, grinning.

Charlotta said, "I have bad news, much worse news, and terrible news."

"Tell me," said the prince.

"Rosencatz and Geldertom are dead."

"I assume that was only the bad news," said the prince, "and it doesn't sound too bad, to be perfectly honest. They were spies, after all. How did they die?"

"That is the much worse news. They died in Slurpees' jaws. They were telling him about how you killed his father. They provided one too many synonyms for the word 'dead,' I'm told."

"Yes. That would do it," Piglet agreed.

"Still, they were only the messengers, and they suffered heavily for it. Now Slurpees will be coming for you. He intends to take your life."

"How do you know this?"

"The mice, of course. News travels fast on a farm."

"Surely there cannot be worse news than that?" asked Piglet.

"There is," said the spider. "Zoophilia is dead. Drown'd."

"Oh no. Was it an accident, by someone else's hand, or by her own?"

"That I cannot say for certain, sire, but the mice whisper that her mind snapped after learning of her father's death. I fear she may have taken her own life."

"Then I have four deaths on my conscience. Tell me, Charlotta, is it all worth it?"

Charlotta didn't know, but Piglet's father did. The ghost appeared in the shadows near the back of the barn.

"Piglet, my son, do not grieve for these fallen. They all knew of Farmer Macbeth's crimes, and they did nothing about it. Finish the deed. Stop whining and get on with it."

"Yes, Father, I will do as you ask. But first, Charlotta and I shall visit Zoophilia's resting place, whether it pleases you or not. If you want your revenge, be silent and be gone."

The ghost departed.

Piglet trotted toward the marshlands where the bodies of dead farm animals were laid to rest. Having no need of coffins, the animals were buried directly in the dirt, and occasionally some of their bones would resurface. Piglet stopped at one marker and nudged a skull with his snout. He pondered the cranium for some time.

"Alas, poor Lorex!—I knew him, Charlotta. A creature of infinite jest, of most excellent sensibilities. He spoke for the trees. The beautiful toofula trees. He lived where the gristle-grass grows and the wind smells putrescent when it blows. You know the place. He was peevish. And boorish. And clownish. And greasy. And he spoke with a voice that was huffish and wheezy. He told me UNLESS someone like you cares a whole awful lot, nothing's going to get better. It's just not."

"Ah, yes. Mr. Lorex. Whatever happened to him?"

"He sold the toofula grove and they chopped it down. He bought a beachfront condo in Sarasota with the profits. I guess he wanted to be buried here though. Huh." He pushed the skull back down into the mud and wiped his trotters together.

"Anyway, it looks like they laid Zoophilia to rest over there. See that upturned earth? Let's pay our respects and get back to the barn. We have an appointment with the farmers, and we can't push it off any longer. It's like my father used to say: If it be now, 'tis not to come. If it be not to come, it will be now. If it be not now, yet it will come—the readiness is all. Since no man of aught he leaves knows, what is it to leave betimes? Let be."

"And what's that supposed to mean?" asked Charlotta.

"I haven't a clue, but it sounds great, doesn't it? Let's go."

"Now dip each of your paws in this liquid, Slurpees. Then all you have to do is scratch Piglet, and he will soon drop dead from the poison even if he wins the fight—which I'm sure he won't,"

Odious added hastily.

"I don't understand why you are assisting me in this," said Slurpees.

"Felonious was my oldest and most trusted advisor. Of course, I wish to help avenge his murder."

"So it has nothing to do with the fact that you fear Piglet's revenge upon you for the death of his father?"

"I don't know what you mean," lied Odious. "Are you ready?"

"Yes. Let's go."

Piglet was waiting in the barn when he heard Slurpees shout from the yard.

"Little pig, little pig, let me in!"

"I'm not playing, Slurpees. I don't want to fight you."

"You should have thought of that before you killed my father, evil pig."

"It was a mistake, Slurpees. I didn't know it was him hiding in the hay."

"I don't care, pig. Come out here and meet your fate like a swine, or show the entire farm what a coward you are. You'll die either way."

Piglet walked outside. The fenced-in area adjacent to the barn was empty except for Slurpees, who was crouching in the far-right corner. Every other animal on the farm was watching from the opposite side of the fence. Upon the center wooden gate sat Farmer Macbeth and his wife, just where Piglet had expected them to be.

The pig addressed his opponent. "It's not me whom you should fight, Slurpees."

"Isn't it?"

"No. It is the lying, pig-eating, murderous bastards sitting on the fence."

"That's funny, Piglet. From all accounts, they had nothing to do with my father's death."

"They had everything to do with it. They started this war by killing the king."

"A war? Really? It seems that your side only has one soldier, Piglet."

"Enough idle talk!" shouted the farmer. "Get on with it! If you're going to fight, then fight. If not, then walk away. It's all the same to me. Just bring it to a close. This is a short story for Pete's sake, not a novella!"

The pig and dog acknowledged the point and started to circle one another.

The pig rushed the dog, head down. A miss.

The dog jumped toward Piglet but misjudged his adversary's speed, landing a foot away from the scurrying pig.

The pig made another pass and head-butted the dog in the rear, but was scratched before darting away.

The dog howled, "You are dead, Piglet."

"Don't be absurd, Slurpees. It's nothing but a scratch."

"My claws are poisoned, pig."

"Well, in that case, here goes nothing. NOW, CHARLOTTA!" The pig lowered his head and charged.

"Hey, you stupid pig!" Slurpees shouted. "You're running in the wrong direction! Are you blind? Has the poison affected you that quickly? I'm over here!"

But Piglet wasn't aiming for the dog. He slammed his head against the wobbly wooden gate upon which the farmer and his wife were sitting. Farmer Macbeth fell into the enclosed area and Piglet immediately started to trample upon his head. Meanwhile, the farmer's wife screamed that something had bitten her leg. A small black object jumped down into the dirt.

"Did you know the black widow spider is one of the most dangerous animals in Wisconsin?" Piglet shouted. To illustrate the point, Gertrude collapsed and started gasping for breath.

Farmer Macbeth yelled, "That'll DO, pig! That'll DO!" He tried to sit up, which was a major mistake. It placed his head at just the right height to connect with Piglet's incoming head-butt. Macbeth's neck snapped, and Piglet collapsed on top of his lifeless form, completely out of breath.

"O, I die, Charlotta," he wheezed. "The potent poison quite o'er-crows my spirit. I cannot live to accept the barnyard crown. See that the truth is told. The rest is silence." The valiant prince expired.

Slurpees trotted up beside them. "It appears you got your revenge after all, Piglet. Well done! And I got mine. The difference is that I'm still alive!" he gloated.

"But not for long," said a small voice in his right ear, which was followed by a very sharp pain. Charlotta dropped down and tried to run, but the dog noticed her, brutally dispatching her with a quick swipe of his paw before collapsing on top of her crushed body.

Within ten minutes, the spider toxin had done its work. All the primary characters were dead, which pretty much rules out a sequel to this story. Not that you were looking for one.

Porky Pig and several of his brothers crowded around their fallen leader. "Goo-goo-goo-good night, sweet pri-pri-pri-prince, and fl-fl-fl-flights of angels sing thee to thy re-re-re-re-rest." Porky waved away the onlookers as they carried the prince's body to the marshlands.

"Th-th-th-th-that's all, folks," he said.

11

Doctor Whozzit

Margot Felderblum stumbled along in the rising desert heat, hoping against hope that the vista from the top of the next sand dune would consist of something other than a series of more dunes, even though such prior aspirations had been bashed again and again. Her food ran out two days ago, and only a few swallows of water remained in the thermos on her belt. *Wouldn't it be great if there were an oasis over the next ridge?* she thought. *Yeah, that's likely,* she thought back. *Maybe there'll be a Marriott and a McDonald's too.*

Margot was beginning to dislike her prefrontal cortex, the area of the brain from which sarcasm originates.

For the past several weeks, she'd been traveling by night and trying to sleep during the day, covering herself with a thin layer of sand to avoid the sun's harmful rays. Now she was afraid that she might never awaken if she fell asleep in her weakened state, so she trudged on this morning in a last-ditch attempt to find salvation.

Suddenly she heard a noise in the air. It sounded like … No, it couldn't be. She must be hallucinating. Were auditory hallucinations even a thing? … There it was again! It was the sound of … a toilet flushing. A very loud toilet.

She arrived at the top of the dune and looked out. Sand everywhere, just as usual.

Except for the bright-blue porta potty standing at the bottom of the hill. That was new.

No way, Margot thought, and for once, her prefrontal cortex could think of nothing to think in response.

She practically fell down the dune in her rush to reach the blue box. Halfway down, her prefrontal cortex woke up again, asking, *What do you suppose you'll find inside that thing, running water?*

Margot half expected the box to disappear as she got closer, but it remained. She touched it. It was solid. Were tactile hallucinations even a thing?

A small card on the door read, "Doctor P. T. Whozzit. The doctor is IN. Knock and enter."

This is nuts, Margot thought, to which her prefrontal cortex simply assented. Nevertheless, she knocked, pushed the door open ... and gasped.

The porta potty was bigger on the inside. Much bigger. Much, much bigger. It was the size of a ballroom, and electronic equipment filled the walls. In the center of the room were some circular control panels and a large rotating *thingy*.

She closed the door and walked around the outside of the porta potty. It couldn't be much more than four feet on a side. She pushed open the door and peeked inside again. The inner walls had to be at least fifty feet wide.

Her prefrontal cortex was sending her the signal to run away when she noticed a jug of water and a plate of sandwiches on the corner table. Her prefrontal cortex shut up. She careened into the impossibly large, impossibly cool interior and grabbed the jug, gulping the water and spilling a good portion of it in the process.

"Do please slow down. Have some sense of decorum, would you?" said a man's voice.

Startled, Margot almost dropped the jug, as she stared at the man in the long checkered coat, pink shirt, black bow tie, and green pants. Words could not describe the shoes, although "horrendous" might've been a good starting place.

"Who are you?" she asked.

"Very close. Points for effort, but no, I'm not Who. My name is Whozzit. P. T. Whozzit, at your service. Baron of time, protector of the universe, and doctor of osteopathic medicine. You can call me 'the doctor.' No, wait. That one's taken. You can call me 'the osteopathic doctor.' No, too difficult to pronounce. How about 'the other doctor'? No, too subservient—"

"Dr. Whozzit?" Margot interrupted.

"Yes! That's a good one. Reasonably short and to the point without violating any of those bothersome copyright laws. My counterpart has been very touchy ever since they gave him his own BBC show in—what, 1963 or so? Frankly, I'm not sure why he merits all the attention he gets. Take me, for example. I have the same job as he does. I've saved the universe on countless occasions, and I didn't even destroy my home planet in the process, unlike somebody *else* I could name—"

"May I ask a question?"

"A question! Yes! I encourage them, actually. Most of the time. What is your question?"

"What the hell is going on? Why is there a porta potty in the middle of the Sahara Desert? Why is it bigger on the inside?"

"That sounds like three questions to me. I thought you only wanted to ask one," said the cat.

"And how can your cat possibly be talking?" Margot asked, pointing to the orange ball of fluff.

"Four questions," said the other cat.

"If I could venture a word—" started Dr. Whozzit.

"You have *two* talking cats?"

"Five," both cats said simultaneously.

"You have *five* talking cats?"

"No," said the second cat. "There are only two of us, and we are not cats. We simply meant to indicate that you had asked five questions."

"Now six," said the first non-cat.

"Yes, now six. Except that two of those have since been answered. Do we subtract them from the total?" asked the second non-cat.

While the two non-cats were considering this problem, Dr. Whozzit said, "Miss Felderblum, may I present Professor Pandemonium and his personal assistant, Floor? They are multidimensional beings from the planet Preposteron IV and are currently taking the form of Earth-felines in order to communicate with us in an inconspicuous manner."

"And they thought that appearing as talking cats would be inconspicuous." The non-cats puffed up and started to say something, but Margot cut them off. "That was a statement, not a question," she said. The non-cats de-puffed.

"Your statement was a bit sarcastic," observed Dr. Whozzit.

"You'll have to take that up with my prefrontal cortex. The two of us haven't been getting along lately. But in fact, I do have another question," Margot continued. "You called me Ms. Felderblum a few moments ago. How do you know my name?"

"Because we've already met. In the future. Well, *your* future, of course. My past. Five years from now, in your timeline. You suggested it might be a good idea if I came back here and saved your life. If I hadn't done so, we never would have met, so I felt somewhat obliged to comply. There's no point in creating an unnecessary time paradox, I always say."

There seemed to be something wrong with this logic, but Margot couldn't put her finger on it. She moved on. "You travel in time?"

"But of course. Time tourism is all the rage. Or it will be in your future, I guess, thanks to Dr. Puffinhead."

"Who?"

The doctor gestured to a framed photograph on the wall. "Dr. Peter Puffinhead, the inventor of the first time machine. He's going to successfully test his time manipulation theory a decade or so from now in Berkeley, California. His theory will be ungenerously scoffed at and he will be shunned by the academic community after causing the death of his unfortunate time-traveling assistant. But his work will eventually form the basis for the creation of the Time Barons, of whom I am one, not to mention over twenty-six television seasons featuring the exploits of one of my co-workers."

"His assistant died while time-traveling?"

"Yes. Well, it was a new theory and there were a lot of kinks to be worked out. It would take a few more centuries until the technology was perfected. Nowadays, it's very safe. Sort of like driving a car in your era. People assume they will get to their destination unharmed. And they do, um, most of the time."

"Okay, Doctor. If you say so. Thank you for saving me, by the way," Margot said as she wolfed down a delicious tuna sandwich. "So now what?"

"Well, we could play a game. I've actually invented a few games in my time. In fact, a board game of mine called *Interminus* was a best seller on planet Malodorous for three years running."

Floor the non-cat looked up. "That was only because you made such a fuss about it before agreeing to save their planet

100

from annihilation by the Cybertortoises," she said.

"Yes," added Professor Pandemonium, "the Malodorian supreme leader made it mandatory for each of his citizens to purchase and play your game, or else face a lifetime of imprisonment."

"Twenty years later, most citizens were still studying the rules," said Floor.

"More than a few chose prison," recalled the professor.

The time baron nodded. "Yes, perhaps I made *Interminus* a little too complicated. I have other games though. Have you heard of *Yahtzee*? That was one of mine. Although the original name I gave it was *I Can Count!* It wasn't doing so well, so I sold the rights to some guy named Milton Bradley. He changed the name and made a fortune. It just goes to show that marketing is everything in gamesmanship."

The human and her three interplanetary hosts stared at one another until Dr. Whozzit finally broke the silence. "Or perhaps we could go someplace and/or sometime else. It's rather boring here in the desert, don't you think?"

"Not if you're a scorpion," said Professor Pandemonium.

"Or a grain of sand," added Floor helpfully.

"Yes, quite," agreed Dr. Whozzit. "But we are neither. So, Miss Felderblum, where and when would you like to go? But please don't choose a time and place from your own past."

"Because doing so could potentially alter the past and create an infinite time loop that could destroy the universe as we know it?" asked Margot.

"No, no, we do that kind of thing all the time. No, it's just that meeting oneself can be a bit awkward and embarrassing. It leads to conversations about how one of you has put on weight or aged significantly, which tends to annoy the older you. The older you typically responds by giving really bad investment advice or by revealing a terrifying event that hasn't happened yet and watching the younger you squirm. It gets worse from there. Best to avoid such encounters where possible."

"Um. Okay. How about we go into the future? Say New York City around a thousand years from now?"

"An excellent choice," said the parody-doctor. "Professor Pandemonium, would you please help me to fire up the Phartis?"

"What did you say?"

"My time machine. It's called the Phartis."

"This time machine. The one that looks like a porta potty on the outside—"

"Yes?" said Doctor Whozzit, getting slightly annoyed.

"You named it the Phartis."

"*I* didn't name it. That's its name. Was there someplace you were going with this line of questioning? Because, just to warn you, the Phartis tends to hold grudges."

There was a hiss of gas from the large rotating *thingy* in the middle of the room that sounded like, well, a hiss of gas. There was an odd smell.

"No, it's nothing," said Margot quickly.

"Super. Off we go then." The time baron and Professor Pandemonium adjusted some settings, and the flushing sound began again. The room seemed to shudder. Then it stopped.

"Excellent. We're here. I give you New York City in the year 3020!" Dr. Whozzit opened the door theatrically.

And they gazed upon a desert.

"This is a different desert, I think," said Professor Pandemonium. "The sand dune on the left was taller last time."

"I don't understand," said the osteopathic doctor as he re-examined the control panel. "These settings appear to be correct."

"Um, we have visitors, and they are definitely not New Yorkers," said Margot from the doorway.

Dr. Whozzit stepped outside to find an army of inverted metallic trash cans with what looked like toilet plungers sticking out of their sides. They were hovering several feet above the sand. There must have been a thousand of them.

"Good lord. Phallics. I *hate* those guys."

The head Phallic floated above the rest and called out, "EXPECTORATE!"

A thousand Phallics started spitting at the Phartis and its inhabitants, shouting "EXPECTORATE! EXPECTORATE!" The desert sands turned muddy.

The time baron held up his hands. "Stop, Phallics! What is the meaning of this onslaught?"

The leader responded, "AS IF YOU DID NOT KNOW, DOCTOR. WE ARE CHASTISING YOU FOR THE ATTEMPTED DESTRUCTION OF OUR ENTIRE RACE,

WHICH YOU WILL UNDERTAKE THIRTY THOUSAND YEARS FROM NOW. GIVEN OUR CONTINUED INABILITY TO EXTERMINATE YOU, WE HAVE DECIDED ON THIS APPROACH INSTEAD. IT IS NOT IDEAL, BUT IT IS STRANGELY SATISFYING NEVERTHELESS."

A few Phallics started chanting, "EXTERMINATE! EXTERMINATE!" until they were shushed by the others.

"Oh, I see, but you have the wrong doctor, I'm afraid. That wasn't me—or rather, that won't be me. I'm the osteopathic doctor. You'll be wanting the BBC one."

The head Phallic turned to his assistant, and there was some frenzied buzzing between them. Finally, it turned back and said, "OUR MISTAKE. EXSICCATE! EXSICCATE!"

There was an ear-shattering sucking sound as a thousand or more Phallics lowered their plungers to the ground and sucked up the moisture from the soil. The desert turned sandy again.

The head Phallic approached and said a little more softly, "I don't suppose you know where we could find the other doctor, do you?"

"No, sorry. We aren't currently on speaking terms."

"Ah, yes. He's quite exacerbating, isn't he?"

"Quite so, yes."

Overhearing this exchange, a few Phallics started chanting, "EXACERBATE! EXACERBATE!"

The head Phallic turned to look at them menacingly. They stopped. The Phallic turned back.

The O-doctor smiled. "If it's any help, I believe that he may be a she in the current season. I mean regeneration."

"Ah, the doctor's a woman now? Where will this all end?"

"It's difficult to extrapolate," said the time baron.

"EXTRAPOLATE! EXTRAPOLATE!" came a voice from behind them. The head Phallic swung quickly around. A bright stream of lightning flew from his plunger, striking the Phallic heckler and causing him to explode into a million pieces. It got very quiet.

The head Phallic turned back and said, "Excuse me, you were saying …"

"Oh, nothing, nothing. By the way, we were on our way to New York City in the year 3020. Would you happen to know in which direction that was, or will be?"

"Oh, yes. You're standing upon it. We reduced the city and its inhabitants to sand after a cabbie made a rude remark to my supervisor. There are still a few odds and ends poking up here and there. If you travel half a mile in that direction, you'll find the top half of the Statue of Liberty sticking out of the beach. It's a great photo opportunity. If you're into it, I even have a monkey suit you can borrow."

"Um, thank you."

Behind him, Margot Felderblum shouted, "You blew it up! Ah, damn you! God damn you all to hell!"

The head Phallic sighed. "It's a very good thing my supervisor isn't here, young lady. Good day, other-doctor. We're sorry to have disturbed you."

"No worries."

Doctor Whozzit closed the door and clapped his hands together. "Well, then. How about a trip to Joplin, Missouri, say a thousand years ago? I know where they make the best donuts in the universe."

"Heavenly Donuts! Heavenly Donuts!" shouted the two non-cats.

"Let's make it 2019," suggested Margot. "The year 2020 kind of sucked."

12

Judy Takes Leave of Her Census

Judy Chekov approached the ramshackle old house cautiously, noting the five-foot-tall weeds in the garden. Some of the windows were boarded, others contained broken panes of glass, and a few two-by-fours propped up the west side of the structure. *There's no way that anyone lives here*, she thought. Nevertheless, the home's address was on her list, and she felt she had a duty to at least knock on the door.

When she stepped upon the first wooden stair, it creaked with her weight, so she moved to the side, hoping that her foot wouldn't go straight through the rotted board, brushing against a cobweb in the process. *This is nuts. I should just turn around and get out of here. Aw, what the hell, I'm almost there. Might as well get it over with.*

Judy approached the door, from which pieces of green paint were flaking off. *I'll probably get lead poisoning if I touch that thing*, she thought. Removing her red scarf, she wrapped it around her hand, then knocked upon the door, which creaked open with her touch.

"Hello," she called. "United States Census. Is anybody home?"

Of course not. She turned to go.

"Come in," a gravelly voice said. "I don't move that well."

Oh, crap.

"I don't really want to come in, ma'am," she replied, hoping it was a ma'am. It was hard to tell. "Can I just ask you a few questions from here? Question 1. How many people were living or staying in this house on April 1, 2020?"

After a long pause, the voice said, "I can't hear you. Come inside."

"I SAID, QUESTION 1. HOW MANY PEOPLE WERE LIVING OR STAYING IN THIS HOUSE ON APRIL 1, 2020?" she yelled.

A longer pause. "What's that, dear? Come in, I won't bite."

Crap.

"Okay, I'm coming in." Judy stepped inside the dark house, leaving the door open in case she had to bolt, and felt along the wall until she found a light switch. Relieved, she flipped it on, but nothing happened.

"Just walk straight back. I'm in the living room."

It's a man. I should get out of here. She thought about trying to shout her questions again, and then she realized that it was too dark to read her crib sheet or take notes. Seeing a dim light ahead, she kept moving.

Something darted in front of her, scaring her half to death.

Just a cat, she thought. *At least I hope it was a cat. I'm being silly. He's just an old man. Let's get this over with.*

She entered the room.

The last thing she saw with her peripheral vision was a figure moving quickly from the right, then she felt an incredibly sharp pain in her back and dropped to the floor. Something wet and viscous touched her hand. She had just enough time to realize that it was her own blood before she lost consciousness.

"That makes twelve," said the voice. "One more."

Three days later, twelve-year-old Bobby Grisham and his younger brother Tom were practicing baseball in the field adjacent to the old house. Tom was at bat, facing the building. He took a swing and missed.

"You throw like a girl!" shouted Tom.

"That's sexist," chided Bobby.

"No it's not!" said Tom, retrieving the ball. "What does

'sexist' mean?"

"It means you're saying something you shouldn't. Anyway, some girls can throw like a guy."

"That's sexist," said Tom.

"No it's not," said Bobby. "I don't think it is anyway. But you can pitch for a while if you think it's that easy."

They switched places.

Tom underhanded a perfect toss and Bobby connected with it, sending the ball in a high arc toward the house. A moment later there was a loud crash as the ball shattered a second-story window and disappeared into the house.

Both boys stood for a moment, dumbstruck.

"That ain't good," said Tom.

"Oh shit," said Bobby.

"That's sexist," warned Tom. "Anyway, you better get that ball. Mom'll be mad if she finds out you lost it."

"I'm not going into that house," said Bobby.

"You have to," said Tom. "You hit the ball, Bobby. It's your fault. If you don't get it back, I'll tell."

Bobby looked at his brother. *Yeah, he'll tell. I guess I'll have to get the ball,* Bobby thought.

Bullshit. That's not what I'm thinking at all.

Bobby walked toward the house.

No, I'm not walking toward that house. Who do you think you are, putting thoughts into my head and action into my feet?

BOBBY WALKED TOWARD THE GODDAMN HOUSE.

HEY, I CAN USE CAPITAL LETTERS TOO, YOU JERK. I JUST TOLD YOU I'M NOT GOING INTO THAT HOUSE, AND THAT'S FINAL.

Seeing Bobby hesitate, Tom decided to get the ball himself and started walking toward the house.

"Stay where you are, Tom! Don't listen to that asshole." *That's a low blow, trying to manipulate a seven-year-old kid.*

Look, Bobby, I'm the narrator, and you have to do whatever I say. It's as simple as that. Now walk toward the damn house.

To hell with that, Narrator. There's a serial killer in there. I'm not going in, and neither is Tom. We're not going to die for the sake of your stupid story.

You're not supposed to know that there's a serial killer in there.

107

Yeah, well, I can read, can't I? He already killed a girl on page [three] of this story. Plus, just look at the place. Even if I hadn't read the earlier scene, who in his right mind WOULDN'T suspect there was a serial killer in there?

A man appeared at the broken window of the house. "Hey, what's the holdup out there?" he yelled.

This damn kid won't go in!

"What do you mean, he won't go in? You're the narrator. Just write him doing it."

I did, but it didn't work! The kid's just standing there, thinking to me that he won't go in!

"What kind of narrator are you? Let's get a move on. I've got an audition for a Stephen King short story this afternoon."

Another figure appeared next to the man in the window. "What's going on?" she asked.

"You're dead, Judy. Go back and lie down," the killer said.

"I got tired of waiting for the story to move on. Then I thought, maybe I don't have to be dead after all," said Judy.

"That ax in your back says differently," smirked the serial killer. "Hey, narrator, you tell her."

Judy Chekov was totally dead. She died three days ago, in fact. Her body lay in a large puddle of dried blood on the living room floor. She definitely was not standing in the window carrying on a conversation with her murderer.

Oh, stuff it, narrator, Judy thought as she stood at the window.

"And, hey," added the serial killer, "would it be too much trouble to give me a name? It's very impersonal to keep calling me 'serial killer' or 'murderer.' How about 'Derek'?"

The serial killer, whose name was Derek, backed away from the window and stopped chatting with his previous victim and the narrator, as it was interrupting the flow of the story.

"Hey, asshole, it's not *me* interrupting the flow. You get that kid in here so I can murder him. But thanks for the name."

"I knew it!" yelled Bobby. "He was going to kill me. There's no way I'm going in there now. I'm heading home. C'mon, Tom."

Tom looked up at the window. "Hey, you up there! Can you please throw our ball back down?"

"Sure, hon," said Judy, tossing the ball out the window. Tom waved as he retrieved it, then he and Bobby started off for home.

108

Hey, I didn't narrate that. What do you think you're doing, Judy?

"I guess you're not the only one who can narrate, you dick," said Judy.

I'm NOT a dick.

The narrator, whose name matched his personality, was called Dick.

Stop that! Narration is *my* function! But, okay, my name *is* Dick as it turns out. Lucky guess.

"Dick, you're just sore because Judy's a better narrator than you are. Go for it, Judy," said Derek.

Dick sat typing at his computer, confused by the bizarre turn the story had taken. While he concentrated on finding a way out of the mess he had created, he didn't notice the lurking hulk in the shadows who rushed at him with an office implement and stapled him to death.

OW! STOP IT, JUDY! OW!

Dick slumped to the floor, dead.

I'm not dead, Judy. How do you kill someone with a stapler anyway? Cut it out.

Fine. But let's agree that I'm not dead either, okay?

Fine.

Fine.

Miraculously, the ax wound in Judy's back was not fatal after all. Instead, it severed a nerve that caused her to lose the ability to narrate.

How's that, Judy? Are we good?

"We're good," said the newly recovered Judy. "Should I continue with the census questions then?"

Sure, why not. I have no idea where this story is going anymore, so have at it.

Judy turned to Derek and said, "Question 1. How many people were living or staying in this house on April 1, 2020?"

"Um, just me, I guess," said Derek. "I'm not positive because it was a bit before my time, if you know what I mean."

"Very good. I'll put down 'one.' Question 2. Were there any additional people staying here on April 1, 2020, that you did not include in Question 1?"

So Question 2 simply asks whether you lied in your answer to Question 1? Seriously?

"Hey, Dick, I didn't write these questions. They're directly from the official census. Look it up. Some brainiac in Washington, DC, actually got paid to formulate that question."

What's Question 3 then? Let me guess. How about, "Are you sure your answer to Question 2 is right?"

"No. Question 3 asks whether you own or rent the place or if you're just a freeloader."

I see.

Derek had been very thoughtful this whole time. Suddenly he asked, "Hey, wait a minute. If she's alive now, does that mean I'm back at number eleven?"

Yes.

"That sucks. I haven't made any progress in this story at all then. What's Stephen King going to think?"

Who cares what he thinks? He's probably going to pick someone or something else to be the villain instead of you anyway. Maybe an evil dog. Or a car. Or a hotel. Or a turd. Or a banana. I don't believe he's written about a monster banana yet, but I could be wrong. He has written about all the others. He can make anything evil.

"No, seriously, guys, I need to show some initiative. What am I going to say when he asks me how many victims I killed in my last story? Eleven doesn't sound like very many. I need an even dozen at least."

"Derek, I don't think you can take credit for any deaths," said Judy. "Those first eleven happened before this story even began."

"Damn. You're right. I'm sunk. I'll be laughed out of King's computer."

"Maybe you can kill the narrator," suggested Judy.

You tried killing me already, Judy, don't you remember? It didn't work. Besides, I thought we had a deal. Maybe you can kill the author instead.

"Aren't you the author?" asked Derek.

No. Normally I would be, but not in this story since I'm acting like a character. The author is different.

"Stop bullshitting me. You're the author, Dick. You've been making all the story decisions. A couple of pages ago it even said you were typing at your computer."

Actually, it was Judy who narrated that part. What does she know? She's only a census worker.

110

"Hey," shouted Judy, "I've had just about all the abuse I can take in this story! First, I get axed in the back, then I get insulted. That's it, I'm out of here! No job is worth this! And for the record, the census questions are stupid."

Judy left the house, slamming the door behind her. Derek watched as she stormed around the corner.

"I'm glad she's gone," said Derek. "Those questions were starting to get on my nerves. Now, where were we? Oh, right. You're the author, Dick. Just admit it and let's move on, alright?"

I am NOT the author, for Pete's sake. Just look at the cover.

"The what now?"

The cover of the book. Whose name is on it? Is it Dick?

"Hang on a sec."

Derek walked toward the book cover and returned a few minutes later.

"Okay, I guess you're right," admitted Derek. "You're not the author, Dick. It's some bozo named Pete. I'm sorry I doubted you."

No problem.

"And there's some weird shit in this book. You ever heard of something called a Phallic?"

Um, I—

"And there are talking animals and teapots and chess pieces and stuff. Crazy."

Derek, can we please stick to our own story?

"Yeah, sure. So maybe I will try to kill the author, as you suggested," said Derek. "Now, how do I narrate?"

Write something as if it just happened, and don't use quotation marks.

"Okay, here goes," said Derek.

The author, whose name was Pete, sat typing at his computer, confused by the bizarre turn the story had taken. While he concentrated on finding a way out of the mess he had created, he didn't notice the lurking hulk in the shadows who rushed at him with an office implement and stapled him to death.

HEY! OUCH! YOU CAN'T DO THAT!

The End.

I SAID, YOU CAN'T—

The End!

13

The Magician's Assistant

I first met "The Great Zucchini" in 1965, following one of his late-night shows in Harlem. After being sawn in half and put back together, his assistant ran screaming from the theater. I got a good view of her face as she sprinted down the aisle. If it was an act, she deserved a Tony Award hands down, but since the girl didn't look like a career thespian to me, I figured there might be a job opening. I was right, as it turned out.

As soon as the theater emptied, I snuck backstage and knocked on the dressing-room door.

"Enter and be amazed," called a voice.

I entered but found nothing too amazing taking place. The Great Zucchini sat at the dressing table, wiping stage makeup off his face. A golden-haired toy poodle sat in the corner of the room, yapping at me.

"Cool it, Copperfield. Take a break," the magician said. The dog stopped yammering and lay down, staring at me. Zucchini glanced up. "Yeah? You looking for an autograph? It'll cost you five bucks. I don't do kids' parties, so don't even ask. Last time, one of the little monsters broke my wand, and his baby brother puked all over my shoes. Never again."

"Actually, Mr. Zucchini, I wondered if you might be searching for a new assistant. I'd like to apply for the job."

Zucchini stroked his white goatee and considered this for a moment. "Debbie may come back," he said.

I shrugged. "You know her a lot better than me, Mr.

Zucchini, but I've never seen a woman run that fast in high heels. She looked like she was being chased by a swarm of angry bees. Unless I'm grossly mistaken, that high-pitched scream was her letter of resignation."

"Yeah. Maybe you're right. Do you have any experience as a magician's assistant? Ever been on stage? Do you perform any magic yourself?"

Aw, crap, I thought. I briefly considered lying but decided he'd find out the truth soon enough. "No," I said. "I've never acted before, and I don't know the first thing about magic."

Zucchini smiled. "Well, that's a relief. I never hire anybody with experience. Those people think they know how things should be, and they're always wrong. What's your name, dear?"

"Susan. Susan Parsnip."

The magician addressed his poodle. "Copperfield, say hello to Miss Parsnip."

The dog responded with a single yap, then walked off to investigate his food dish.

"He'll know you now. If you play your cards right, he may even allow you to pet him someday."

"I'll try to live up to his expectations," I said.

"Yes. Now then, Miss Parsnip, what kind of work experience *do* you have?"

"I, um, worked as a bank teller for a few years until the bank went belly-up—but don't get me wrong. They didn't go belly-up because of me. Before that, I was a waitress at a diner."

"Very well, my dear. My next show starts at seven on Wednesday night. If Debbie doesn't return by then, you've got the job. Be at the backstage door by six, and wear black stockings and high-heeled shoes. I'll supply the costume. We generally do six shows a week. You get seventy-five bucks per show, in cash. If you decide not to declare it to the IRS, that's your business. Sound okay to you?"

"Yeah, thanks, but won't I need to practice first? How can I walk onstage without any preparation?"

"You let me worry about that, my dear. Everything will be fine if you remain calm and simply follow my instructions."

"Okay, Mr. Zucchini," I said, thinking to myself, *If it's that easy, why did Debbie run out screaming?*

114

I showed up backstage at a quarter to six on Wednesday. Copperfield was apparently unimpressed with my entrance and didn't bother to get up. Zucchini handed me a costume and said he hadn't heard from Debbie. She didn't even stop by to get her money for the last show.

I changed my clothes behind a partition and stepped out. Zucchini gave me a once-over and said, "Yeah, that'll do."

"Yap," added Copperfield.

"I still don't understand what I have to do, Mr. Zucchini."

"Don't worry about it, my dear. Mainly you're there to look nice and to take some of the audience's focus off me. There are only three things you need to know." He paused for dramatic effect.

"And they are?" I asked.

"Number one, magic is real."

"Sure it is, Mr. Zucchini. I'm with you. Don't worry, I won't spoil the illusion. But don't I need to know where the secret compartments are and all that?"

"No, no, you misunderstand me. I'm not asking you to *pretend* that magic is real. I'm asking you to *believe* it. I do not deal in illusions. There are no secret compartments in my show. No wires, keys, mirrors, or hidden panels. *My … magic … is … real.* I know that 99 percent of professional magicians use some form of trickery to fool the audience. They're nothing but charlatans. Please don't ever suggest that I'm one of them. Do you understand me?"

"Magic is real. Check," I said. *What a fanatic*, I thought to myself at the time. That was before I knew better.

"Number two, follow my instructions to the letter. When I tell you to remain still, REMAIN STILL. I can't emphasize this point enough. You need to trust me. This is very important. You may be acutely uncomfortable at times, particularly when we get to the sawing-in-half part, but I shall not let any harm come to you. Which brings us to number three."

"Which is?"

"Don't panic. As you so aptly put it, if you run screaming

115

from the stage, I will take that as your letter of resignation. Are we clear on everything?"

I nodded. "Magic is real. Follow instructions. Don't panic."

"Yes. I believe that covers it."

There was a knock on the door, and a voice outside shouted, "Five minutes!"

"That's our cue," said Zucchini with a wink. "We're on. Copperfield, stay."

The seats in the theater were only half-filled, but Zucchini didn't appear to mind. He started with a card trick. "Go and select someone from the audience," he told me. "It doesn't matter who."

I picked an attractive woman from the sixth row. She followed me onto the stage, and Zucchini fanned the cards in front of her. "Pick a card, any card, and show it to the people in the first row. Don't let me see it," he told her.

The lady did so. I saw she had chosen the seven of hearts.

"Good," said Zucchini. "Now take the rest of the deck and put your card inside. Shuffle it well, then spread the cards upon the table, faceup. I shall inspect the cards without touching them and tell you which card you picked."

When the cards were laid out, Zucchini approached them with his hands behind his back, inspecting the tableau. "But madam," the magician said, "are you trying to trick me? Your card is not here."

The woman insisted that she had returned it to the deck.

"See for yourself then." Zucchini backed away. I'd swear on a stack of Bibles that he never touched the cards. The lady from the audience bent over the table, and I watched her paw through the deck. The seven of hearts wasn't there.

"You're right," the woman said. "It's missing. I don't understand. Where is it?"

"Let's find out. Will the person who catches this tennis ball please come forward?"

Zucchini placed his right arm over his eyes. With his left hand,

116

he tossed the ball into the back of the auditorium. A man caught it and walked toward the stage.

When he reached the bottom of the steps, Zucchini said, "That's far enough. I don't wish to have contact with you. Please take out your wallet. In view of the first row, examine its contents and remove anything that doesn't belong."

"There's a playing card in here that I've never seen before. The seven of hearts."

The applause of the audience almost drowned out the woman's confirmation that this was indeed the card she had chosen. Both volunteers retook their seats.

I figured both people must've been plants, but I didn't know how Zucchini had arranged to get them selected. I'd chosen the lady at random, and Zucchini's aim with a tennis ball couldn't have been that accurate, could it?

Anyway, The Great Zucchini had the audience's attention from that point forward, performing one magic trick after another. Even standing right next to him, I could never figure out how he did any of them.

Then he told me to get the disappearing box from the side of the stage, so I wheeled it out. It was an upright wooden container, about seven feet tall with a door on one side. Zucchini had me turn it around so the audience could see it was solid on all sides. Then he asked for a volunteer to stand behind the box during the trick, to confirm that there was no way for me to sneak out the back.

He opened the door and whispered to me as I stepped in. "Be still, and don't panic. It's better to keep your eyes closed. Breathe normally. I'll have you back in a jiffy."

I stood facing the audience and closed my eyes. He shut the door, and a moment later there was a strange little "pop" sound. Even with my eyes shut I could tell it was dark. Darker than it had any right to be, I thought, but I figured that was just my imagination. I reached out to touch the side of the box to steady myself, and my hand didn't touch anything.

I opened my eyes and saw that it wasn't totally dark. There were tiny little pinpoints of light all around me.

Stars.

I started to panic and breathed faster. Then I realized that I shouldn't be able to breathe at all. Since I was, I couldn't be floating in outer space. I forced myself to be calm and closed my eyes.

Just when it seemed like it had been way too long, there was another "pop." I felt a rush of air and I detected the presence of light.

I opened my eyes and was standing in the box facing the audience. People were clapping. The Great Zucchini appraised me with a curious look in his eyes and offered his hand. I grasped it and stepped out of the box.

"Take a bow," he whispered, so I did. Then I recalled that Debbie had been wearing a strange expression at this point in last week's show—probably the same one that now adorned my own face.

Suddenly, I wasn't looking forward to being sawn in half and I considered sprinting toward the exit doors. As if he knew my innermost thoughts, Zucchini took hold of my hand and whispered, "Don't worry. It won't hurt, and you won't be harmed in any way. I *promise.*" He squeezed my hand.

I'm not sure why I believed him, but I stayed.

Being sawn in half wasn't half-bad. I mean, it was actually kind of neat once you got over the disconcerting feeling of watching your own feet sticking out of a box on the other side of the stage. Yeah, they were my feet alright. They wiggled and twisted whenever I moved them. I could understand why Debbie ran out screaming after this, but I had no similar inclination. I was not in the least bit of pain, and I trusted that Zucchini would put me back together, good as new. In fact, if I closed my eyes, I felt like I was completely normal. It made no sense that I was in two pieces. I decided it was better to go with it and disbelieve what my eyes were telling me. It had to be some kind of weird illusion.

Had to be.

I could tell my calm demeanor during the trick impressed Zucchini. I even forced a few smiles at the audience, determined to make a go at my new career. No screaming banshee, I.

The magician reconnected me as promised, and I suffered no ill effects. I climbed out of the box, and we took our final bows. As the curtains closed in front of us, The Great Zucchini turned to me and said, "Well done, Miss Parsnip. Welcome to the show."

"Please, call me Susan."

"I shall. And you shall call me Barry—when we're offstage, that is. May I invite you out for a celebratory beverage, Susan?"

"I wouldn't say no."

Four gin and tonics later, Barry Zucchini decided to tell me his life story.

"My mother was a witch," he began. "Not your run-of-the-mill bitchy type of witch, you understand. No, she was the real deal. She was a spell-casting, potion-making, wand-twirling, truth-divining type of witch. I knew she was powerful and looked up to her. Perhaps I also feared her a little, but she was never anything but kind to me."

I took a sip of my drink and asked, "Did she wear a pointy black hat and ride a broom?"

He took my question far more seriously than I had intended it. "She had a black hat, I believe, but it was round and flat on top. Not pointy at all. As far as I know, she only used the broom for sweeping the floor. Never for transportation. I don't know why she'd consider traveling on a wooden stick when she could simply teleport herself at will to anyplace she'd like to go."

"I was joking, Barry."

"Oh. Yes. I see. Stereotypical witch behavior. Haha. Not even remotely accurate in the real world, of course. Ha."

"And your mother taught you magic?"

"Yes. It took quite a few years, as you might imagine. Teleportation is particularly difficult. You need to have a good understanding of fourth-dimensional geometry, which is terribly hard to learn when your brain is wired to deal with only three dimensions."

"When I was in the disappearing box, I saw stars all around me. Did you really teleport me into outer space?"

"Not exactly. Your body never moved from its coordinates in three-dimensional space. I simply shifted it ten feet dweebward."

"Dweebward?"

"Yes. Every time you add a spatial dimension, you add two axes of movement. For example, if you're a point on a one-dimensional horizontal line, you can only move left or right. If you're in a two-dimensional plane, you can also move forward or backward. And if you're in three-dimensional space, you can also move up or down. Four-dimensional space has two additional directions, but you can't see them in three-dimensional space. I call these directions dweeb and frump. I moved you ten feet dweebward. You can think of it as an alternate universe. Except it isn't."

"Huh. Is it dangerous?"

"Not if you don't stay there for long, but there's no air to breathe in a vacuum. If I didn't bring you back, you'd soon suffocate."

"But I *was* breathing!"

"That's because I transported the air inside the box along with you and prevented it from dispersing into space. You would have used it up eventually. Not to worry though. I'd never leave you there for that long."

"Wow. But you can also transport things in three dimensions, right? Like the seven of hearts? You sent it to that guy's wallet?"

"That's very perceptive of you. Yes. Cards are easy to transport because they don't take up much space."

"Wow. Can you transport people to other places on Earth too?"

"Yes, but I'd need to be sure there's nothing in the way on the receiving end. It's fine when I can see the destination. That's why popping the lower half of your body into a box on the same stage is no problem for me. But let's say I wanted to transport you to Piccadilly Circus in London. If someone happened to be standing in the spot where I sent you, things would get a bit, well, messy. Two physical objects trying to inhabit the same space generally don't get along, if you see what I mean."

"I get it. Transporting people on Earth is a no-no then."

"I didn't say that. There are ways to do it. You just have to be careful. For example, certain spaces around the world are guarded by local witches and kept empty. If you want to go there, you first send a small object, like a pebble or a pea. If the object reappears, it means the witches will keep the space empty for you for the next five minutes."

"So as long as you know the space is unoccupied, you can send a person anywhere?"

"Yeah, that's the gist of it."

"That's awesome. Aside from transporting things, what else can you do?"

"Ah, well, sometimes I can see the future, but only bits of it, and I can't choose what I see."

"Have you seen my future?"

"If I did, I wouldn't tell you. It's against the rules."

"The rules?"

"Witches have rules, like any profession. They're quite simple. First, do no harm."

"Like the doctor's oath."

"*Exactly* like the doctor's oath. Hippocrates was a witch."

"Ah."

"Second, do not use magic for personal gain."

"But you get paid to perform it. Isn't that against the rules?"

"No, I checked with the Witches' Council. As long as people think it's just an act, it's okay to take their money."

"I see. But if they knew the magic was real, they couldn't pay you to do it."

"That's correct. Nor can I make any financial profit from knowing the future or from selling potions or spells."

"And you can't tell other people about their future?"

"No, because telling them might alter it, which is generally held to be a bad thing."

"Is it *necessarily* a bad thing?"

"I don't know. We err on the side of 'do no harm,' as a rule."

"And what if not telling causes harm?"

"That would be an interesting conundrum, Susan."

"Should you be sharing all this with me, Barry?"

He took another drink. "No. Certainly not, my dear. If anyone asks, my excuse will be that I was drunk, and as my new assistant, I trusted you implicitly."

Barry lifted his glass to tap mine, and we both drank to that.

Almost immediately, I betrayed his trust.

I didn't mean to. But I should have foreseen what would

happen when I told my younger brother Fergus about The Great Zucchini's abilities. He couldn't wait to inform Ralph Dodgy. And that's when the trouble started.

I'd had problems with Ralph before. When I got the job as a teller with First Transcontinental Bank, Fergus was quick to brag about it to his lowlife childhood friend, and Ralph began to brainstorm ways he could use my position inside the bank to his advantage. I managed to give good reasons why each of his harebrained schemes to defraud the bank wouldn't work, but every few months Ralph would be back with another idea. I finally told him flat out that I was not going to help him rip off my employer and that I'd report him if he tried anything. That shut him up for a while.

You might be wondering why I put up with him at all. It's a good question. The answer is that he was my brother's only friend, and I was afraid of what might happen if he walked away. Fergus had always been a bit mentally challenged. In grade school, Ralph was the only kid who would give him the time of day. Initially, I suspected this was because Ralph figured he could manipulate Fergus, which was true, yet over the years a bond developed between the two of them. Although I didn't like Ralph, I grudgingly had to admit he was a good friend to Fergus, at least up until then. So I tolerated him. Until the robbery incident.

It happened about six months after I told Ralph to go to hell. I knew something was up because my brother became secretive and uncommunicative for several weeks. Then one night he asked me to stay home from work the next day. When I asked why, he just smiled and placed his finger on his lips. He left the apartment, presumably bound for Ralph's.

I did what any big sister would do: I searched his room. It didn't take me long to find a plastic Bugs Bunny mask and a loaded gun. Horrified, I threw the mask in the garbage, removed the bullets, and hid the gun in the attic. Then I walked out and used a pay phone to leave an anonymous message with the police about a robbery attempt tomorrow at First Transcontinental. I called the bank manager and left a similar warning on his voicemail, disguising my voice as best I could. When that was finished, I returned to the apartment and waited for Fergus to come home so I could tell him what I'd done.

They had no choice but to call off the heist. Fergus didn't talk to me for several weeks, but I think he knew that I'd done it for his own good. Ralph didn't come round to the apartment after that, but he remained friends with Fergus, for better or worse.

Once Ralph heard that The Great Zucchini might be the real deal, his little criminal mind started spinning. He showed up on my doorstep with a bunch of flowers and a bottle of scotch, telling me he wanted to bury the hatchet. Fergus urged me to let him in. A few minutes later, when Ralph asked about my new job, I knew that Fergus had told him about Zucchini.

Not surprisingly, Ralph wanted to meet the magician. I put him off, but one night I spied him and Fergus sitting in the late-show audience. Immediately following the final curtain, they came knocking on the dressing-room door. I gave in and introduced them to my boss.

Copperfield the poodle seemed indifferent to my brother, but when Ralph approached to shake Zucchini's hand, the little dog started running around in circles and yapping like it was the end of the world. Zucchini had trouble getting him to calm down.

That dog's a good judge of character, I thought.

True to form, Ralph was his usual undiplomatic self. "That was a great show, Mr. Zucchini. Tell me, you can't really move objects around with your mind, can you? It's all some kind of trick, right?"

Barry puffed up and grew red in the face. "My magic is real, Mr. Dodgy. I defy anyone to prove otherwise." He folded his arms.

"Alright, alright. No need to get all worked up about it. I'm just saying your tricks are very good, is all. I can't figure out how you did them."

"They are demonstrations, not tricks. I performed them using magic."

"Is that so? Well, why don't you prove it then? Can you transport me to the other side of the room?"

"I don't perform on request, Mr. Dodgy. I'm not a trained seal."

"I'll pay you five bucks if you can do it."

"Keep your money, Mr. Dodgy. You look like you need it more than I do."

"What's that supposed to mean?" Ralph's hands balled up

into fists.

Even my brother realized that this encounter was going south. "Um, Ralph, maybe we should get going," he suggested. "It was very nice to meet you, Mr. Zucchini." Fergus turned to go.

Ralph stood his ground. "I'm not leaving this room until I have proof this old bird can actually do magic."

Sensing the heightened tension in the room, Copperfield started yapping again.

"As you wish," said The Great Zucchini. He snapped his fingers, and Ralph disappeared. Fergus screamed. Copperfield stopped yapping and trotted back to his water bowl.

"Where did you send him?" I asked.

"To a place that's always empty at this hour."

"In New York City? Where could that be?"

Zucchini smiled. "Let's just say I don't think we'll be bothered by Mr. Dodgy again."

Knowing Ralph Dodgy, I figured that Barry was dead wrong.

I later found out from Fergus that Ralph materialized inside the crown of the Statue of Liberty, which was closed for the night. Ralph had to wait until dawn before there was enough light to climb down the 162 steps to the main lobby. Then he paced for several hours before a very surprised park ranger unlocked the doors.

We didn't hear any more from Ralph for a few weeks. When I asked Fergus what his friend was doing, my brother said he didn't know. Ralph wouldn't answer his phone or door.

I knew this was a bad sign. Ralph was planning something, and he didn't want Fergus to find out what it was. He must have been worried I'd throw a wrench into his plans again. He was right about that. Knowing it would have something to do with Zucchini, I warned Barry to watch out for him, but Barry thought I was crazy to worry about it.

One night after the show, we returned to the dressing room to find an envelope addressed to Barry propped up on his vanity table. Barry opened it and became very still.

124

"Copperfield?" he called.

There was no response. Not a single yap.

"Copperfield!" he yelled.

Nothing. He sat down heavily in the chair and handed me the letter. It was typed in all capital letters. I'm not sure why Ralph bothered. It's not like we didn't know it was from him.

TO THE GREAT ZUCCHINI:

I HAVE YOUR DOG.

IT'S SAFE FOR NOW.

IF YOU DO WHAT I WANT, THE MUTT WILL BE RETURNED TO YOU UNHARMED.

IF NOT, THE DOG IS DEAD.

I WILL BE IN TOUCH SOON. DON'T DO ANYTHING STUPID WHEN YOU SEE ME.

P.S. IF I MAKE ANOTHER TRIP TO THE STATUE OF LIBERTY, OR IF ANYTHING ELSE HAPPENS TO ME, YOUR DOG WILL NOT BE FED AND IT WILL DIE.

I put down the note, praying that Fergus wasn't involved in this. I stared at Barry.

"Can't you magic him back?" I asked.

"Not without knowing where he is," said Barry. "Do you have any idea where Dodgy might have taken him?"

"Not offhand," I replied. "I'm sure he's not in Ralph's apartment though. That's the first place we'd look."

"We should check anyway."

"Yeah. I'll talk to my brother about it."

"Susan, you don't think Fergus is mixed up in this, do you?"

"No. Absolutely not," I said, hoping I was right.

"I can't believe Ralph would steal a puppy," Fergus said. "That doesn't sound like him at all."

No, he doesn't steal puppies, but armed bank robbery is fine with him, I thought.

Seeing that my brother was moderately distressed, I decided not to press the point. "Do you think he could be keeping the dog in his apartment?" I asked.

"I ain't been inside Ralph's apartment since he visited Miss Liberty, but I been standing outside a few times. If he had Copperfield in there, I'd have heard him. The dog, I mean."

"Can you think of anyplace else he might have taken it?"

"Um, no. I'll try his apartment again and see if he'll talk to me."

"Okay, Fergus, let me know if you find anything out."

"Yup, will do, Sis."

Zucchini and I had a show that night, so I left shortly afterward. I arrived backstage and was surprised to find the magician in a heated argument with Ralph.

"... and I tell you again, I can't send you into a space that I haven't seen beforehand. It would be incredibly dangerous. Even if it's unoccupied, you could materialize inside a wall or a table or some other object, which would kill you instantly."

"You sent me to the Statue of Liberty!"

"*Because I've been there!* I know what the space looks like. I know it's empty at night. There's plenty of room to work with and no objects that could impale a person when they pop in."

"What if I'm willing to take that risk?"

"Then you're an idiot. I still wouldn't do it. I don't want to live with the death of somebody on my conscience. Not even you. Oh ... hello, Susan. Can you please try to talk some sense into this moron? He wants me to magic him into a bank vault, unseen."

"Hey," said Ralph, "are you forgetting I have your dog?"

"I know you kidnapped my dog, and if you kill him, it will be your doing, not mine. I can't control what awful things you may do, but I can definitely refuse to run the risk of taking a life myself. Besides, if you were to die, then my dog would presumably follow."

I decided to intervene and buy us some time. "There is a simple solution to this problem. Go and see the space, Barry."

"And how am I to do that?" Zucchini asked.

"It's easy. Go to the bank tomorrow and ask to rent a safe deposit box. They'll bring you right into the vault."

"No," said Ralph. "The heist needs to happen tonight. If I leave you two alone, how do I know you won't warn the bank and the police ahead of time? Right, Susan? You're not going to screw up this job like you did the last one."

"First of all, Ralph, since you're not involving my brother this time, I don't care what you do. Second, ratting on you won't get Barry's dog back. And third, what exactly would we tell the cops? That you're going to suddenly appear inside a locked vault, steal some stuff, and then suddenly disappear with the loot? Come on."

Ralph was not completely stupid, even though some of his actions begged the question. He calculated the relative risks and agreed to a one-day postponement.

"I'll be back tomorrow night. Same time. You'd better be ready."

"Wait just a minute. How do I know my dog is even still alive?"

"I thought you might ask that. Here, have a look."

Ralph reached into his jacket pocket and pulled out a Polaroid photo of Copperfield sitting on a copy of that morning's paper.

"Satisfied?" Ralph sneered.

"Bring another photograph tomorrow. Better yet, bring the dog. I give you my word I will keep my end of the bargain."

"No way, Zucchini. I'll bring the photo, but you'll get the pooch when I've got the loot. Not before."

As he walked out, Ralph turned to me and said, "Tell Fergus I'm sorry I ain't been able to see him lately. He can swing by after this gig tomorrow night."

"I'll tell him," I said, *when hell freezes over*, I thought.

Ralph left, and I looked at Barry. "Well, we have one more day to find Copperfield. Can I have that photo?"

"I'm not sure what good this will do." He tossed me the picture.

"I don't either, but it's a clue. Anyway, let's get ready. We've got a show to do."

The next morning, Zucchini went to the bank to get a safety deposit box and check out the vault. Meanwhile, I showed the photo of the dog to Fergus, hoping it would trigger a breakthrough. It was admittedly a long shot.

A long shot that paid off handsomely.

"I recognize that purple wall color," Fergus said. "That's Aunt Martha's place."

"What?"

"Ralph's aunt Martha. I met her a few times. She lives in Hoboken, New Jersey. Wood floor, purple walls. Yeah, that's her place."

"I don't believe it," I said.

"Why would I lie to you, Susan?"

"No, Fergus, I mean that it's pretty amazing how you figured out where Mr. Zucchini's dog is by just looking at that photo."

"Oh. Yeah. It's at Aunt Martha's place."

"Do you know the address, Fergus?"

He furrowed his brow. "Um. No."

"How about her last name?"

"Oh! Oh! I do know that. It's Martha. First name Aunt, last name Martha."

This was not exactly the answer I'd been hoping for. I hoped Martha might have the same last name as Ralph, but there was no telephone listing in Hoboken for a Martha Dodgy. I got off the line with the operator and put my head in my hands.

"How come you're upset, Sis?"

"I want to recover Barry's dog, but I'm not sure where Aunt Martha lives."

"Oh! Oh! I know that. She lives in Hoboken."

"Yes, Fergus, but where in Hoboken?"

"Oh! Oh! I know that!"

"I thought you didn't know her address."

"I don't. But I know where she lives."

"You're saying you can find her place?"

"Oh! Yes! You can get there from the train station. You walk straight, then turn left at the candy store, then right at Woolworth's, then—"

"Hold that thought, Fergus. Let's go."

It cost a small fortune, but in the interest of time, we hired a cab to take us to Hoboken. Starting from the train station, Fergus gave the driver directions. We ended up at a slightly disheveled apartment complex and asked the cabbie to wait.

Martha knew Fergus, and she buzzed us in. We could hear Copperfield's yapping before we even reached her third-floor apartment. When she opened the door, the aroma of chocolate chip cookies made our mouths water.

Aunt Martha grabbed Fergus by the hand and pulled him inside. I followed.

"Fergus, it's so nice to see you! What a pleasant surprise! And who is this lovely lady with you?"

"Oh, this is my sister, Susan. Susan, this is Aunt Martha."

"Pleased to meet you, ma'am," I said.

"I just pulled some cookies out of the oven. Come and sit down."

Fergus started to move toward the table, but I put up my hand. "I don't want to be ungracious, Aunt Martha, but we have a cab waiting downstairs with the meter running. We only stopped by to pick up the dog."

"Oh, really? Ralph was here this morning, and he didn't mention anything about that."

"Just a change of plan, ma'am. The dog's owner came back from vacation early, and Ralph asked us to come over and retrieve him."

"Oh, and we were beginning to get along so well."

"Yes, and thank you so much for watching him. We'd best get moving though. I'm sorry. Next time we visit, we'll stay longer."

Aunt Martha helped us to attach Copperfield's leash, and she wrapped up some cookies for our journey. We thanked her again and headed back to the city with the dog in tow. I dropped off Fergus at the apartment and continued to the theater where I paid the driver and gave him a couple chocolate chip cookies.

Barry was thrilled to be reunited with Copperfield, who kept up a constant stream of yaps as he ran back and forth around the dressing room.

"Thank you for finding my dog, Susan. Now, my dear, what shall we do about the nefarious Mr. Dodgy?"

"We need to send him away, or he'll just keep trying to find a way to get what he wants."

"That's what I thought as well. Still, he's your brother's friend, is he not?"

"I'll deal with Fergus, but Ralph is getting more and more dangerous."

"Very well. I will take care of it."

"You won't harm him, will you?"

"Of course not. Not physically, anyway. Now please take Copperfield out of the room. Ralph will be here soon, and I don't want him to know that I have recovered my dog. Come back in an hour."

I took Copperfield for a long walk, and we relaxed in a park. When I returned to the theater, Barry informed me that we shouldn't expect to see Ralph for quite a long time, if ever again.

"Where did you send him?"

"Ah, you remember I told you about certain spaces around the world that are kept empty for popping people in and out? I sent him to one of those."

"Where, exactly?"

"It's a small village near Lake Tanganyika in Central Africa. And oh, would you mind disposing of these?" He handed me a bag. I looked inside.

"Wait. You sent him to Africa without his clothes?"

"More importantly, I sent him without his wallet. Don't worry, it's warm there, and the locals won't let him freeze or starve. I figured this was the best way to slow down his return. He has no money and no identification. I expect he'll be gone for several years at least."

I wasn't sure we'd heard the last of Ralph Dodgy, but I was pleased that he'd be away for a while.

Fergus was livid when he heard his friend had been sent to Africa, even though he understood that Ralph had stepped over a line with the puppy kidnapping. Still, he insisted that Ralph never would have harmed the dog. I wasn't so sure, but I declined to argue the point. Fergus soon got over his anger with me, but he vowed to never speak to Barry again. For the longest time, he'd quickly leave the apartment whenever my boss showed up, but his anger at Zucchini eventually passed. Fergus was a softy at heart.

Over the next few years, the show was pretty successful. We even did a few road tours, hitting smaller theaters in out-of-the-way towns across the Midwest. I thought we could have done

130

even better, and I suggested that maybe Barry should up the ante by performing more spectacular demonstrations. He wasn't interested. He said he just wanted to make a decent living and that the other true magicians around the world would be upset if he drew too much attention to himself. He told me there'd be "negative repercussions" if he became famous doing real magic. He was nervous even discussing it, and I quickly dropped the topic.

Three years after the pupnapping incident, I saw someone who looked like Ralph crossing Madison Avenue downtown. He was thinner and had a darker complexion than I remembered, but I was pretty sure it was him. He boarded a bus before I could catch up to confirm.

Barry was dismissive when I told him. "I'm sure you were mistaken, Susan. Even if it was Mr. Dodgy, I expect he's learned his lesson. We won't be hearing from him again."

The following week, my fears materialized in the form of Ralph Dodgy, who stood in my apartment doorway holding a gun in his hand and a crazed look in his eyes. Fergus had opened the door before I could stop him.

"Back up. Both of you."

"I'm glad to see you again, Ralph," said my brother. "Are you okay? I've been worried about you."

"Shut up, Fergus."

Ralph pointed the gun at me. "Where is he, Susan? He's not performing at the same theater anymore."

"Ralph, why can't you just let it go?" I asked.

"Let it go? That creep made my life hell. He sent me naked to the middle of Africa!"

"Because you kidnapped his dog and threatened to kill it if he didn't help you rob a bank!"

"The magician must die. I'm going to plug him before he sees me. The bullet will come from out of nowhere when he least expects it. I'm going to kill his dog too. NOW, WHERE IS HE, SUSAN?"

The hand holding the gun was shaking badly, and I feared for my life.

What happened next occurred very fast. Fergus lunged at Ralph, who swung the gun around and fired, hitting my brother in the shoulder. Fergus fell to the floor, and Ralph turned the gun back to me. I snapped my fingers.

Ralph disappeared.

The gun and the clothes he had been wearing dropped empty to the floor.

I rushed to my brother.

"What? How did you do that?" he asked.

... eight ... nine ... ten, I counted to myself then snapped my fingers a second time.

"Barry has been teaching me a few things," I said. "It turns out I have a knack for magic."

"Where did you send him?"

"Back to Africa. But first, I sent him five feet dweebward and left him there for ten seconds. That should have been enough to scare the living daylights out of him without killing him. Hopefully, it will convince him not to try this again."

"Dweebward?"

"It's in the fourth dimension. Sort of an alternate universe, but not really ... Oh, never mind. Let's get you to the hospital."

Thankfully, my brother's wound wasn't life-threatening. We got rid of Ralph's clothes and gun, telling the police that Ralph Dodgy had gotten into an argument with my brother and shot him, then ran away. When the police searched for him, they found the small studio where he was living, but Ralph never returned to it.

Barry was extremely upset by our close call and apologized for not taking my warning more seriously. He insisted that my quick thinking had saved his life and said he would somehow find a way to repay me. I told him not to worry about it.

We continued our show, which we now billed as "The Great Zucchini and Parsnip." We became moderately famous but not *too* famous.

Copperfield passed away in his sleep ten years later. Both Barry and I were heartbroken over it, but the poodle had a good life.

Several years later, The Great Zucchini was diagnosed with

132

stage four lung cancer. It turns out that magic can't prevent aging or disease.

Fergus and I watched over Barry as he lay in his hospital bed. The doctors had told us the end would be coming soon. Barry asked me to hand him the deck of cards on the table. He fanned them out and said, "Choose one and don't tell me what it is."

I selected the four of clubs.

"Here. Take the rest of the cards and shuffle it into the deck."

I did so.

"Now look for your card and show it to me."

I flipped through the deck.

"It's not here," I said.

"Yes, I know," he replied. "I expect it will turn up someday. Wait for it, my dear. But right now I need to be going. It has been a pleasure and a privilege to work with you, Susan."

I took his hand and tried to hold back my tears as Fergus placed his hand on my shoulder.

"Give my regards to your granddaughter," Barry said.

"I don't have a granddaughter. Or a daughter. Or a husband, now I come to think of it," I said.

"You will," said the magician.

I smiled. "Hey, you're breaking the rules. I thought future telling was off-limits."

He smiled back. "I owe you. Plus, I've never been great at following rules, Susan."

He closed his eyes. Five minutes later, he stopped breathing and the machines started beeping. Doctors and nurses rushed into the room, but there was nothing they could do.

"He never finished his card trick," said Fergus.

"It wasn't a trick, Fergus. It was a demonstration. I expect to see the four of clubs again. It's simply a matter of time. And magic."

14

Interview

Mr. Dingle pressed the intercom button on his desk. "Miss Gibbons, please send in the next applicant."

"Your final appointment just called to cancel," said Miss Gibbons, "but there's a walk-in here. I'm not sure if—"

"Send him in, please."

The door opened, and an extremely large, muscular man entered wearing a skin-tight, highly reflective suit that looked like latex but wasn't. The outfit was uniformly black except for the image of an orange wooden club on the torso. The man carried a club that appeared to be the one pictured on his chest. His face was masked.

"Ah, I see you have coronavirus protection," said Mr. Dingle. "Very good, very good. Shall I wear my mask as well?"

"As you wish," said the applicant.

Dingle opened his desk drawer and removed a cloth mask adorned with amateur drawings of bunnies. He put it on and smiled, although you couldn't see the smile on account of the bunnies.

"My daughter made this. Fifth-grade project," he said.

"Very nice," said the applicant.

"Please, take a seat." Mr. Dingle took out a pen and a form. "Well, then. Name?"

"I am Kron. Destroyer of Worlds."

The room itself seemed to tremble as he spoke, but Mr. Dingle didn't notice.

"Nice to meet you, Mr. Kron. First name?"

Kron paused. "Almighty," he said.

"Almighty. That's an unusual forename. I suppose people call you 'Al' for short?"

"No."

"Okay, Al. That's interesting. And 'Destroyer of Worlds' was your previous job title?"

"Yes."

"Company name?"

"I was employed by the Seven Harbingers of Universal Chaos. Their headquarters are in the Galaxy of Ohmigod Three."

"Can you spell that galaxy name for me, please?"

"It's like the expression 'Oh, my God' with no spaces and an 'i' instead of a 'y.'"

"Yes. Got it. Thank you. Interesting work, was it?"

Kron shrugged. "It paid the bills."

"What is your age?"

"Kron is older than your solar system but younger than the universe. I have lost track of the years, which are as inconsequential as the fleeting stars. Six billion, perhaps? Give or take a few hundred million."

"Um, okay, I'll put down '60.' That seems close enough for our purposes. I understand that you wish to apply for a job as a greeter at one of Crappie-Mart's 3,500 grocery and fishing supply outlets?"

"Yes. The one downtown, right here in your Earth city of Poughkeepsie."

"Why?"

"Why what?"

"Why are you applying for this position, Al?"

"It's embarrassing." Kron looked away.

"Tut, tut, Al. Just tell me. I need to put something down on my form."

Kron coughed. "Ah, well, I may have accidentally incinerated my home planet. Unfortunately, my island lair and all my universal possessions were on it. Not to mention six billion or so of my fellow Grocks. The Grocks who happened to be off-planet at the time were very upset with me. Since then, I cannot bring myself to destroy another world. Therefore, I am in need of money and a place to live."

136

"Ah. I'll put down 'retired' then."

"Yes. That is accurate," said Kron.

"Now, Al—"

"Call me Kron."

"Very well, Kron. Let me ask you some hypothetical questions. If you were hired, what would you say when a new customer entered the store?"

"I would say, 'Welcome to Crappie-Mart, home of edible plants and tasty skinned animals, as well as a splendid selection of equipment you may use to capture and kill defenseless aquatic creatures. Behave respectfully while you shop, or I shall introduce you to my thunder-club.'"

To emphasize this last statement, Kron lightly tapped his club on the ground. The building shook. A gaping hole in the floor appeared, and the man in the office below looked up in surprise and horror as he dusted small pieces of metal and concrete from his shoulders. A bookcase toppled over, spewing its contents across the room. Several framed photographs fell off the walls, their glass shattering into tiny pieces. A sound of gushing water suddenly emanated from the adjoining bathroom.

"Sorry," Kron said.

Mr. Dingle didn't appear to notice. He made a note. "Welcome to Crappie-Mart. Yes, excellent. Now, what would you do if you noticed a customer was shoplifting?"

"I would use my trustworthy thunder-club to pulverize the worthless being until his or her blood filled the floor and his or her bones were dust." Kron paused for a second. Mr. Dingle's frown suggested that this hadn't been the correct answer.

"Then I would obtain a mop and clean up the mess," Kron finished, and sat back, satisfied.

Mr. Dingle just stared for a moment. Finally, he said, "Um, yes, I'm sure that would be the first impulse of most of our greeters, but the *correct* answer is that you would alert the store manager, who would call the police."

Kron frowned. "That seems most inefficient."

"Yes, I understand, but can you bring yourself to do it? Instead of … instead of what you just said?"

"If that is your wish. It is your store, after all."

"Excellent. Excellent." Mr. Dingle made a note. "Now, what if a woman nearby was having a medical emergency? A heart attack, for example?"

Kron thought hard, wanting to get this one right. "I would lay my hand upon her chest and use my healing powers to repair her anatomy. Then I would ask her not to do that again, as it might upset the other customers."

"Um, you have healing powers? Are you certified, by any chance?"

Kron beamed. "I am a Class 1 Galaxial Lifeforce Provider. I completed my training on the planet Preposteron in the Proxima Hyperbole system when their primary star was still a cloud of swirling dust." Then he slumped a little. "Although to be completely honest, I haven't used my life-giving skills in several eons. My previous employment tended to focus in the other direction."

"Ah, so you are a first responder! Outstanding! One last question, Kron. When can you start?"

"I am free tomorrow."

"Excellent. Well, Mr. Kron, you're hired. My assistant will guide you through the necessary paperwork." Mr. Dingle stood and extended his hand.

Kron rose from his chair and said, "I do not clasp appendages of lesser beings."

"Ah, yes. Of course. Risk of coronavirus. Silly of me." He pushed the intercom button. "Miss Gibbons, we are extending an offer of employment to Mr. Kron. Would you be so kind as to help him with the paperwork?"

Miss Gibbons entered the office and directed Kron to an adjacent conference room. As she turned to leave, she whispered, "So the interview went well then?"

"Best candidate I've seen all week," said Mr. Dingle.

15

A Picnic on Mars

The red disc grew slowly larger in the viewing window as the spaceship converged with its orbit. Sandra Duncan couldn't pull her eyes away. *Very soon I'll be walking on that planet*, she thought. *First woman on Mars.*

The individual who was about to become the first *man* on Mars looked over her shoulder. "That's some view, isn't it? It's almost worth having to spend the last six months cooped up in this tin can, eating processed food and listening to Jerome's ancient new wave music."

"You know it's *totally* worth it, Michael. Not to mention the six-month trip back. I'd do it all again to get the chance to set foot on another planet."

Michael Summers put his finger to his lips "Shush, Sandra. Jerome might hear."

"Jerome *can* hear," came a voice from the cockpit. "Haven't we already established that sound carries unusually well in this capsule? Now I'll say it again: you don't need to dance around the topic of your surface excursion. It doesn't bother me that I'm staying in the mother ship while you prance around like idiots on the ground. Someone has to cart your sorry asses home. And for the record, new wave music is the bomb."

Michael turned to respond. "It's the bomb? What does that even mean? Is that an '80s expression, Jerry? Because that was a half-century ago. It's 2037 now. Get with the times."

Devo's "Whip It" began playing, and Michael put his hands

over his ears.

Sandra smiled. "You know it annoys him when you call him Jerry," she whispered.

"And that's why I do it," replied Michael. "I'm not oblivious."

Ares Mission Commander Michael Summers maintained a running diatribe with Jerome Freeman. It was all an act, designed to relieve the tension of living together in a confined space for such a long time. *It was mostly an act,* Sandra thought. There had been a few occasions during the trip when tempers threatened to flare, but Michael and Jerome were both consummate professionals and never let their disagreements get out of hand. *Truth be told, there were times when I had to count to ten as well.*

Plus, Sandra believed, Jerome did have a particularly tough job. To fly six months out here and six months back without an opportunity to step onto the planet must be hard. Yet *someone* had to pilot the command operations module (COM for short) when it separated from and later re-docked with the Mars excursion lander (lovingly called MEL) that would take Sandra and Michael down to the planet's surface. Jerome never complained about it though.

"It's the job," Jerome said. "There are millions of people who would give their right arm to do what I'm doing." And he was right.

Michael looked at his watch and said, "Hey, isn't it about time for your next transmission?"

Sandra nodded. She had agreed to broadcast a series of science lectures from space, targeted at children in middle school and above. There were to be seven episodes: three on the trip to Mars, one from the surface, and three on the way back. She positioned herself in front of the camera and got ready to record.

"Hello, I'm Sandra Duncan, and this is another episode of *Notes from the Red Planet*. Our spacecraft, *Ares 1*, is getting very close to Mars. It's easy to see why the Romans named this world after their god of war. The reddish color makes the planet appear angry and forbidding, but the pigmentation is simply due to the presence of iron oxide in the soil. Incidentally, NASA named this the Ares mission because Ares was the name of the Greek god of war. Personally, I think it should have been named Pax for the Roman goddess of peace, but they didn't give me a vote.

"Since we're traveling much faster than the planet, we'll need

140

to slow down to avoid passing it. In a few hours, we'll fire our retro-rockets and get into position for a stable orbit. Pretty soon after that, Michael Summers and I will get into the Mars excursion lander, which we call MEL for short, to make our way down to the planet's surface.

"We'll have only three days and two nights down there before we need to start back to Earth. You'll remember from our last episode that the distance to Mars varies a lot because Earth and Mars revolve around the sun at different speeds. Objects closer to the sun have to move faster to maintain a stable orbit. Earth speeds by Mars every six months, and the closest they come to each other is about 35 million miles. But when the two planets are on opposite sides of the sun, the distance between them is over 250 million miles. We have to make our trip back to Earth when the planets are close to one another, which is about now, since they get close every six months and it took us six months to get here. If we miss this launch window, we'll have to wait another six months for the next one. That would be unfortunate because we don't have an extra half-year's supply of food and water. Don't worry though. We won't miss it.

"MEL will drop to the surface pretty fast, so we'll need to slow down a lot to make a soft landing. We'll deploy a parachute, but that alone won't be enough because the atmosphere around Mars is pretty thin. As we get closer to the ground, Commander Summers will fire MEL's retro-rockets. They'll reduce our speed, and we'll gently set MEL down.

"Once we're on the planet, Commander Summers and I will take a little time to let our bodies get used to gravity again. Even though Mars's gravity is only about a third of Earth's, it will still take a bit of adjustment since we've been weightless for six months. Once we're acclimated, we'll do some exploring. I'm so excited for the chance to be the first woman on Mars!

"The NASA folks chose a terrific landing spot close to the base of Olympus Mons, the highest mountain in the solar system. It's three times as tall as Mount Everest, and it used to be an active volcano. Although its slope is gradual in most places, we won't be climbing to the top, unfortunately. It's way too far to walk in our spacesuits. But the mountain should make for some fantastic photos.

"My next broadcast will be from the surface of Mars. I'm

really looking forward to that one, as you might imagine. See you then! End transmission."

As usual, Michael and Jerome gave her a floating ovation when she was done.

"Oh, cut it out, guys. Stop the applause."

"But you're a star," said Jerome. "When we get back, everyone will know your face. Poor Michael and I will fade into the woodwork. No one will recognize us."

"Oh, yeah, you'll be practically invisible, I'm sure."

"I kind of wish that were true," said Michael. "I can't stand all that media attention."

"Bullshit, Michael," said Jerome. "You know you love it."

"Well," Michael admitted, "maybe a little."

The entry into Mars's orbit went smoothly. The retro-rockets fired, and the spacecraft slowed to just the right speed to allow it to circle the planet without falling in. *Ares* would complete a full revolution around Mars every ninety minutes.

After one orbit, the time came for their descent. Michael and Sandra hugged Jerome. "You won't be too lonely up here, I hope," Sandra said.

"Are you kidding me? I've been waiting for this day for six months. I get the COM all to myself. It's party time! Duran Duran at full volume!"

"That's rad," said Michael. "Just make sure you don't head home without us."

"I wouldn't think of it, dude. You still owe me a hundred bucks for that bet we made. I need to collect."

"What bet?" asked Sandra.

"Oh, nothing," replied Michael sheepishly.

"I bet that you'd refer to yourself as the first woman on Mars during one of your broadcasts. He said you wouldn't."

"Oh. So *that's* why you guys watched me do every transmission, huh?"

"No, no," said Michael. "We would have watched anyway."

142

"But it did add a little excitement," said Jerome.

"Not that your shows weren't riveting," said Michael.

"Fascinating," added Jerome.

"And educational," finished Michael.

"Enough!" laughed Sandra. "But seriously, do you think I shouldn't have said it? Was I being too vain?"

"Don't be absurd, girl," said Jerome. "You *are* going to be the first woman on Mars. You should milk it for all it's worth."

"As long as you remember whose boot hits the ground first," said Michael.

"Oh, I thought you'd be chivalrous and hold the door for me, Commander. Ladies first, right?"

"Not in this case, Sandra. We've got to follow protocol."

"Said the first man on Mars," mocked Jerome. "Anyway, I hate to break this up, but it's time you get the hell out of here. Godspeed, my friends."

After another set of hugs, Michael and Sandra climbed into the Mars excursion lander.

As he closed the hatch, Michael said, "See you in three days."

"Not if I see you first," said Jerome. He sealed MEL's door, then floated back into the COM and closed the inner hatch.

Inside MEL, the commander took his seat next to Sandra and said, "That guy always needs to have the last word."

"Speaking of words, Michael, what do you plan to say when you step onto the planet?"

"My first words will be 'Drink Pepsi.' They offered me $500,000."

"You're going to use man's first landing on another planet as an opportunity to advertise a soft drink?"

"For half a mil? You bet I am."

"You're not."

"No, don't be silly. Did you honestly think I'd sell my soul for only half a million? I could auction those rights off for a *lot* higher. I'm no dummy." Michael clicked the communications link to Earth. "Houston, this is *Ares 1*. Captain Duncan and I are in the Mars excursion lander. We are about to detach from the command operations module. Over."

"I'm not sure why you bother. At this distance from Earth, it will take them ten minutes to respond," said Sandra.

"And that's why we don't wait for orders from them unless

it's a SINE."

"A sign of what?" Sandra asked.

"No, a SINE. Like sine wave. It's an acronym for super-important non-emergency. Still, they like to be kept informed. Makes 'em feel important and all. Hey, Jerome, you there?"

"I'm here, big guy." Jerome's voice came to them clearly over the radio. "You ready to detach?"

"Ready when you are."

"Okay. Approaching the zone now. Seven minutes to detach."

"Roger that."

Seven and a half minutes later, the Mars excursion lander separated from the command operations module. When they were sufficiently far apart, MEL fired a short burst of propellant that sent them hurtling toward the planet. The descent took about forty minutes, and halfway down they lost radio contact with Jerome as the COM swung around to the opposite side of the planet.

There was some heat and buffeting due to friction with the atmosphere, but far less than they'd later experience on the descent to Earth. Michael started a running commentary to advise Earth on their progress. They'd hear it five minutes later.

"Olympus Mons sighted. The landing area will be to the south."

As they grew closer, the parachute was deployed, then a few minutes later the reverse thrusters were ignited.

"Approaching target landing area. The surface appears smooth."

"Landing gear engaged ... Now at 3,000 feet."

"Roll 20 ... Stable ... Small crater below ... Shifting to port ... Elevation 2,000 feet."

"Now 1,000 feet ... Looking good ... 500 ... 200 ... 75 feet ... Touching down."

"Houston, this is Olympus Base. MEL has landed. We have arrived safely on Mars."

Ten minutes later, the radio crackled. "Olympus Base, this is Houston. Roger your landing. There's a big celebration happening all around the world down here. Congratulations to the entire *Ares* crew. Take a moment to revel in your achievement ... Okay, guys, that's long enough. Now get back to work and perform your post-landing checklist. After that, we have you scheduled for two hours of downtime. Try to get some rest—you've got a big day ahead. As you know, a day on Mars is only slightly longer than a day on Earth. We estimate local Mars time when you receive this message to be 10:25 a.m. Your first two-hour excursion is planned for 2:00 p.m. local time. We'll give you a wake-up call at 1:00 p.m. Darkness falls at 6:10 p.m."

"Roger that, Houston. Talk to you in a few hours."

"Are you really going to be able to sleep?" Sandra asked.

"I seriously doubt it. Nevertheless, we should try to relax as much as possible. The next few days will be tiring, and we need to be at our best. First, though, let's go through the post-landing checklist."

"Roger that, Commander."

Two and a half hours later, the speakers began playing "Start Me Up" by the Rolling Stones. Jerome's voice followed with, "Wakey, wakey, guys! I'm back, and I can't say how pleased I am to find out you touched down without a hitch."

Michael wiped his eyes, surprised that he had fallen asleep after all. "Hey, Jerome. How was your swing around the planet?"

"I've done two loops while you've been getting your beauty sleep. The dark side of the planet is boring. You've seen it once, so you know. It's too dark to see anything on the surface. It's just a big black void. I did get a glimpse of Jupiter, but we're still pretty far away so it's not much bigger than it would look from Earth. I took advantage of the darkness and radio silence to get some much-needed shut-eye—without your snoring, I might add."

"I don't snore."

"Ask Sandra."

"You snore," confirmed Sandra.

"Thanks for that," said Michael. "Someone on Earth is recording these conversations for posterity."

"We just call 'em as we see 'em, man," said Jerome. "Enjoy the rest of your day."

"You too, Jerome."

An hour later, the two astronauts were ready to make history by becoming the first humans to walk on Mars. As previously determined, the mission commander was the first to step out of MEL. He abandoned the potential for millions in advertising fees by saying, as his foot touched the Martian dirt, "Imagination and courage brought us here. With such guides at our side, there is no place we cannot go."

For her part, Sandra said as she stepped off the ladder, "Mars, we bring you greetings and peace from your neighbor, planet Earth."

Sandra stepped away from MEL and beheld her surroundings. *If NASA had been searching for the most photogenic spot on the planet, they chose well*, she thought. The surface was an alien desert with a reddish complexion, the horizon dominated by Olympus Mons, which towered skyward for nearly fourteen miles. They were too close to see it in perspective, of course. It had a diameter of 370 miles, roughly the width of France. Most of the volcano had a mild incline of about five degrees, as she had mentioned on her broadcast. What she'd neglected to say was that its southern edge was a sheer cliff rising as high as five miles from the Martian surface. *Minor detail*, Sandra thought. *I'll discuss it on my next transmission.*

They'd landed about four miles south of the mountain's edge and the cliffs towered above them. Sandra laughed at the thought of someone even attempting to climb Olympus Mons from this vantage point. There was a far more gradual approach on the southwest side, without any cliffs to scale. In fact, a person approaching it from that direction might not even realize they were climbing a mountain. Yet it would take a week or more to walk to the summit, and scientists believed that the surface was covered with a thick layer of dust which might make progress difficult.

Noticing an odd shadow on one of the cliff walls, Sandra pointed it out to Michael. After some discussion, they decided to send a drone camera to the location for a better view. They prepared the drone for takeoff and would launch it when they were back inside MEL. In the meantime, they had plenty of work to do: collecting rock and soil samples, taking a slew of pictures, and setting up equipment to monitor radiation, atmospheric conditions, and seismic activity. The two hours slated for their walkabout passed quickly, and both astronauts were reluctant to return to MEL when it was over.

Once they were safely back inside, Michael sat down and reached for the drone controls. The small aircraft lifted off, and Michael sent it speeding toward the wall of Olympus Mons. Video from the drone appeared on MEL's monitor and was simultaneously streamed back to Earth.

It took about six minutes for the drone to cover the four miles between MEL and the cliff. As it got closer to its objective, Michael and Sandra became more excited.

"There's no reason for a shadow to be there," Michael said. "There's nothing nearby to cast it."

"That's because it's not a shadow. It's a cave," said Sandra.

"I think you might be right," said Michael as he stared at the image. "It could be a lava tube."

Olympus Mons used to be an active volcano, and some scientists speculated it might become active again in the future. Lava tubes can form when the lava near the top cools and hardens, leaving the molten magma below to keep moving below the surface. If the 'upstream lava suddenly starts moving in a different direction, the magma inside the tube can drain out, leaving an empty cave.

As the drone neared the target, Michael slowed it down and scanned the cliff face. The shadow was clearly a cave.

"Well spotted, Sandra. This is awesome."

"You know we have to go out there and check it out, right?"

"Um, I'm not sure about that. It's a long walk, and the cave is a hundred feet or so up from the base of the cliff. It might be too risky. Not to mention that it's not in the schedule."

"Screw the schedule, Michael. Caves could be a possible harbor for bacterial life. There might still be evidence of heat-seeking bacteria on the cave walls or floor. Think of it—we could confirm the existence of life on Mars!"

"Yeah, I see your point, but this is one of those SINEs I mentioned earlier. A super-important non-emergency. We need Houston to weigh in on it."

"They'll debate it for a day and a half and then tell us it's too dangerous," moaned Sandra.

"In which case, we won't go. There'll be other missions.

147

Anyway, I'll transmit the suggestion. Maybe we'll get lucky. Right now, let's use the drone to identify the best approach to the cave in case they give us a green light."

They spent the next hour scanning the cave and the surrounding cliff wall. The drone found a narrow ledge leading to the entrance that might be climbable, assuming it was solid enough. When they'd seen as much as they could, Michael flew the drone back to MEL and radioed Houston with a request to do a manned exploration.

Ten minutes later the intercom blared, "Olympus Base, Houston here. Thanks for the video feed from the drone. We're analyzing it now, and we'll get back to you with a response to your request for a manned investigation. In the meantime, please keep to the existing schedule of activities. Night will be falling in about an hour. It's going to be a cold one, guys, so bundle up. We'll check in with you again at 5:00 a.m. Mars time."

Night on Mars fell suddenly because, unlike Earth, the thin atmosphere didn't disperse light. As soon as the sun dropped below the horizon it became pitch-black outside, and because the atmosphere lacked much capability to store heat the temperature quickly plummeted from over sixty degrees Fahrenheit to minus one hundred.

Sandra noted the temperature and looked out the capsule window. Just above the horizon, she could see Phobos, the larger of Mars's two moons, which was much dimmer than Earth's moon. Sandra couldn't see the other one, Deimos. Since it was only eight miles wide, she figured it would be nearly impossible to spot with the naked eye.

"I can see why NASA didn't schedule any moonlight walks for us," Sandra said.

"Yeah, night on Mars is no picnic, that's for sure."

"Do you think people will colonize this planet someday?"

"Oh, it'll happen, yeah. They'll eventually build a permanent outpost, but it'll have to be continually supplied from Earth, so it'll be extremely expensive."

"What about the idea of terraforming?"

"Whether we can terraform this planet to make it suitable for terrestrial life is an interesting question. It would likely take thousands of years, even if we had the technology—which we currently don't, despite all the theorizing that goes on about it."

148

Sandra considered this, then asked, "Have you ever read Kim Stanley Robinson's novel, *Red Mars*?"

"Of course. It's brilliant. I also read the sequels, *Green Mars* and *Blue Mars*. The first book was the best, I thought."

"I must admit that after viewing Mars in all its glory earlier, the idea of transforming it into some kind of alternate Earth smacks of hubris, if not lunacy."

"Yeah, but two hundred years ago, someone seriously suggesting that man would walk upon Mars would have been committed to an asylum," said Michael.

"True. You up for a game of chess? I brought my miniature magnetic board."

"You're on. No betting this time, Sandra. I only gamble when I have a chance of winning."

After the game, Sandra recorded another episode of *Notes from the Red Planet*. She described how exciting it was to touch down on the surface with MEL, and even more so to set her foot upon the Martian soil. She explained the workings of some of the equipment they set up outside and why these measurements mattered to planetary scientists. She talked about Olympus Mons and its steep cliffs. She discussed the drone flight and the cave, but Michael nodded with satisfaction when she diplomatically refrained from mentioning their request for permission to visit it. NASA definitely wouldn't have taken kindly to that.

When it was over, Jerome radioed in his approval, and he and Michael applauded.

It was their first night on Mars, and time for bed.

At 5:00 a.m., the astronauts woke up to the sound of "Spaceman" by Harry Nilsson.

"Oh, Lordy, where'd you dig that song up from, Houston?" Michael asked.

Ten minutes later: "It was a recommendation from your buddy Jerome."

"Of course it was," mumbled Michael.

"I'm afraid we've got some bad news and some worse news for you," the transmission continued. "Which do you want first, Commander?" There was a slight pause. "Belay that. I'm advised we can't wait ten minutes for you to answer that question. I'll give you the bad news first. Your request to visit the cave is declined. Repeat, do not attempt to visit the cave. It was determined to be not worth the risk. I'll give you ten seconds to confirm before I continue."

"Shit," said Sandra.

"Not unexpected," replied Michael. He clicked the microphone and said, "Olympus Base confirms, Houston. No Martian spelunking. Over."

In a moment the transmission continued. "Okay, Olympus Base, I assume you confirmed that. Now here's the worse news. There's a sandstorm headed your way. ETA 2:00 p.m. local Martian time. Wind speeds of up to fifty miles per hour. We recommend you batten down the hatches and protect the external equipment as best you can. It will probably last about three hours, assuming no changes to its trajectory and size."

Now it was Michael's turn to say, "Shit." He depressed the mike button. "Roger that, Houston. We will prepare for the storm. Over."

"Should we be worried?" asked Sandra.

"Worried? No, not particularly. It's mainly a nuisance. It means we have to cut back the schedule. No wonder they denied the cave excursion."

"Fifty-mile-an-hour winds sound pretty bad."

"Yeah, but thanks to Mars' thin atmosphere, the winds don't carry much force. The storm will blow dust everywhere and it may disrupt communications for a few hours, but it shouldn't cause much actual damage as long as we secure the equipment."

An hour later, the sun was up, and the astronauts were ready to do another surface excursion. They went outside and completed the scheduled morning tasks, then covered the surface equipment with tarps and staked the ends into the ground. They brought some of the more sensitive electronics back into MEL, including the drone. After checking in with Houston, they relaxed and waited for the storm.

"*Ares* COM to Olympus Base. You there, Michael?"

"Roger that, Jerome. Go ahead."

"Hey, I've got some more bad news for you, buddy. I've been visually tracking the storm from up here, and I've detected some lightning flashes. You'd better power down whatever you can until it passes."

"Roger that, Jerome. Thanks." Michael started flipping some switches.

"I didn't even know Mars *had* lightning," said Sandra.

"It's pretty rare, and the energy levels are much lower than in lightning strikes on Earth. Still, I imagine a direct hit could do some damage to our circuitry."

"What can we do about that?"

"Just pray it doesn't hit us."

When the storm came, the dust flew everywhere. They could no longer see out the viewing window. MEL shook slightly, but Michael was right. The force was pretty low—nowhere near the strength needed to do any real damage or tip MEL over. They listened for thunder but didn't hear anything apart from the sound of sand particles hitting the spacecraft.

Thirty minutes in, they lost radio contact.

Two hours in, they were jolted by a loud cracking sound, and the cabin lights went out.

"Oh shit," said Michael. "That was a lightning strike. We've been hit."

"Michael! What's that smell?"

"Electrical fire! Help me find the source!" Michael grabbed the extinguisher and started ripping off panels.

"Here! It's over here!" Sandra called out. "I see smoke!" They removed the cover panel, releasing a black vapor from melting wiring, but thankfully there were no flames. Michael sprayed the area and the smoking stopped.

"That was a close call," said Michael. "Be on the lookout for other issues. We should advise Houston."

"Still no signal. We'll have to wait until the dust settles. Wow, I can't believe I just said that. Anyway, what's the damage look like?"

"It will take a while to figure it out. Hand me the emergency manual and help me work through the checklist."

It took several hours to assess the situation, by which time the storm had passed.

Michael was lying on MEL's floor, examining an open panel box. "Well, that's it. The wiring from the main fuel cell is fried. I'll have to repair or replace it. We can't ignite the burners for lift-off without it. Is the radio working yet? I'll want Houston's advice on this."

Sandra picked up the microphone. "Houston, this is Olympus Base. MEL was struck by lightning during the storm, and it damaged the wiring from the main fuel cell. We are assessing options for repair and replacement and request your advice. Over."

They sat back to wait ten minutes for the reply but only a few seconds passed before they heard, "Olympus Base, this is *Ares* COM. Are you okay?"

"Yes, Jerome, thanks. We're fine. Unfortunately, some of the wiring is in bad shape."

Jerome and Michael discussed the problem for several minutes until the Houston controller broke into their conversation. "Olympus Base, this is Houston. We received your report of electrical damage. Please provide all relevant facts and your diagnosis, and signal to us when you are done. We will then analyze the situation and get back to you with further questions and our thoughts on next steps. Over."

Knowing Houston was in the loop, Michael provided all the data he had on their status. He signaled when he was finished, and they sat back to wait for Houston's response.

Ten minutes later they received an acknowledgment that Houston had received the information and was working on it.

An hour after that they were still waiting.

"Shouldn't we request a status update?" asked Sandra.

"There's no point," replied Michael. "They know we're waiting. When they have something to say, they'll contact us."

It took another forty-five minutes.

"Olympus Base, this is Houston. Grab a pen and paper, guys.

152

This will be a long message."

There was a pause, presumably to allow them to get something to write on—as if they hadn't been ready two hours ago.

"Okay, Olympus, we recommend you replace the faulty wiring from the fuel cell."

With what? Sandra wondered. They didn't have nearly enough spare wire.

"We know you don't have sufficient wiring in your repair supplies to do this. You will have to salvage wiring that is being used for nonessential systems. We believe you will have enough to complete the job. What follows is a detailed list of the location of such wiring and instructions for retrieving it."

Oh, great, Sandra thought, *and what about the fact that most or all of these wires will be of lower gauge than the main fuel cell cables?*

"We are aware that the wire you will be using is a lower gauge. We believe it will still be sufficient to trigger ignition. You will need to stand by with your fire extinguisher to ensure that the wiring does not flame out afterward."

Holy crap, Sandra thought. She glanced at Michael, who was playing it remarkably cool under the circumstances.

"Okay, Olympus Base, get ready. Here are the details."

The message droned on for another twenty minutes. Michael and Sandra scribbled furiously as if their lives depended on it. Because they did.

They worked through the night, stripping wire, soldering, twirling the strands together, and wrapping them in duct tape. It was cramped, feverish work, but they kept at it. They had no time to despair. Not if they wanted to survive.

Jerome called in periodically to check their status and offer encouragement. Not too often, though, as he didn't want to slow them down. The lift-off was scheduled for 11:00 a.m. Mars time. Failing that, they would have subsequent launch windows every ninety minutes, which was based on how long it took the

153

command operations module to circle the planet and get into position for an intercept.

But at some point, Sandra knew, Jerome would be ordered to leave orbit without them. If he waited too long, the orbits of Mars and Earth would diverge too much, and the command operations module would be unable to get back home.

Sandra wasn't sure how much cushion for possible delays had been built into the flight plan. One day? Two? It couldn't be much, she knew. Every day that passed added another million miles to their trip home, which meant they'd need to burn more fuel, and they were carrying a limited amount. Michael probably knew the answer, and Houston definitely did, but so far they weren't volunteering that information. Sandra figured it would be premature and defeatist to ask. It was what it was. One crisis at a time.

So they worked on, until it was finally done with thirty minutes left to spare. After completing the preflight checks, Michael readied himself at the lander controls with Sandra next to him holding the fire extinguisher in her lap. They'd want to put out any flames before they reached zero-G because a fire in a weightless environment is a hellish thing.

They prepared for the final countdown and held their breath.

3 ... 2 ... 1 ... Ignition. Michael pushed the button.

There was a loud "pop," and the replaced wiring split open and burst into flames. Nothing else happened. Sandra extinguished the fire quickly, but they could both tell it was game over.

Michael relayed the news to Houston and the command operations module. There was a pregnant silence, then Jerome said, "That's all right, guys. Just try again. I'll be back around in ninety minutes."

Sandra and Michael examined the burned wiring. It was beyond repair. Sandra looked at Michael and said, "There's not going to be a plan B, is there?"

"No. I don't think so, Sandra. I'm so sorry."

Houston sent another message a few minutes later, saying they were sorry to hear that their first solution hadn't worked. They would revert shortly with further thoughts.

An hour later, Houston confirmed there was no more wiring available to strip out. Everything still left was essential for the flight back into orbit and docking with the command operations module. They insisted that their best minds were working on the problem, but Sandra could tell from the controller's voice that they were out of ideas. Right now, she figured, the head honchos at NASA were debating how soon to instruct the COM to leave Mars without them. They'd want to wait as long as reasonably possible, to make it seem as if they were doing everything they could to rescue the two brave astronauts on the surface. Sandra knew there was no possibility of a real rescue, though. If Michael and she couldn't get this thing off the ground, they were dead.

Sandra had been watching Michael's face, which was beginning to show signs of despair. Suddenly she said, "Let's go to the cave."

"What? Now? Are you serious?" he asked.

"Do you have any hope at all that Houston is going to find a way to fix this?"

"No. Not really."

"Nor do I. So instead of sitting here waiting for a solution that doesn't exist, let's do something useful. Let's explore the cave and see if we can find any indications of life on Mars. I don't know about you, but for me, a discovery like that would make this trip worthwhile, regardless of whether we get home."

Michael thought about it. "That's a crazy idea," he said. "It's an awesome, crazy idea. Let's suit up." Just before they were ready to leave, he picked up the microphone. "Houston, this is Olympus Base. While we wait for your response, we've decided to make an excursion to the cave. We will be back in several hours and will contact you immediately upon our return. Olympus Base out."

Sandra was glad the COM was currently out of communication range on the other side of the planet. She didn't want to hear Jerome tell them what uncooperative morons they were being. They exited MEL before Houston could order them to stop.

155

Although the atmosphere was still hazy with dust from the storm, there was plenty of light to see by, and the walk to the base of the cliff was fairly easy. They had to circumvent a few small craters but none of them presented any difficulty. They found the ledge that they had seen on the drone footage and carefully began to climb to the cave entrance, now clearly visible.

It took some effort. Sandra almost lost her footing at one point, but Michael had been quick to steady her. A tumble here could result in a ruptured suit, which would be disastrous. They arrived at the cave door without further incident.

It was dark inside the cavern and they turned on the flashlights built into their helmets. Sandra walked to one of the cave walls and chipped off some samples. "There are some small striations in the rock that could be due to microorganism activity. This could be important. I just wish we could get this sample back to Earth."

"Holy shit," said Michael. "Am I going crazy? Tell me I'm not. Or tell me I am because I don't know which is better."

"What are you going on ab—Oh my God, Michael! Is this some kind of joke? Did you bring that thing with you?"

"You know I didn't. How could I hide *that* from you on the long walk out here? It was just *sitting there*."

They both stared at the picnic basket.

The basket that could not possibly be there.

In a cave.

On Mars.

"Open it," Sandra said.

"You open it," Michael said.

"You're the commanding officer."

"And I command you to open it."

"Michael!"

Sandra watched as Michael approached the picnic basket and slowly lifted the lid, ready to jump back if necessary. She knew it was impossible for anything to be alive inside the basket, but she also knew it was impossible for the basket to be there at all— so what did *she* know about what was possible?

When it was open, Michael stared at the contents. "No ... frigging ... way."

Sandra stepped forward, and they both looked down.

Inside the basket were two letter-sized envelopes. Underneath the envelopes were several coils of high-gauge wire.

"We've gone insane," Michael said. "That's the only logical explanation."

"And we're both having the same delusion?"

"Must be."

"Well, hell, Michael, let's pick up the basket and see if our mutual delusion can get us off this goddamn planet before NASA decides to send our ride home without us."

Michael closed the top of the basket. He picked it up by its convenient carrying handle, and they began the walk back to MEL.

"How on earth are we going to explain this?" Michael asked.

"We can't say anything about it. They're going to say we're crazy. No one will believe this. Hell, *I* don't believe this."

"Then how do we explain where the cable came from?" he asked.

"We say we found it stuffed behind one of the access panels. We don't know how it got there."

"How do we explain the envelopes?"

"We don't. We examine them when we get off this planet and try to figure out what it all means."

"How do we explain the picnic basket?" he continued.

"We don't. We leave it outside MEL and forget we ever found it. I don't want to go straight to an insane asylum when we return to Earth. Do you?"

When they got back to MEL, they contacted Houston and indicated that the cave visit had been successful and that they were carrying samples that might indicate the past existence of microbial life on the planet. More importantly, on a second search of MEL, they found some spare high-gauge wire behind one of the access panels. They were connecting it now.

Ten minutes later the speakers transmitted, "Olympus Base, I was instructed to give you hell for making that unapproved excursion, but after hearing your message, I don't have the heart. Congratulations on your find at the cave. Hopefully, the samples will confirm your assumption. Moreover, we are extremely excited and frankly a little confused about your discovery of the high-gauge wire. No one down here was aware that it was on board, but we are sure glad that you found it. If possible, please depart Mars at the next blast window, which should be twenty-five minutes from the time you receive this message. Over."

Michael laughed. "You can bet they're going bonkers down there right now, trying to figure out how that wire got on board." He connected the new wires.

When the COM returned to their side of the planet, Jerome was overjoyed to hear the news. The replacement cable worked like a charm, and MEL blasted off without incident. Once they were in orbit and waiting to intersect with COM, Sandra picked up the two envelopes.

"You won't believe this, Michael. This letter is addressed to both of us, by name."

"You're right. I don't believe it. What's it say?"

"It says, 'Please forgive the use of a picnic basket. It's all I had handy at the time. I hope I purchased the right kind of wire. Congratulations on your success and have a pleasant journey home. Z.'"

"Z? Who the hell is Z?"

"I haven't a clue. The other letter is addressed to ... Susan Parsnip! Oh, my God!"

"What? What's the matter? Who's Susan Parsnip?" asked Michael.

"She's my ninety-three-year-old maternal grandmother. Parsnip is her maiden name. This just gets weirder and weirder. Should I open it?"

"Hell, no, you shouldn't open it! It's addressed to your grandmother, and this Z person just saved both our lives. You will deliver this letter in person to your grandmother, and I want to be there when you do. If that's okay with you, I mean."

Six and a half months later, Sandra and Michael sat at Susan Parsnip's dining room table and enjoyed a cup of tea and a slice of chocolate cake. They told Susan the story of the picnic basket and handed over the envelope.

Susan took a letter opener from the side table and inserted it into the fold with a shaky hand. She opened the envelope and removed a slip of paper.

"My dear Susan," she read aloud, "I hope you are well and that life has treated you with the respect you so greatly deserve. I know you have a wonderful granddaughter at least. First woman on Mars! Isn't that something? Anyway, I think you will agree that we are officially even now. My best wishes for your life and afterlife. Always remember: magic is real. Yours truly, Barry."

As she finished reading, Susan noticed there was something else in the envelope.

It was a playing card.

The four of clubs.

"Grandma? I hope you have an explanation for this," said Sandra. "Michael and I have been debating whether to seek psychiatric treatment."

Susan smiled, looked at her granddaughter and her friend, and began to tell her story.

"I first met 'The Great Zucchini' in 1965, following one of his late-night shows in Harlem. After being sawn in half and put back together, his assistant ran screaming from the theater ..."

159

16

Old Hand Game

In May of 1972, Samuel P. Rockefeller was watching the Mets lose another ball game when the telephone rang authoritatively. He briefly considered ignoring it but his many years of experience as a spy compelled him to answer the call. *Maybe this is a national emergency*, he thought. *Perhaps they need me back in the field.*

Sam had recently retired from a national security agency so secret it didn't even have initials. Only the president and the highest echelon of his advisors knew the agency's name and that it existed at all.

Sam put down his can of Pabst Blue Ribbon and extracted himself from the La-Z-Boy recliner, which he considered to be the second-best investment he had ever made. His best investment was currently displaying a Pep Boys Auto Parts commercial.

Sam Rockefeller had never been particularly gifted at financial transactions, a fact his ex-wife and her lawyer frequently bemoaned. As it happened, they didn't know the half of it, which suited Sam just fine.

He picked up the receiver. "Yeah? This is Sam. Make it good, I'm in an important meeting right now."

A familiar voice on the other end replied, "Is that right? And would the other participants in this meeting happen to be Dr. Pabst and Professor La-Z-Boy?"

"You know me far too well, Roger."

"Yeah, either that or else you failed to find at least one of the spy cameras we placed in your apartment."

"Another one? Damn it. I knew I should've checked behind the crack in the crown molding."

"Don't worry. You can disable it after this call if you like. We have more. Anyway, Rock, I'm phoning to inform you about a little job we'd like you to do."

Sam Rockefeller despised the nickname "Rock," but he'd given up trying to get people to stop using it decades ago. It was a natural fit, given his last name and muscular build. And in the case of some jerks, like this guy, telling them he disliked it would just encourage them to use it even more.

"Um, you know I'm retired, right? Can I refer you to the second paragraph, first sentence above?"

"I know, I know, Rock. But guess what? Your retirement doesn't mean shit to the agency. Check your exit contract. If we have an assignment for you which is, and I quote, 'in the national interest,' unquote, you're *required* to come back and get the job done."

"Yeah, and what if I say no?"

"Well, as I read this contract, which just happens to be sitting in front of me, paragraph 73 says, 'Refusal to serve your country when asked can result in revocation of your government pension and other retirement benefits.' I'm guessing that would be a bad thing for you. Am I right?"

"Why can't some younger agent handle this?"

"We need an old hand on this job, Rock. Someone with plenty of experience. You were requested for this job specifically, by the chief himself. He said this assignment was in the national interest and so you couldn't refuse."

"Crap. What's the job?"

"A simple termination. You've done dozens of these, Rock. Execute this assignment with extreme prejudice."

An assassination, thought Sam. *Goddamn it.*

"Who's the target?"

"You've clearly been away too long, Rock. Even if I knew who it was, which I don't, I couldn't disclose the name over an unsecured phone line. Just check your mailbox as soon as you hang up the phone. You'll be compensated for your time and expenses at the standard rate, plus a $10,000 bonus payable when the job is completed. Check with Laurie and she'll make travel arrangements and get you whatever supplies you need. It was great talking with you, Rock. You know where to find me if you need anything."

"Yeah, Roger, thanks for calling. And let me tell you just how pleased I am to be serving my country again after all the goddamn crap you put me through before I left—"

The phone line went dead.

Roger Roshambo always had been an asshole, Sam thought as he walked to the mailbox. Inside was a plain manila envelope. He ripped it open and removed an eight-by-ten black-and-white photograph, on the back of which were the target's name, aliases, known addresses, places frequently visited, a deadline for completion, and other relevant data. The top of the page was marked, "Memorize and Destroy."

Before reading the details, Sam turned the page over and looked at the photograph.

"Oh, shit," he said.

Halfway around the world, Yvonne LePapier entered the La Cave bar in the Montparnasse section of Paris and made her way to the back room where two guards checked her credentials and allowed her to enter. A small, mustached man was sitting at the only table with an open bottle of wine and two glasses. He nodded as she entered and poured the wine.

"*Bonsoir, ma cherie*," he said.

"*Bonsoir, monsieur*." She smiled as she took her seat.

"Shall we speak English? I'm making a trip to Orlando with the family next week, and I need to practice."

"Yes, of course. As you wish."

"Also, I asked for guards who don't know English. They are hard to find. Everyone seems to speak this ugly language nowadays. Not that I think these men would risk their jobs by listening in, mind you."

"Why all the secrecy tonight, Henri?"

"I have a confidential assignment for you, my dear. A job requiring finesse, discretion, and the use of your special skills."

An assassination, Yvonne thought. *Interesting.* She took a sip of the burgundy.

Henri was not in any particular rush, and they worked through the bottle of wine slowly, discussing the current politics within the SDECE.

The Service de Documentation Extérieure et de Contre-Espionnage was the French equivalent of the CIA. It had a somewhat checkered history, particularly during the presidency of Charles de Gaulle when it became embroiled in a series of scandals including the kidnapping of a left-wing Moroccan on the streets of Paris. They turned him over to the Moroccan government, which subsequently tortured and killed him. Two years ago, President Georges Pompidou appointed Count Alexandre de Marenches to head the agency, charging him to clean it up. De Marenches proved to be extremely competent and reduced the staff of the SDECE by fifty percent, refocusing it on intelligence gathering and away from political intrigues and assassinations.

But apparently, some assassinations are still okay, LePapier thought.

When the bottle was empty, Henri stood and offered his hand.

"It was lovely to see you again, my dear."

They shook. "Same here, Henri."

He reached down into his briefcase and pulled out a sealed manila folder, which he handed to her. "Even I do not know the contents of this envelope, my dear. Please open it after I have left the room. I will direct the guards to wait ten minutes so you are not disturbed, then they shall depart. I hope to see you again soon."

"*Au revoir, Henri.* Enjoy your visit to Disney World. I've heard it's fabulous. I have some friends who attended the grand opening last year."

"I did not say I was going to Disney World."

"But you are, aren't you? Young Marie and Phillipe would surely raise havoc if you didn't."

"*Oui, oui. C'est vrai, bien sur. Bonne nuit, Yvonne.* It has been a pleasure."

After Henri had gone, Yvonne ripped open the envelope and

stared at the photo inside.

"*Merde*," she said. After reading the information on the back, she used the candle on the table to set the document aflame. When it was reduced to ash, she finished her glass of wine and left the room.

Sergei Nozhnitsy enjoyed his job at the KGB. He particularly liked to see the look on people's faces when he told them where he worked. Unfortunately, he often had to go undercover and hide this information, posing instead as an accountant or a mineworker or some such menial. *Bah*, he thought. *How can people do such work? Give me a job where I hold people's lives within my control. Give me employment that causes powerful men to grow weak with fear and headstrong women to become obedient and submissive. Long live the KGB!*

Sergei's coworkers had nicknamed him "the scissors" for several reasons, not least of which was his surname "Nozhnitsy," which means "scissors." But he was also highly proficient with sharpened weapons of any kind, from sickles to swords, rapiers to razors, daggers to darts, and scimitars to scissors. Moreover, in his younger days, he was a skilled practitioner of martial arts. His flying-scissors kick—performed by leaping into the air and simultaneously striking the victim in the chest with one of his legs while the other leg bashed into the back of their knees—was particularly effective in bringing down an opponent. Truth be told, now that Sergei was in his mid-fifties, he hadn't been practicing his martial arts moves as much as he used to. Still, you wouldn't want to meet him in a darkened alleyway—or anywhere, for that matter, especially if you happened to be his current assignment.

On a fine, clear morning in May, unusually pleasant for Moscow, Sergei walked along Arbat Street, thankful that the muddy slush from the last few months had finally disappeared. There was a special Russian word for it: *slyakot*. The gunky mixture was a pedestrian nightmare that reappeared in Moscow at the end of each winter. It took forever to melt, and when it finally did, the dirty water had nowhere to go since most of Moscow's streets lacked adequate drainage. Omnipresent potholes could cause a person to find their leg submerged halfway up the tibia without warning.

Although KGB headquarters were located in the Lubyanka Building (the basement of which was the site of the dreaded Lubyanka Prison), Sergei felt fortunate to have an office in the Ministry of Foreign Affairs, a short walk from Arbat Street. Part of his duties involved keeping an eye on the diplomatic corps, particularly those comrades who had travel privileges to Western countries. He had foiled several defection attempts and two large smuggling schemes.

Some illegal trade was allowed, of course—it was one of the perks of a diplomatic job—but if a comrade became too greedy, the KGB was liable to step in. In practice, there was a certain amount of leeway in determining exactly where the line was drawn. Senior diplomats were allowed more discretion to enjoy illicit profits, but the threshold for acceptable graft could fluctuate based upon one's political standing. A diplomat who fell out of favor with the Kremlin could suddenly find that behavior once countenanced was now deemed anti-Soviet, earning him a one-way ticket to Siberia. The most intelligent comrades avoided going too far afield of the standards of acceptable corruption, knowing that doing so could come back and bite them later.

The Ministry of Foreign Affairs was located in one of the "seven sisters" buildings. Designed in the Stalinist style, these looming skyscrapers were built between 1947 and 1953 and were dotted around the city, intended to serve as highly visible reminders of the majesty of the USSR. The Moscow State University building was the tallest, at 240 meters. Two of the other sisters were hotels, and the remaining three were used for a combination of residential and office space.

Sergei's official title at the ministry was Director of Security and Special Projects, but pretty much everyone knew he was KGB. Breezing past the queue of people waiting to be frisked, interrogated, frisked again, and hopefully granted permission to enter the building, he gave a curt nod to the soldiers guarding the main doorway. They knew him on sight and would not contemplate questioning him, much less frisking him. He rode the elevator to the twenty-fifth floor, silently hoping that one of

166

the frequent power outages didn't interrupt his ride.

He unlocked his office door to find a note on the desk that read, "New Assignment." Another KGB operative had been sent here last night. Sergei walked over to the wall safe, dialed the combination, and opened it. Inside was a sealed manila envelope with a small X drawn in one of the corners.

An assassination, Sergei thought. *About time.*

He ripped it open and stared at the photograph inside.

"*Nyet. Nyet. Nyet.*" Sergei shook his head and spit into the trash receptacle.

Returning to his desk, he opened the bottom drawer from which he removed a glass and a bottle of Stolichnaya. He opened the vodka and poured himself a hefty shot, draining it quickly and slamming the glass down on the desktop.

"Der'mo[1]," he said.

Three days later, Yvonne LePapier received a telegram that read, "Looking forward to visiting Aunt Marie and Uncle Pierre at their home in Lyon. Has it really been four years since we last met? Dress appropriately and bring no gifts. Rupert."

Yvonne took out her cigarette lighter and set fire to the paper, dropping it in the ashtray when the flame approached her fingers. The message was a request for a meeting at a safe house near Dijon four days from now at the usual hour of 3:00 a.m. "Dress appropriately" indicated she should be especially careful not to be tailed. "Bring no gifts" meant to come unarmed.

Fat chance under the circumstances, she thought. Still, it was a point of honor within the spy community that a mutually designated safe house was a place where all who entered were protected from harm. She had no intention of using her concealed weapon unless someone else made the first move, in which case she hoped she'd be fast enough to avoid a sudden death.

Four days later, Yvonne cautiously approached the remote cabin in the woods outside Dijon. Even though she had been

---

[1] Crap.

friends with these two men for over twenty-five years, her recent assignment had thrown their relationship into question, and she couldn't afford to take any chances. If the others had heard any whispers about her assignment, they'd be feeling the same insecurity. All three of them would have to be extremely careful not to make any sudden movements tonight.

She gave the usual secret knock at the door and a voice said, "Enter."

Rock and Sergei were sitting at opposite ends of the table with their hands placed flat on the top.

This is bad, Yvonne thought. Making sure her hands were clearly visible as she approached her chair between them, she sat down and put her hands flat on the table as well.

"Hello, Yvonne," said Rock pleasantly.

"Good evening," said Sergei with a slight, formal bow.

Yvonne forced a smile she hoped looked genuine. "Gentlemen. It's nice to see you both again."

"Who are you trying to kid, Yvonne? You could cut the tension in this room with a knife," said Sergei.

"Yes," said Rock, "and you know all about knives, Sergei, as we've come to respect. Well, I called for this meeting, and so I will begin. First, though, can we all agree that no violence will take place tonight, no matter what information is disclosed?"

"*Oui, d'accord,*" said Yvonne.

"*Da, soglasovano,*" said Sergei.

"Me too. Okay then. I recently received a disturbing assignment, and I'm wondering whether the two of you were charged with a similar task. I am now—very slowly—going to reach for a piece of paper with my left hand."

"Understood," said Yvonne.

"Proceed," said Sergei.

They both watched him like hawks. Using two fingers, Rock carefully removed a paper from his inside jacket pocket, unfolded it, and placed it upon the table.

It was a photograph of Sergei.

"Shit!" exclaimed Sergei.

"*Ooh, la,*" exhaled Yvonne.

Yvonne watched carefully, but Sergei made no sudden movement. It was almost as if he had expected this.

"Alright," said Yvonne. "I will go next. I have been instructed to terminate you, Rock."

Rock simply nodded. He and Yvonne looked at Sergei.

"Da. Da," Sergei said, leaning back slowly. "I've been ordered to kill you as well, Yvonne. No offense."

"None taken," said Yvonne.

The three spies stared at each other for a few moments.

"I have reason to believe that these simultaneous assignments are not due to coincidence," said Rock.

"Oh, you think?" said Sergei.

"Even if that's true, what do we do about it?" asked Yvonne. "I've never refused an assignment, and I'm not sure what would happen if I tried."

"I have never refused either," offered Sergei, "but unfortunately I *do* know what would happen."

"Nor I," said Rock, "although technically, I'm retired now."

Sergei snorted. "Ha! You haven't been retired, Rock, but you certainly will be if you decline your assignment. I'm familiar with how your initial-less agency operates, and it's the same as the KGB. We are simply more open about it."

"Why do you think this is happening, Rock?" asked Yvonne.

"I suspect that none of these three assignments have official backing from our respective agencies. They were manufactured and slipped to us by someone who wishes us to kill each other until there is only one of us left."

"Why?" asked Yvonne. But she already knew the answer.

"Someone found out about the gold, of course," said Sergei. "They don't wish to fight all of us at once, so they thought they'd have us do the difficult work for them. Two of us will die. Then they'll approach the last man standing—"

"Or woman," added Yvonne.

"Or woman," agreed Sergei, "and pressure them to reveal the location of our treasure before killing him or her."

"This makes sense. Yet how can we prove it?" asked Yvonne.

"We can't," admitted Rock. "No one at our respective agencies would ever confirm an assassination order, even if it's legitimate. *Especially* if it's legitimate. That's the beauty of this plan."

"Da. I agree. There's no way to tell for sure whether these orders are properly sanctioned. So what do we do?"

"As I see it, we have two options," said Rock. "Option one,

we carry out the assignments and may the best man or woman win—but not here and not tonight. We must allow each other the courtesy of getting away from the safe house and planning our respective operations."

"*Da*, agreed," said Sergei.

Yvonne nodded her acceptance, asking, "And option two?"

"We ignore the orders and accelerate our planned retirements, simultaneously trying to figure out who, if anyone, has set us up."

The three spies looked directly at each other without speaking for several minutes, carefully weighing the pros and cons of each option. Then the meeting continued, and each of them spoke his or her piece while the other two tried to determine whether the words they were hearing were the truth, a lie, or (most treacherous of all) a subtle mixture of both. They had been measuring each other's words for many years, but that didn't make it any easier.

It was June of 1945, and Germany had declared an unconditional surrender the previous month. The war in Asia was ongoing, but it seemed to be only a matter of time before it would be brought to a close as well. In another two months, the atomic bomb would be dropped, and the world would enter a new era, not necessarily for the better.

Troops of many nations were camped all over Europe and were slowly beginning to make their way home. While they waited for their return orders, Allied soldiers and partisans celebrated.

In a small town called Avallon, about 100 miles southeast of Paris, three people in their mid-twenties sat in a French wine bar, huddled around a table littered with several empty bottles. U.S. Army Lieutenant Sam Rockefeller poured another glass for his newly made friends from Russia and France. (Russia was still an ally at this point, although the strains between Stalin and the West were already apparent.)

Colonel Sergei Nozhnitsy savored his wine and secretly

dreaded the return trip to Russia. He had heard a rumor that Mother Russia had not been treating her triumphant heroes with much warmth upon their homecoming, particularly those who had direct contact with foreigners. He hoped his march home wouldn't end with a government-sponsored train ride to Siberia.

Across from him was a smiling Yvonne LePapier who had distinguished herself as a leader of the underground French resistance. Now that the war was over, she was actively on the lookout for Frenchmen who had collaborated with the enemy, all of whom were desperately scrambling to change their identities and cover up their wartime treachery.

"You know what I'd like to see before I leave this country?" asked Sergei.

"A woman's bedroom?" asked Yvonne.

"*Nyet, nyet* … unless you're offering, perhaps?"

"*Non. Non. Pas moi*, but I know some girls …"

"*Spasibo, nyet.* I'd like to explore some of the caves near here. In Arcy-sur-Cure, I think they call it."

"Are you sure those are the kind of caves you want, *mon cher*? They are cold and depressing. Now, these girls I know, on the other hand …"

"I agree with Sergei," said Rock, his voice a little shaky after his excessive wine consumption. "Let's go to the caves. Can you take us there, Yvonne?"

"Well, I suppose …"

"Good. It's settled then. Let's meet here at 9:00 a.m. tomorrow and head out. I will commandeer a jeep for the trip." Rock stood up, but a second later, he sat back down again. "Let's, um, make that 11:00 a.m."

The next morning the trio set off for the mountains where they discovered several small caves suitable for exploration. After an exhausting day of spelunking, the sky began to darken, and they returned to their jeep. Just as the vehicle was about to reach the main road, Sergei said, "Rock, pull over. There's something in the ditch."

Rock stopped the jeep, and they jumped out. Down in the ditch was the wreckage of a German transport truck lying on its side. The driver was dead, and the bodies of several Gestapo policemen were strewn around the area, some in pieces. Flies were everywhere.

"What a mess," Rock said. "They must have driven over a land mine. I'll need to report this."

"Let's look inside the truck," said Sergei.

"It could be booby-trapped," said Yvonne.

"Not likely, if all these guards were inside," said Rock, "but it probably won't be pretty. You should stay back, Yvonne."

"Are you kidding? Whatever it is, I've seen worse. Lead on."

They clambered down and peered inside the truck.

"Holy shit!" said Rock.

"*Mon Dieu!*" exclaimed Yvonne.

"*Blin!?*" muttered Sergei.

Inside was a pile of gold bars, along with the bodies of two Gestapo.

Rock whistled. "They must have been taking this to a storage site when the truck blew up. The Krauts' top brass have been hiding cash and artwork all around Europe, hoping they'll be able to retrieve it later."

"You still want to report this, comrade?" asked Sergei.

"You mean, report that we found an overturned German truck full of bodies and no cargo? Yes. Yes, I do," said Rock.

The three allies looked at each other, then looked at the gold, then looked at each other.

"I'll drive the jeep up closer," said Rock.

"Sergei and I will begin unloading," said Yvonne.

They transported the bricks to one of the small caves they had found, which took the rest of the night. A few days later, Yvonne found them a more secure storage location, and they spent another night transporting the treasure to its semi-permanent home. Several years later, the comrades moved it to an even better spot.

There were one hundred and fifty gold bars in all, each one weighing 400 ounces, or twenty-seven pounds. Each brick was worth about $200,000, making the total value in 1945 around thirty million U.S. dollars.

They were smart about it, leaving the gold untouched for a decade, figuring that the French and Americans were still on the lookout for wartime booty. Then they began selling off three or

---

[2] According to Google, 'blin' translates as 'pancake,' but it's also a mild curse word in Russian.

four bars per year. With the right equipment, gold is relatively easy to melt down, so they divided each brick into smaller, more manageable pieces and sold it off through black-market contacts they had developed. They deposited the cash into numbered Swiss bank accounts and were careful not to visibly overspend their money. Eventually, each of them obtained some false identity documents and used them to purchase a retirement property in a foreign country with no extradition treaty. The spies planned to divide the remaining gold and all disappear simultaneously. After being pushed out of the agency, Sam suggested that the time for this had come, but the others weren't ready.

A week following the Dijon cabin summit, Rock was the first to complete his assignment. On May 28, 1972, *Pravda* reported that Sergei Nozhnitsy, a decorated Hero of the Soviet Union, was tragically killed in a freak building collapse. Rock passed along the news clipping to Roger Roshambo without comment.

"Rock crushes Scissors," Roger quipped. A few days afterward, the bonus payment mysteriously appeared in Sam's Chase Manhattan bank account.

Unfortunately, Samuel P. Rockefeller never got to spend the bonus money. He never even got the chance to argue with his ex-wife's lawyer about whether he was legally entitled to spend the bonus money.

The following week, Rock was seen entering his apartment at 7:00 p.m. by two agents who had been tailing him ever since he returned from Europe. The agents had a good view of the only door and windows. They were absolutely certain that Rock never left the apartment.

At 7:25 p.m., the agents both dropped their coffees in their laps when Rock's apartment exploded.

Thankfully, because the adjacent apartments turned out to be empty at the time (and the coffee was not very hot), no one was hurt—no one, that is, except for Samuel P. Rockefeller. He was quite dead, as was confirmed the next day based upon the dental pattern of his charred remains. Roger Roshambo and the two coffee-stained agents viewed what was left of his body.

"This is LePapier's work," Roger said to his agents. Disgusted, he pulled the white sheet over the corpse's crispy head. "Paper covers Rock," he said. "I'm sorry, Sam. I'll avenge you. Have no doubt of it."

Roger drove to the office and asked Laurie to book him a flight to Paris with an open return.

A team of initial-less agents had been tracking Yvonne LePapier's movements for several weeks. Per their instructions, they reported the addresses she visited but did not follow her inside. Of particular interest to the agent in charge were any self-storage sites or remote locations she visited.

One night in late July, the spies followed Yvonne to a storage facility located thirty miles south of Tours, watching with binoculars as she unlocked the chains securing one of the units and carried a canvas bag into the room. A few minutes later she exited with the bag, now apparently heavier, relocked the door, and drove off. They reported her movements as usual.

The following night, Roger Roshambo drove to Tours after confirming with his operatives that LePapier was safely tucked in for the night. He arrived at the storage facility and broke open the lock with some heavy-duty bolt cutters. He opened the door and stepped inside, feeling for a light switch on the wall. He found it and flipped it on. Two men in black suits and sunglasses were sitting in the back corners of the room, pointing guns at him.

A female voice behind him said, "Don't even think about trying to use the door, Mr. Roshambo. I have no qualms whatsoever about shooting you in the back where you stand. This I will do immediately if you make any sudden movements."

Roger took a breath to speak, but the voice said, "Don't talk and don't turn around. Please follow my next instructions to the letter, remembering there are three guns trained on you and we

174

are all excellent shots. First, drop the bolt cutters and kick them back toward me. Good. Now, with two fingers, remove your gun and gently toss it into the middle of the room. Well done. Third, remove your shoes and kick them toward your gun. *Bon.* Now, put your hands on the wall. Spread your legs and bend forward. That's it. Thank you."

Roger felt a man's hands frisk him roughly from behind. It was a thorough, professional job.

"Turn around slowly now, Mr. Roshambo."

Roger did and found himself face-to-face with Samuel P. Rockefeller, whose fist immediately connected with his nose and his chin in quick succession. Roger dropped to the floor.

"Stay down," Rock barked.

"I thought you were dead. How…?"

"My death was staged. Several years ago, I acquired the apartment below mine under a false name and cut a trapdoor into my floor. I dropped down and was well away via the back door before setting off the blast."

"Then whose body …?"

"Does it matter? It was one I had dental records for, which I substituted for my own in the files. He was already dead, by the way, and not by my hand."

"Ah. And I suppose the Russian's death was also faked?"

"Of course it was," said Sergei from the corner. "Did you think I'd be foolish enough to let this American amateur kill me?"

"Amateur, my ass," said Rock. "If I'd wanted you dead, I'd—"

"Stop it, boys," interrupted Yvonne.

"How did you know it was me?" asked Roger.

"We didn't. Not for sure, anyway. We knew it had to be someone fairly senior in one of our agencies. We decided to let them think their plan had worked, then we waited to see which rat showed up. The smart money was on you, particularly after you made that crack about Rock crushing Scissors. That was a stupid slip. You told me you didn't know who my target was, remember? But how did you find out about the gold?"

"It was just a fluke. One of my other operatives happened to see you enter a Credit Suisse branch in Zurich a few years back. He mentioned it in passing and it got me thinking. Why would you need to visit Credit Suisse? After some digging and

175

surveillance, I discovered you'd been routinely meeting with these two foreign agents. I eventually pieced the story together. I just never knew where the gold was hidden."

"And you still don't. Goodbye, Roger." Rock pointed his weapon at Roshambo's forehead.

"Wait! You can't kill me! Two agents are watching this location right now."

"Bullshit. You wouldn't want to share the gold with anyone, or risk being caught. You're here alone. No one will be looking for us. When they finally discover your body, the only prints they'll find here will be yours."

Roger finally noticed their gloves and hairnets.

"Besides, Roger, in case you've forgotten, Sergei and I are already dead. Yvonne will soon join us in the Great Beyond. Or Brazil, perhaps. I don't recall which country she chose to retire in. Oh, and before you die, I just want you to know that whether or not you turned out to be guilty, I always thought you were a complete flaming asshole."

Before Roshambo could respond, Rock squeezed the trigger and placed six bullets into his head.

"Waste of good bullets," said Sergei.

"Yeah, but I'm rich. Let's go. Don't you still have to assassinate someone?"

"*Da.* I always complete my assignments, even after death." Sergei smiled at Yvonne. "Are you all packed, my *printsessa?*"

"Ready when you are, comrade. Let's go give those agents outside my house a fireworks show they won't forget."

The three old hands left the building and put a brand-new lock on the door.

17

Three Modest Wishes

nce upon a time, a young woman named Katie lived in a long-long-ago era in a far-faraway land in a more-than-slightly-more-liberal-than-not political climate. She aspired to build fairytale castles, and she studied diligently to learn the appropriate depths of different types of moats, the best parapet locations from which to tip boiling-hot caldrons of oil onto the heads of the unfortunate besiegers below, and the minimum safe height for tower prisons such that a young maiden locked up in her chastity penthouse wouldn't be bothered by pesky handsome princes trying to scale her castle keep.

This morning, Katie was taking a break from her work as court architect with a leisurely stroll along the forest path. She had gained some renown for her successful design of a new distribution center for "Tarts on Carts," a philanthropic organization that delivered fresh pastries daily to the kingdom's poor via mule-drawn carriages.

As construction of the Tart Cart project neared completion, Katie debated whether to bid upon a new job commissioned by the local dragon. The dragon wanted an impregnable cavern in which to store his gold and precious jewels. Katie considered sealing the cave opening with a stone so heavy only a dragon could budge it, but decided this wouldn't be secure enough. If she took the assignment, she'd want to look into one of those new "automagic" doors that opened only when the correct enchantment word was spoken. She'd need to subcontract that piece of the job for sure. A guy in Gaul named Ope Ensezimi specialized in those things. She decided to send him a request for proposal by special express tomorrow. With any luck, she'd have his response within two or three months.

So distracted was Katie with these thoughts that she unknowingly left the safe path and wandered deep into the heart of the forest. When she finally refocused on her surroundings, she couldn't remember the way out and idly wondered whether the gingerbread house she'd designed for Witch Hazel was around here someplace. She hoped not. After the unfortunate Hansel and Gretel incident a few years back, she never wanted to see that thing again.

Perhaps if I had designed it to appear a little less appetizing, the children never would have entered, Katie thought. *But that's what the client wanted, and I was desperate for work at the time. Still, you have to draw the line somewhere. Maybe I'll pass on the dragon job after all.*

Trying to refocus on the more immediate problem of getting back to the safe path, she noticed a beautiful golden box sitting next to a tree with a note pinned to the top[1] that read, "Open me."

Well, why not? thought Katie[2].

Had Katie's parents been nearby, they would have gladly supplied at least a dozen reasons why one should not open a strange box that appeared out of nowhere in the middle of a deep, dark forest, particularly if it had a note pinned to the top that read, "Open me."

But Katie was Katie, and Katie was nothing if not curious.

Curiosity held her fast and whispered sweet nothings into her ear until she opened it.

Inside was a pineapple.

Katie took it out. Pinned to the pineapple was a note that read, "Rub me."

Well, why not? she thought[3].

Before Curiosity had even begun to whisper, Katie started rubbing the exotic-looking fruit, being careful because pineapples are a bit touchy and should never be rubbed the wrong way.

---

[1] The note was on top of the box, not the tree, which was fortunate since Katie's tree-climbing skills were mediocre at best.

[2] This was a typical response for Katie.

[3] I told you.

178

Smoke began to pour out of the top of the pineapple. Katie knew this was not normal behavior for an edible fruit of a tropical bromeliaceous plant and wondered whether she had made a mistake.

Just at that moment, in a far-faraway town, her parents felt oddly vindicated for no apparent reason.

The smoke became thicker. Katie dropped the fruit and prepared to run, but Curiosity held her back.

Out of the smoke suddenly stepped a man dressed in flowing robes with a ruby-studded turban on his head.

Terrified, Curiosity let Katie go, and it ran off into the woods in search of a cat.

For her part, Katie wasn't terrified in the slightest. She waved Curiosity goodbye for now and turned to greet the new arrival. "Hello!" she said chirpily. "I'm Katie!"

"Greetings, Katie. I am Eric, Genie of the Pineapple. Wow. It feels great to be finally out of that thing. What time is it anyway?" He stretched and yawned.

"Um, it's long-long-ago," said Katie, slightly surprised by this course of events.

"Oh, I was imprisoned in the fruit in the year 'very-long-long-time-ago.' No wonder I'm stiff. Don't mind me while I do some stretching exercises. It's really cramped inside a pineapple, but on the plus side, you can have all the piña coladas you can drink. Now, what can I do for you?"

"What do you mean?"

"Oh, I haven't explained the rules yet, have I? Silly me. I'd lose my own head if it wasn't stuck on." He quickly reached up and put his hands on his head. "It is stuck on, right? I haven't left it inside the pineapple again, have I? That happened once, and the client ran away so fast I never even got to tell him about the wishes. It was one hell of a bad day, I can tell you. The United Brotherhood of Genies were highly displeased. It's considered very bad form to be released and not to perform at least one wish-granting in return. I still get hate mail. It's very hurtful. Genies can be cruel."

"What's this about wishes?"

"Oh, oh, yeah. Now, how does it go again? Alright, alright. I've got it. Ready?"

"Ready," said Katie, laughing.

There was another burst of smoke and Eric said, "I am Eric, Genie of the Pineapple. You are hereby granted three wishes. Now listen closely. The following rules are non-negotiable, and I will only say them once unless you ask me to repeat them:

1. You may not wish for more wishes.
2. You may not wish for knowledge of the future.
3. You may not wish to change the past.
4. No time travel either; that's covered in a completely different short story. Try page 19.
5. You may not wish for others to fall in love with you, although I can see that such a wish would be totally unnecessary in your case, looking like you do. Oh, wait. I'm off-script. Let me go back. Blah, blah, blah ... fall in love with you.
6. You can't wish for other people to have wishes. Did I mention that we're really serious about the three-wish-limit thing?
7. Wishes that are considered evil, depraved, uncool, or just plain stupid may be denied, and you will lose that wish for trying to slip one of those by. Incidentally, wishing to live forever falls into all four of those categories. Wishing for world peace falls into none of them, but you still won't get it so don't bother asking.
8. If you wish for anything with a brand name, we reserve the right to substitute a generic equivalent.
9. You can't wish to un-wish a wish. Take some responsibility for your decisions, for Pete's sake. (Sorry, my dear, that's not directed against you specifically. It's just part of the script.) And last but not least,
10. Tipping your genie is not required, but it is greatly appreciated.

"Please sign your name in the smoke to signal your agreement with these terms."

A pad of smoke appeared in front of Katie, who signed her name in it. The smoke disappeared.

"Well, now, with the preliminaries out of the way, we're ready for your first wish. Please proceed."

Katie thought for a while. "I wish …"

"Yes?" The genie raised his arms over his head, and a cloud of smoke appeared. There were occasional sparks of lightning within the cloud.

"I wish …"

"Please don't keep me in suspense, my dear," the genie said. "This is actually quite tiring."

"I wish for a pair of sunglasses. Something fashionable, but not too pricy."

Eric put his arms down, and the smoke cloud disappeared. "You *do* realize you're not paying for these wishes, don't you? We won't bill you afterward."

"I know, but I'm quite happy with my life. Except for a chronic shortage of sunglasses."

"Huh," muttered Eric. "Ray-Bans okay?"

"Sure, that would be nice," said Katie. "But don't go out of your way."

"It's the least I can do, princess." Eric raised his arms. There was a smoke cloud with lightning and all that, and … poof! … a pair of Ray-Bans appeared.

Katie tried them on. "A perfect fit," she said approvingly.

"I'm glad you like them," said Eric. "And now for your second wish?"

Katie scrunched up her pretty face as she gave this question some serious thought. "I have it!" she finally exclaimed.

Eric grinned and raised his arms. The smoke cloud reappeared.

"I wish for a pet tortoise," Katie chirped.

Eric's grin and cloud both faded as he dropped his arms. "A tortoise? Seriously? Because they're not necessarily the most affectionate of creatures, are they? How about a dog? Or a cat? I think we have a few elephants in storage as well. Or perhaps—"

"No, my mind is made up. I wish for a pet tortoise."

Eric shrugged and raised his hands. Cloud. Lightning. Poof. Tortoise.

"Oh, he's lovely!" cooed Katie. "I'll name him Arnesto."

"Ernesto is a nice name."

"Not Ernesto. Arnesto."

"That's nice too, I suppose. I should mention that it's a she-tortoise. Does that make a difference to you? Because I could

181

exchange it."

"No need for that, Eric. I'll call her Nessie."

"I believe that name is already taken by a creature in the Loch Ness," said Eric.

"So what?" Katie pouted. "Lots of people have the same name, don't they ... *Eric*?"

"Okay, Nessie the tortoise. Got it. And for your final wish?" Eric raised his hands. Cloud. Lightning.

"I wish for ... a yurt."

Eric lowered his hands. The cloud disappeared.

"What on earth is a yurt?"

"It's a place in which to live. A large round tent with wood or bamboo support walls. It's used as a dwelling by several distinct nomadic groups in the steppes of Central Asia, according to Wikipedia."

A loud ringing noise emanated from the pineapple.

"Anachronism alert," said the genie, who waved a hand at the annoying fruit. The ringing stopped.

"What?" asked Katie.

"Um, this is *long-long-ago*, remember? The Internet hasn't been invented yet."

"Oh. My bad," said Katie. "But why didn't the alarm ring when we talked about the sunglasses? The Ray-Ban company wasn't formed until 1937."

The ringing began again.

"You're too late!" Eric said to the pineapple. "Stop it. And pay more attention next time." The ringing stopped.

"Anyway, I know what a yurt is now," said Eric, "but wouldn't you rather have a castle? Or a mansion on your own personal island? Or a small cottage? Cabana? Bungalow? Cabin? Shanty? Houseboat? Hut? With a pool, perhaps?"

"No, thanks. A yurt will do nicely. No pool. Cleaning them is way too much work."

"Very well then." The genie raised his arms. Cloud-lightning-poof. And just like that, they were standing inside a spacious yurt—spacious for a yurt, that is.

"This is lovely. Thank you, Eric."

Eric bowed. "My pleasure, lady." He looked at Katie.

"Now what?" asked Katie.

"What?"

"What happens now, I mean? That was my third wish."

They both stared at one another until Eric finally said, "Actually, I'm not sure. Usually, the person wishes for something extravagant but the wishes come out wrong and they have to use the third wish to cancel the other two—completely ignoring rule nine, I might add—and they end up with nothing. The story ends at the punch line. It's kind of like a joke, you see. That hasn't happened here because you made three relatively modest requests."

"So here we are," said Katie.

"Yes," said Eric, glancing around nervously.

"You don't have to return to the pineapple then?"

"Not if I can avoid it. It's really quite cramped in there, as I said before. It's even smaller than your yurt."

"I see," said Katie.

They looked at one another for a while. Nessie took a nap.

"This seems a little awkward," said Eric.

"Uh-huh."

"Perhaps I should go," said the genie.

"Well, I … okay."

Eric started to turn to smoke, then he thought better of it. "Listen, are you busy tonight? Maybe we can go out for a Starbucks."

The pineapple rang.

"Or something," Eric corrected.

Katie smiled. "Sure. That would be nice. I'll see you later, Eric."

She had received her fourth wish after all.

183

18

Death on the Beach

The room smelled of disinfectant, sweat, and sickness. It was a warm Friday in Houston, and the hospital air conditioning either required maintenance or else some soulless administrator had deliberately set the temperature too high to save money.

Robert Morticallo didn't seem to mind. He just breathed in and out as the respirator operated. He hadn't opened his eyes since the accident.

He shouldn't even have been driving at the age of ninety-two, thought his son William. *What was he thinking? Now we're paying $3,000 a day to keep him alive. Would he even want that?*

William glanced over at his sister Ruth and her husband Tom. Ruth looked tired. She'd been spending too much time here during the past several days. Tom was sipping a cup of coffee and appeared to be somewhat bored.

The doctor walked in and examined Robert for a few minutes, then approached the family. "Well," he said, "there's been no change since yesterday. Mr. Morticallo's brain function has ceased. The machines are the only reason he's still breathing. There's nothing more we can do. Unlike a coma, from which a patient can sometimes awaken, there's no coming back from brain death. I'm very sorry. At this point, it's up to you as the holders of his medical proxy to decide when to turn off the machines and let him go."

William grabbed Ruth's hand, and his eyes asked her the

question. She nodded, then turned away.

"Turn it off," said William quietly. "It's time."

The doctor walked over to the machine and switched it off.

"How long will it take?" William asked.

"It should be almost immediate," said the doctor.

"Shouldn't he have stopped breathing?" asked Ruth, who was standing at the bedside.

With an expression of surprise, the doctor swung around and placed his stethoscope against Robert's chest.

"This ... isn't ... possible," he stammered.

Robert opened his eyes and said, "Mmm Mmm Mmm Mmm Mmm Mmm!"

The doctor removed the respirator.

"That's better," said Robert. "Now what the hell happened? Where am I, where's my goddamn car, and what the hell are all of you standing around *here* for?"

One person who certainly *wasn't* standing there was me. At the moment of the fortunate Mr. Morticallo's recovery, I was relaxing on Lido Beach, Florida, about 850 miles to the east, soothed by the hypnotic crash of the waves upon the shore. I had left my working robe and scythe in my hotel room and was enjoying the sun's rays upon my body. The hotel's reclining beach chair was very comfortable, and a gentle, refreshing breeze was coming in from the gulf. *Life is good,* I thought, draining the remains of my piña colada and thinking of that song "Escape" by Rupert Holmes. I signaled to the cabana boy for a refill.

He walked over a few minutes later with a fresh glass on a tray. "I'll put this on your tab, Mr. Azrael. Enjoy."

"Add five bucks for yourself, Ramon," I said.

"Thank you very much, sir." He turned and walked back to the cabana, taking the empty glass with him. I could tell he was starting to wonder about my ability to drink multiple alcoholic beverages without displaying any ill effects, and I resolved to slow my consumption rate. But these things were so darn tasty!

A mother and her six-year-old son walked by my chair.

"Mommy, I want to swim in the ocean!"

"I told you before, Johnny, we can't go in. The red tide is here now. The water is filled with tiny little creatures that would make you sick, so you're going to have to swim in the pool, sweetheart."

"Don't wanna pool! Want the ocean!" He stamped his little feet in the sand.

I sat up and waved my hand toward the Gulf of Mexico. Billions of algae suddenly decided that being alive wasn't something they particularly wanted to do anymore. The water slowly lost its reddish hue as the current pulled the deceased algae out to sea.

I smiled at the mother. "It's okay now. You can take him in the water."

She looked a little confused for a moment, then she said to her son, "It's okay, Johnny. The creatures went away. We can swim in the ocean now." They walked to the shoreline, laughing.

I drained my drink and waved to Ramon. *What the hell*, I thought. *It's a vacation, after all.*

I love Florida.

On the other side of the Atlantic Ocean, Ian Wilson's black cab swung into the driveway just off Kensington Gardens near the High Street and the driver whistled. *Posh neighborhood*, he thought. *Very posh. This rider should stand me a nice tip—unless he's a bloody git.*

A man was standing at the side of the road with a suitcase and a carry-on bag. "Tha's wha' I'm talkin' abou'!" said Ian to himself. "It's an airport run, innit?" He came to a stop and rolled down his window. "Good day, sir. Where to, guv?"

"Heathrow," said the man. "And I'm running late. There's an extra fifty quid in it if you can get me there in twenty minutes." He opened the passenger door, threw his bags inside, and got in.

The cabbie pulled onto Kensington High Street. "Ah, I'll try me best, guv, but traffic can be a bitch this time o' day."

187

"I know. That's why I'm offering fifty quid."

Congestion on the High Street made for slow progress. Spying his passenger in the mirror, Ian said, "I'm gonna try to use the backroads to get over to the M4. Hang on, guv." He made a sudden left turn onto Allen Street. "SHITE! WHERE THE BLOODY HELL DID *HE* COME FROM?"

The cabbie slammed on his brakes, but to no avail. He struck the pedestrian full-on, launching the man into the air and throwing him over the cab. Unfortunately, he came down right in front of another car that hit him decisively and sent him flying into the plate-glass window of Waterstone's Bookstore. Glass flew in all directions as the unfortunate victim impacted headfirst, finally connecting with a bookshelf before his limp body crumpled to the ground.

Ian pulled the cab over to the side of the road and got out, saying, "No, no, no, this can't be happening." He met the other driver, who was similarly stunned, and they started to discuss what to do. Meanwhile, Ian's passenger got out with his bags and ran to the High Street to hail another cab.

"Bloody git," muttered Ian. "He's a material witness."

The sound of falling glass came from the bookstore behind them. The two drivers turned to see the victim standing up and carefully brushing glass shards off his jacket. He waved to them. "Hallo? I'm fine, guys. Perfectly fine. I don't even seem to have any bruising. It's the oddest thing, innit? Damned lucky, I'd say."

On Saturday I reached page ninety-five of Terry Pratchett's book *Mort* and couldn't stop chuckling. What an imagination. Sir Terry was only sixty-six when he passed away, as I recalled. A shame, really. Ah, well, they all have to meet their maker sometime. Or meet me at least. I reached for my mai tai, debating whether the switch in cocktails had been a good decision. I watched the sunset and noticed three people on horseback approaching along the shoreline. I shaded my eyes. It couldn't be *them*, could it?

Yes. It could.

I probably should have recognized them sooner, based on the color of the horses. White, black, and red. Maybe the cocktails were starting to affect me after all.

They stopped in front of my beach chair, declining to dismount.

"You look like death," said the figure on the red horse.

"Does that surprise you?" I asked.

"No, not particularly, but I do wonder why these humans don't seem to have caught on. Shouldn't they be screaming and running away in fear?"

"Oh, they see what I wish them to see, which at the moment is a balding Jewish man in his mid-fifties drinking a piña colada. No, forgive me, a mai tai." I took a sip. "Would you like one? I can call Ramon over."

"No, thank you," said War.

Famine raised her hand. "I'd like to try one, please." War gave her a dirty look.

I waved Ramon over. "How about you, Pestilence?" I asked.

The figure on the white horse said, "Will it be sterilized?"

"Um, no, I don't believe so."

"Good. Okay then. Sure. Why not?"

I turned back to War and coaxed, "Come on now, my friend. Don't be stubborn."

"Yes, yes, alright," said War. "Just a small one."

Ramon arrived. "A round of mai tais for my friends and me, Ramon, if you please."

"Of course, Mr. Azrael. On your tab?"

"Indeed. Charge it to suite D—eighth floor. Thank you, my boy."

Ramon walked away. As soon as he had gone, I asked, "Well, comrades, I assume this isn't a social visit. Has the end of the world come already? If so, I'm very disappointed. I'd been planning for another few thousand years at least. It would've been nice to get a little advance notice. I've got some stock market investments that will take a few days to liquidate. I hope I'll be able to get that done in time."

"There's no need to liquidate anything. The End of Days is still a ways off," said Famine.

"As far as we know," added Pestilence. "The Big Guy plays his cards close to the vest sometimes."

189

War jumped off his red steed and said, "Now what's all this about a work stoppage, Azrael? Are you having problems with management? Because if so, we'd like to know."

"No, no, nothing like that. I simply wanted a few days off, is all."

"I see. Still, I wish you had told us first. Don't you realize the grief you've caused us?"

"Grief? How so?"

"Good God, isn't it obvious? You can't have a war without death. It isn't *done*. It's not *civilized*. I've had to allow truces to be called all around the globe. The newspapers are picking up on it, and they're wondering where all this peacemaking is coming from. The cease-fires don't make sense because there's no reason to stop the fighting."

"Well, a cease-fire does prevent unnecessary deaths on both sides of the conflict," I suggested.

"And when has *that* ever been a sufficient reason to call a halt to some good old-fashioned bloodshed?" War crossed his arms and turned away in a huff.

"I agree with War," said Pestilence. "Armed conflict without death is just silly. The same goes for me. What's the point of creating a worldwide contagion if at least some of the people who are infected don't die?"

"Yes, and it won't be long before people realize that starvation no longer has negative consequences," added Famine.

War turned around. There were tears in his eyes. "Let's face it, Azrael. Without you, our lives are meaningless. O Death, where is thy sting?"

"Oh, stop it, all of you. You're being melodramatic," I said. "Ah, here come the cocktails. Thank you, Ramon. Take another ten for yourself."

Famine and Pestilence got down off their horses and grabbed some beach chairs. Ramon handed them their drinks. War remained standing, but he accepted the glass and took a sip.

"Mmm, quite tasty," he said.

"Thank you, sir," said Ramon. He walked back to the cabana.

"Now, look," I said. "I'm not quitting my employment. I simply want a long weekend off. Is that so bad? I've been doing this job for over 3.7 billion years without a break. Except for the occasional office party. Heh heh. Do you remember the night

Lucifer got drunk and brought the comet down upon our heads? What a practical joker."

"Wasn't that the one that wiped out the dinosaurs?" asked Pestilence.

"Oh, I remember!" said Famine. "The skies darkened, and the plants died out. The herbivores had nothing to eat. When they starved to death, the carnivores soon followed."

"Oh yeah. And the few who were left fought each other to the death for the remaining food," recalled War. "It was global chaos." He sighed, and finally took a beach chair.

"Good times, good times," said Famine.

We four comrades stared out at the water, reminiscing.

After a time, War said, "Thank you for the beverage, Azrael. It was surprisingly refreshing."

"Don't mention it," I replied.

"Now will you please *get back to work*?" asked Famine.

"No. I'm not ready yet," I said.

"But you're messing things up for all three of us," said Pestilence.

"You uncooperative bastard! You're returning to work even if we have to drag you there ourselves!" threatened War.

The three of them got out of their beach chairs and approached me menacingly.

I raised my hand and commanded, "STOP!" in my iciest tone. They stopped. "You know my power. I can kill with a word. Or a look. Don't test our friendship."

They stepped back.

"You ... you can't kill *US*!" War stammered. "*We are anthropomorphic beings.* We can never die!"

"Who said anything about killing *you*?" I glanced at the horses.

"You wouldn't," said Pestilence.

"Wouldn't I?"

"You couldn't," said Famine.

"Yes, I could," said I. "If I so choose."

"I think this whole thing has gotten out of hand," said War. "Why don't we move along now and let our dear friend Azrael enjoy the rest of his weekend?" They mounted their horses.

"A wise choice," I said. "No hard feelings?"

"No, of course not," said War.

"No harm, no foul," said Pestilence.

"We just wanted to make sure you were all right," said Famine.

"I am Death," I said. "What could possibly happen to me? Fare thee well, fellow horsepersons."

They spurred their horses and galloped away into the distance.

Ramon stopped by. "Can I get you anything else, Mr. Azrael? I'm going on break in a few minutes."

I carefully considered my options and ordered a tequila sunset.

After two days with a mortality rate of zero, the humans appeared to be getting the message. Oddly, it wasn't universally perceived as good news.

"A world without death? Overcrowding and resource scarcity imminent," said *The New York Times*.

"Clergy and morticians demand a return to mortality," said *The Washington Post*.

"Real estate prices skyrocket," said *The Wall Street Journal*.

"Where has all the toilet paper gone?" said *USA Today*.

"The end of the world: What happens when Earth becomes uninhabitable and we still inhabit it?" inquired *The Economist*, whose cover featured a cartoon of a planet covered with angry, anguished people.

"Up to our necks in cockroaches? If bugs can't die either, we've got big problems," said *Insects Illustrated*.

As mankind adjusted to the thought of not dying, many individuals became bolder. Crime rates increased. Thrill-seekers took bigger risks, which many of them soon regretted. Although death was temporarily off the table, people failed to account for the possibility they could still be hurt. Quite badly hurt. And for the moment, death was no longer a release for the risk-prone, the unlucky, or the incredibly stupid.

Sunday was another fine day on Lido Beach, and I enjoyed the gentle breeze as I sipped my mojito. An anthropomorphic entity could get used to this kind of thing. Still, after reading this morning's newspaper, I knew I'd have to get back to work very soon. Leave it to the humans to turn temporary indestructibility into a curse. They were wrong about the bugs though. I wouldn't let those things multiply without restraint. I might be the Grim Reaper, but I'm not a sadist.

The truth is, I don't spend much of my time dealing with plants, microscopic organisms, or animals other than man. I let nature take its course with the lesser living entities—which isn't to say I won't step in now and again, like with the red tide the other day.

I looked out at the gulf, which was fairly calm today. A few swimmers and body surfers were enjoying the algae-free waves. Off in the distance was a bearded man walking on top of the water, coming this way. None of the humans paid him any attention. He reached the shoreline and made a beeline for my chair.

"Hello, Boss," I said as he arrived. "I wasn't expecting to see you here in Sarasota."

God shrugged and said, "I'm everywhere."

"Of course you are. Pull up a beach chair. Hey, Ramon!"

Ramon trotted over. He was making pretty decent money this weekend, thanks mainly to yours truly.

"I'd like a death in the afternoon," I said when he arrived, "and put whatever my esteemed friend is having on my tab, including $10 for yourself."

"I'm afraid I'm not familiar with death in the afternoon," Ramon replied.

I looked at his youthful form. "No, of course you're not. The drink was invented by Ernest Hemingway. A flute of champagne with a jigger of absinthe."

"I ... I don't think we have any absinthe."

"Yes, you do, my boy," said God. "It's right behind the gin. Go look again." God pointed. I knew that even if the absinthe hadn't been there before, it was there now.

"Um, okay ... and you're having?"

"I'll take a three wise men," said God. "Equal parts Johnnie

Walker scotch, Jack Daniels bourbon, and Jim Beam whiskey. On the rocks, please."

"Haha. Three wise men. Got it. I'll be just a few moments." He trotted to the cabana.

"So what brings you to Florida?" I asked.

"I'm everywhere," God repeated, "but I did wish to speak with you."

"About …?"

"This little vacation of yours is causing me a spot of bother, Azrael. The birth angels are asking why they can't have some time off as well. The tooth fairies are complaining about working conditions and they're picketing in front of the Pearly Gates. And Santa's elves are threatening a work stoppage—that one is particularly vexing to me since they already get 335 days off each year. I told them this was God's kingdom, not France, and if they didn't get in line I'd give their cushy jobs to the tooth fairies and solve two problems at once. I never did see the point of collecting baby teeth anyway. That was one of Lucifer's ideas before he fell."

"I'm sorry about all that. The other three horsemen of the apocalypse aren't happy with me either. I suppose I didn't foresee all these impacts when I requested some time off."

"I did," said God. "I'm all-knowing, you know. Since you've been a good, steady worker over the past several eons, I decided to grant your request anyway. I hope you enjoyed your vacation. Now, do you feel sufficiently relaxed to return to work? If you don't restart soon, we'll become hopelessly backlogged."

I didn't respond immediately since Ramon was arriving with the drinks. We took them from the tray, and I said, "Thank you, Ramon. Would you be so kind as to total my cabana bill? I'll be checking out today. I need to return to work."

"Yes, sir. I've enjoyed serving you, Mr. Azrael. I hope we'll meet again very soon."

"You shouldn't," I said, "but thank you for the thought."

19

Night Fishing

Roderick Petters turned the car onto the lake access road just as the sun was setting, its golden rays illuminating the trees on the other side of the deep blue water. However, the beauty of the scene was lost on Rod, who had other things on his mind ... and in his trunk.

As he approached the boat launching area, Rod saw two policemen in the process of pulling their patrol craft out of the water. *Oh shit*, he thought. *Not now. What the hell are the cops even doing on this small lake? There's no way to turn around without arousing suspicion. I'll have to talk to them.* He pulled his vehicle off to the side to allow them plenty of room to exit, then got out of the car and waved. One of the officers waved back as they finished loading their motorboat onto the trailer and drove it out of the water. Then they both started wiping the boat down.

Although he didn't want to, Rod figured he'd better make the first approach. Sauntering over to them, he said, "Evening, Officers."

The older of the two men glanced up and nodded. "Good evenin', sir. Plannin' to do a little night fishin'?"

"Yes, indeed. Seems like it should be a perfect night for it."

The officer looked up at the sky. "You got that right. After a hot day like this, those fish'll be huddled at the bottom of the lake where the water's cooler. They'll rise to the surface as the temperature drops. What are you goin' after?"

"Oh, I'm not particular. Bass, I suppose. Or bluegill."

The officer nodded. Rod noticed his name tag. Thompson.

195

The younger man finished wiping down the boat and joined them. "Evening, sir. Would you mind if we took a quick gander at your fishing license?"

The older policeman smiled. "Officer Blackhawk is all business, I'm afraid. But if you wouldn't mind …"

"Of course. I figured you might ask. Got it right here." Rod handed him the document, and Officer Thompson gave it a quick glance then handed it back.

"Yep, everythin's in order. You got a workin' cell phone with you, sir?"

Rod thought it a strange question, but he said he did have a phone.

"Would you mind checkin' it to see if you've got a signal up here?"

Rod pulled the phone out of his pocket and looked at it. "I've got two bars."

"Should be good enough to make a call. Would you do me a favor, sir? If you see anythin' out of the ordinary tonight, would you give us a shout? Here's my card." He handed it over, and Rod glanced at it before putting it in his pocket.

"Sure, Officer Thompson, but what do you expect me to see?"

The officer peered at him. "You new in town, sir?"

"Yes, I drove up from the Twin Cities this morning."

"So you ain't heard of the recent troubles then?"

"What troubles?"

"A few fishermen have gone missin' in these parts. Three in the last two months."

"We found their cars at the boat landing and their empty fishing boats in the water," added Officer Blackhawk, "but so far there's been no trace of the men."

"At this lake?"

"Two here. One at Lake Wabana," replied Officer Thompson.

So that's why they're here, thought Rod.

"Don't suppose you'd consider doin' your fishin' in daylight?" asked Officer Thompson. "The disappearances only seem to happen at night."

I need the darkness, thought Rod, *but I'll be sure to get out of here as soon as the job is done.*

"I guess I'll take my chances, Officer. I'll be sure to call if I

196

notice anything."

"Alright then. We can't stop you. Just stay alert, sir."

"Will do."

The policemen nodded and walked to their car. Rod waited until they had left the area before starting back to his vehicle. He swung the car around and carefully backed the trailer into the water, then he unhitched the motorboat and tied it to the dock.

Scanning the sky, Rod saw that the light was fading, but not quickly enough for his taste. He didn't want to load the boat until it was fully dark. Then he'd need to do it quickly, just in case those cops came back.

He sat in his car and smoked a cigar, waiting for night to fall.

Two hours later, he decided it was time. There was enough moonlight to see by, but hopefully not enough for anyone to be able to observe him from a distance. Not that other people were around, but in these situations you couldn't be too careful.

After positioning the car as close to the dock as he could, he got out and opened the trunk, then carried his fishing pole and tackle box to the boat. Next came some rope and two cored cinder blocks. Rod walked back to the car and stood still for a moment, listening for any nearby car or watercraft noises. Finally, he reached into the trunk and lifted out a large black duffle bag. Grunting under the weight, he dragged the six-foot-long sack down the dock, hopped into the boat, and carefully pulled one end of the bag inside. Then he lifted the other end and set it gently down. So far, so good. He scrambled onto the dock and rushed back to the car, closing the trunk and parking it quickly to the side. He rushed back to the boat, untied the ropes, and pulled the cord to start the engine. Nothing happened.

"God damn it, don't quit on me now," he muttered and pulled the cord again. The motor roared to life. He sat down and guided the boat out to the middle of the lake.

It was a perfect crime, he thought. *I'm in the home stretch now.*

Things hadn't been right with his wife, Dolores, for a long

time. Rod suspected that she blamed him for their failure to have children, which clearly wasn't his fault. Still, their marriage was beset by plenty of other problems that *were* at his door, not the least of which were his drinking and womanizing. Still, she had taken him for better or worse, hadn't she? When she told him she was planning to file for divorce, he was floored. How could she leave him? More to the point, how could her money leave him? Without her, he could kiss the mansion on Summit Avenue in St. Paul goodbye, along with her various properties in Hawaii, California, Switzerland, and Italy. He promised her the moon and swore he'd change his behavior, but he knew it was just a matter of time before his marriage and cushy lifestyle were history. He didn't know what to do. Then he met Cynthia.

Cynthia Sanders—a younger, prettier version of Dolores—worked at the Starbucks near his gym, and her resemblance to Dolores was uncanny. The first time he saw her he was struck speechless. He turned on the charm, found her to be receptive, and started courting her. Given his wife's current disposition toward divorce, he was more circumspect than usual to keep the affair secret.

Right from the start, Rod told Cynthia that he was married, figuring his plan would never work if Cynthia didn't trust him implicitly. He went out of his way to please her, buying expensive gifts and taking her on lavish trips whenever he thought he could safely get away with it. He let several months pass before hinting at the possibility of removing Dolores from the picture. Had Cynthia been unwilling to help him, he would have been in a real quandary. As fate would have it, she went along.

The plan was simple. Rod convinced Dolores to join him for a few weeks' vacation in Europe, and they purchased their tickets. A week before their departure, he told her he'd need to delay his own flight for work reasons but suggested she go on without him. She agreed, and they informed friends and relatives about her upcoming trip.

The flight left for London a few hours ago, but Dolores wasn't on it due to an unexpected appointment with the Grim Reaper. Well, unexpected by *her* anyway. Last night, Rod struck Dolores on the back of the head with a lead pipe, loaded her body into the car's trunk, and drove to Cynthia's. He gave his mistress some cash, his wife's passport and phone, the keys to the

European flats, and some old postcards Dolores had sent him from a solo trip several years ago. Rod had steamed the cards to remove the old postage stamps.

Cynthia flew to London using his wife's passport and checked in at the Ritz as Dolores Petters. As she traveled around Europe, she'd mail back the corresponding postcards from each stop. She'd also make several phone calls to him from various locations to corroborate her travel itinerary. After two weeks, she'd return to Minneapolis using Dolores's passport, after which "Dolores Petters" would simply disappear. By the time Cynthia returned, Rod would have already flown to South America for an extended business trip, thereby ensuring he would not be a viable suspect in his wife's subsequent disappearance.

After Cynthia left for the airport, Rod hitched up his boat and drove to northern Minnesota, throwing the lead pipe into Lake Mille Lacs on the way. Once he'd disposed of the body, he'd be free and clear. Cynthia was the only loose end. He'd refrained from giving her any details of the murder or his plans for disposal of the body, so even if she turned on him later, she wouldn't be able to lead the police to any physical evidence. Still, Cynthia was a potential risk. Something would have to be done about that, and soon. He'd give it some thought during his South American trip.

Once Rod arrived at the center of the lake, he killed the engine and grabbed a length of rope, passing it through the holes in one of the cinderblocks and the handles on the end of the black bag. He wrapped it carefully around the bag and block, looping it through several times. When the block was securely attached to the bag, he tied off the rope, sat up, and scanned the lake. He thought he saw a small light in the distance, and his heart stopped for a moment. The light didn't reappear, and he decided it was just his imagination.

He lifted the unweighted end of the black bag over the starboard hull, tipping that side of the boat toward the water. He fed a length of rope through the handles of the bag and looped it three times around. Then he passed the rope through the holes in the second cinder block and lifted it carefully over the hull to rest on top of the duffle bag. He secured the block to the bag and wound the cord around several more times before finally tying it down.

With one end of the bag and its attached weight now hanging over the side of the boat, Rod moved to the center and bent down to pick up the other end. He stood up and carefully balanced the bag on the edge of the boat for a moment, then in one swift movement, he lifted his end and pushed it over the side. There was a loud splash, and the boat rocked significantly before settling down.

Rod looked over the side at the dark water and said, "Goodbye, Dolores, and good riddance."

When he raised his head, he noticed the light again. This time it was followed by the sound of an outboard motor being started.

"Shit," he muttered. He stepped to the stern and pulled the engine cord. Nothing. He pulled again. Nothing.

He picked out the outline of a fishing boat in the moonlight and watched as it came closer.

Beginning to panic, Rod tugged at the starter cord again. It snapped back and cut into his hand. Blood dripped onto the boat. The motor remained quiet.

"Hello!" shouted a voice.

Calm down, Rod thought to himself. *The evidence is over the side. There's nothing to worry about.*

"Ahoy!" Rod said as the motorboat drew alongside. It contained two men who had apparently been granted more than their share of testosterone. They were smiling, which only made them appear more threatening. The first man was dirty and unshaven in tattered clothes, his short sleeves exposing two extremely muscular arms covered in tattoos. More tattoos adorned his neck. The other man, who looked like a heavyweight wrestler, had a sizable scar running down the left side of his face. There was a shotgun propped up next to his seat.

"We heard a big splash and wanted to make sure you were alright over here," the tattooed man said.

"Oh, I was just throwing a fish back, that's all."

"Izzat so? Seemed like an awfully big splash for a fish," tattoo man said.

"And I can't help notice that your fishin' rod is still in its case," said the wrestler. "Were you fishin' with your hands?"

"Um, I just put it away," said Rod. "I'm done for the day."

"Didn't catch much, did ya?" tattoo man sneered as he peered into the boat.

"You wouldn't be dumpin' stuff in our fine lake, now would you?" said the wrestler.

"Because we really wouldn't take kindly to that," added tattoo man.

"Not kindly at all," said the wrestler.

"I wasn't dumping," Rod said.

"Uh-huh. You got a fishin' license?" asked tattoo man.

"Of course."

"May we see it, please? We're legally appointed conservation officers for this area."

My ass, you are, thought Rod. *Still, I just want to get out of here.* He handed over his license.

Tattoo man peered at it. "This license is expired. It's no good." He ripped up the paper and threw the pieces in the lake.

"Hey!" Rod shouted.

"There's a $200 penalty for fishin' without a license. Payable now. Cash only," said the wrestler.

"But that's nothin' compared to the penalty for dumpin'," added tattoo man.

"Yeah, the cops don't like that kind of thing. They might even send some divers down to see what you dumped," said the wrestler.

"You guys are nothing but scam artists," said Rod.

The wrestler's hand moved a little closer to the shotgun.

Rod thought better of his objection. "I'm sorry. I don't want any trouble," he said, slowly reaching for his wallet and avoiding any sudden movements. He opened it up and pulled out $200.

"We'll take another $100 to forget about the scam-artist crack," said tattoo man.

Rod resisted the urge to respond and handed over $300.

The wrestler grabbed the shotgun and pointed it at Rod. "Maybe you'd best give us all of it, asshole."

As he handed over his wallet, Rod thought back to the three missing fishermen and wondered if another empty boat would be found on this lake tomorrow. Tattoo man removed the cash and Rod's drivers' license and threw the wallet into the water. It sank to the bottom.

"Hey, what about the credit cards?" said the wrestler.

"Them things is an invitation to get caught," replied tattoo man. "They're better off in the lake."

"What about him?" asked the wrestler.

"He ain't gonna say nothin'. I'm guessin' he don't want whatever he just dumped to be dredged up," said tattoo man, holding a flashlight to the drivers' license and squinting at it. "Ain't that right, Roderick Petters of 1215 Summit Avenue in St. Paul?"

"That's right," said Rod, sweating profusely now.

"Have a pleasant evenin'," said tattoo man.

The wrestler grimaced and spit into the lake. He started their engine, and they went back in the direction they came from.

Rod exhaled, feeling he'd just come very close to death. He waited for the sound of their engine to recede, then he moved to the stern and pulled the cord again.

Nothing. *Shit. I need to get out of here.*

There was a sudden noise right behind him, and Rod's heart skipped a beat. He turned to see a fish flopping back and forth in the bow.

I'll be dammed. The thing must have jumped right into the boat!

Rod approached the fish, which was incredibly ugly. He'd never seen one like it before. Then again, he wasn't really a fisherman, so what did he know?

Strange, it seems to have some kind of fishing line in its mouth. The line trailed over the side of the boat into the water.

It must have been in the process of being hauled in by someone when the line broke. Anyway, whatever. It's your lucky day, Nemo—not that anyone would want to eat a fish as ugly as you.

Rod reached down to pick up the creature and toss it back into the water. As soon as he lifted it, several sharp quills suddenly popped out of the fish and pierced his hands. Rod was too startled to even scream.

The fishing line tightened and tugged him toward the starboard hull. Now he screamed, but not for long. Rod lost his footing and was pulled over the side.

As he was dragged deeper into the inky darkness of the lake, he thought he glimpsed a light ahead. When he saw the source of the light, he tried to scream again and inhaled a lungful of water.

The luminous thing at the bottom of the lake was not even remotely human. Nor was it a fish.

Whatever it was, though, it had a fishing pole, and it knew how to use one.

202

The next morning, Officers Thompson and Blackhawk found Rod's car still parked near the dock. After launching their boat, they did a circuit of the lake and found the abandoned motorboat. When they found the bloodstain near the stern, they radioed in for the divers.

20

You

eah, this one's all about you. I've been waiting for you to reach this point in the book. It certainly took you long enough.

Well, okay, the truth is I don't actually know how long it took since, from my perspective, I'm writing this *now*, and you'll be reading it *later*. I wrote that first paragraph without any certainty about when you would see it. Would it take a week? A month? A year? I dunno. But read it you shall. I will make sure of it somehow.

Sure, plenty of *other* people may read these pages as well, but this story certainly isn't about *them*. It's about *you*.

I'm not going to address you by name. That way, if my plan succeeds, the cops won't be able to use this writing as evidence of premeditation. If they ask me, I'll say it's just a story. That it wasn't about *you* specifically.

But it is.

As I write these words, I'm still not sure if I will send you a copy of the book directly or wait to see if you obtain one on your own.

Everybody else who reads this will think it's just another offbeat story in a collection of offbeat stories.

But you know better, don't you? You know who you are, and so do I. The trick is to figure out who *I* am.

Maybe I'm this book's author. Maybe I'm not. That's for you to uncover … if you can.

Maybe I wrote this story and showed it to the book's author. Maybe he liked it, and I permitted him to publish it as his own. Maybe I even paid him to do so.

So who am I? Think back. Way back.

Do you remember the time you almost killed a guy? Well, that was me.

You say you don't recall such a thing? That it never happened?

It did happen. Of course, I don't rule out the possibility you didn't even realize what you'd done at the time. After all, I'm not a mind reader, am I?

But even if you weren't fully cognizant of your actions, you did it. You're responsible regardless. You will pay.

Let me refresh your memory. A dark road in a wooded area. Late at night. You were driving a bit too fast.

I don't know whether you'd been drinking, but you were at the wheel. The license plate and your face are the last things I remember seeing before I lost consciousness. The images are etched into my memory.

I was riding a bike when you sideswiped me. Maybe you didn't see me. The bike didn't have any reflectors, which was my bad. Maybe you didn't even realize you'd struck me. Either way, I don't care. It was still your fault.

I know it was you. I saw you as your car rushed past. I saw your license plate. Then I careened off the road and flew off the bike. My head connected with the trunk of a tree. I wasn't wearing a helmet. My bad, again.

The only reason I'm not dead is that a good Samaritan happened to see me from the road the next morning. She brought me to the hospital where I remained in a coma for many years. Far too many years. You robbed me of a good portion of my life.

Several months ago, I woke up. The doctors called it a miracle. I call it karma. It's payback time for you, my oblivious, self-centered friend.

As soon as I awoke, I recalled the car's license plate. I spent weeks tracking you down. Once I found you, I thought about how best to achieve my revenge. I did a lot of research on you, friend. It's truly amazing what you can uncover on the Internet.

We all have secrets. Some are hidden better than others. Not yours though. You really should pay more attention to computer security.

But no worries, I won't reveal your dirty secrets here.

Probably.

Because I haven't finished writing yet, and who knows? Maybe I'll change my mind about this content before it gets published.

So, "What now?" you may ask.

Like I said earlier, it's payback time.

I'm coming for you.

I'm going to show you what a serious head injury feels like.

And if I'm very, very lucky, you won't die.

You'll be comatose.

Did I mention that I know where you live?

Pleasant dreams, you.

21

𝕳ousebound

John woke up feeling like his entire body had been hit with a sledgehammer and wondered whether he had come down with the coronavirus everyone was talking about. He'd need to distance himself from Maureen and the kids. Maybe go get tested someplace.

Maureen was still sleeping peacefully beside him. Since it was Saturday, there was no rush to get up. He lay motionless for another twenty minutes and started to feel a little better. He was still sore, but the pounding in his head had stopped. With more effort than was usually required, he eased himself up. *I was fine when I went to bed last night*, he thought, *but I sure feel like crap now.* It was still dark. The clock on the nightstand read 5:48 a.m.

He stood up and grimaced at the pain. With legs like lead, he stepped slowly to the bathroom and threw some water on his face. He examined his reflection in the mirror and started. *No way! I've grown a beard and mustache overnight. How is that even possible?*

He headed downstairs and noticed the drawn curtains. *Strange,* he thought. *I wonder why Maureen covered all the windows.* He moved to the kitchen and popped a K-cup into the Keurig machine and turned it on, the aroma of the dripping coffee comforting him. When it was ready, he sat at the counter, relishing the first sip.

He heard noises upstairs and realized Maureen was awake. A few minutes later she came down the stairs, looking beautiful as usual, albeit a little lethargic.

"My God. I feel like I've been run over by a truck," said

Maureen.

"Yeah. I'm in the same condition. Coffee helps a little. I'll make you a cup." He stood up.

"Thanks, hon. Hey, why did you close all the curtains?"

"I thought you did that."

"No … at least, I don't think I did."

John turned around with a freshly made cup of coffee. Maureen looked up and said, "Oh God, John, your face!"

John smiled. "I know. I'll shave it off in a minute."

"But how can that happen overnight?"

"Damned if I know, love. Here, this should help clear your head."

She took a sip. "Mmm. Yeah. Thanks, it hits the spot." She reached for his hand. "Your fingernails could use a trim also. Mine too. Weird." She took another sip. "John, do you think we both have COVID? What are we going to do about the kids?"

"I don't know. Let's just take it slow. We should probably get tested for it later today. Did you check on them before you came down?"

"Yeah, they're both sleeping peacefully. Could you open the curtains please?"

"Sure."

John pulled the cord and uttered an out-of-character expletive.

"John?"

"Come and see this."

Maureen approached and looked at the window. "What the hell?" she said.

John pulled back some more curtains. "It's the same all over. All the windows are covered with some kind of plastic sheeting."

"I don't understand."

"I'll go outside and check it out." He opened the front door and froze in place. "No frigging way."

Maureen stepped behind him. "What the hell *is* that, John?"

"It's a large metal container, like an air lock. It covers the whole doorframe. There's another door on the opposite end." He stepped inside and fiddled with the latch on the outer door, then banged his fists against it. "It's no good. It's locked from the outside. It's solid metal. I can't open it."

"My God, this is insane. I'm scared, John. What's going on?"

210

"I don't know. Let's check the kitchen door."

The back door, which opened outward, wouldn't budge. Something appeared to be blocking it—presumably more of that plastic.

"I'm calling the cops," said John. He pulled out his cell phone and was surprised to find it turned off. He pushed the power button, and it came to life.

"That's odd," he said after a few moments. "There's no phone signal. And no Internet."

"Let me try mine," Maureen said, but she got the same result.

John placed his phone on the table. "I'll check the kids' phones in a little while. I expect it'll be the same though. Something must be blocking the signal. Maybe it'll clear up later."

"Do you think it's got to do with the virus, John? Maybe it's some kind of emergency measure?"

"That's hard to believe, hon. They couldn't have known we were sick. And how could they do this overnight? Why didn't we hear anything?"

"Let's check the news anyway."

They proceeded to the living room and turned on the flat screen. The picture showed a rotund man wearing a blue shirt and captain's hat arguing with a thin man in a red shirt, white pants, and a floppy white hat. They were standing on a beach next to a wrecked pleasure boat.

Maureen pointed the remote control at the screen and changed the channel. It was the same show. She flipped quickly through the options, growing increasingly agitated.

"This is impossible. Every channel is broadcasting the same episode of *Gilligan's Island*! Even CNN and Fox News!" She turned it off.

"No, hon, leave it on. Just turn the sound down. Maybe they'll start broadcasting again later this morning."

Maureen complied. The professor was demonstrating his bicycle-powered washing machine.

"I'm going to check the upstairs windows," said John.

"Okay, but stay out of the kids' rooms for now, alright?"

"Sure. If all the other windows are covered, there's hardly any reason to check theirs anyway."

"I'm going to make a few masks for us to wear, just in case."

"Sounds good. We can't be too careful."

John ascended the stairs, noting to himself how unusually strenuous the climb was. A minute or two later he came back down, a frown upon his bearded face.

"It's the same thing upstairs. All the windows are covered by some sort of shielding. I managed to slide one of the panes open and felt the surface of the stuff. It seems to be a very smooth, hard plastic, and it's firmly attached. It wouldn't budge when I hit it."

"Oh my God, John. Do you think we've been put into quarantine?"

John scratched his head. "I don't know, Maureen. I wouldn't have thought our government would do that, even if they could," he said, thinking, *Unless we have a disease that's too dangerous to let escape, in which case we're in a world of hurt. Still, why would they mess with our phone and Internet reception?*

John's musings were interrupted by a shrill scream from upstairs. "Mom! Dad! Help me! I'm really sick!"

"We're coming, Will!" shouted his wife as they both heavily climbed the stairs. They entered their six-year-old son's room and stopped dead in their tracks at the door. Something was definitely wrong.

Will was sitting up in his bed.

He was older.

Not *way* older. Maybe he'd grown about a year's worth? But he sure didn't look like this when they put him to bed last night.

And it wasn't his imagination, John knew. Will's clothes were too tight. They no longer fit his body.

John turned to his wife and saw from her face that he didn't need to point it out. She knew, and she was trying—unsuccessfully—to come to grips with it.

Because it simply made no sense.

"Mom, my body doesn't feel right. It's all sore and heavy."

Maureen broke out of her lethargy and rushed to Will's side. "It's okay, honey, Mommy and Daddy have it too. It's just a little virus. You're going to be fine. Come on downstairs with us."

"I need to pee."

"Right, then, a quick stop at the potty."

Maureen looked up at John. She didn't need to say a word.

"I'll check on her right now," said John, already heading toward their daughter's room. He opened the door and entered,

212

proceeding to Penny's bedside.

Yes, it was the same. Penny was twelve, so the changes were less obvious but they were there. Her face was fuller, slightly more mature. Her pajamas seemed a size too small.

While John watched, Penny opened her eyes, looking confused for a moment. Then she croaked, "Dad? I don't feel so good."

John sighed. *No need for those masks.* "You're okay, sweetheart. It's some kind of virus, we think. The whole family's got it. You'll feel a little better after you've been up for a while. Come on downstairs, okay? Your mom's going to make us breakfast."

Penny nodded. John kissed her on the forehead and walked out.

It was starting to get light outside, but the translucent plastic covering on their windows was too cloudy to allow them to see out. The family ate their breakfast in relative silence, an unusual occurrence. Normally, the kids would be teasing one another but they knew something was wrong today. Then the questions started.

"Why are the windows covered up?" asked Penny.

"Why is *Gilligan's Island* on all the TV channels?" asked Will.

"What happened to us last night?" asked Penny.

"We don't know," said John, figuring it was useless to lie. "I believe we may have been asleep for a long time. Maybe because of this virus we seem to have. I'm sure we must be getting better now."

"How long did we sleep?"

"I ... I don't know."

"C'mon, Dad. I could see the changes to my face in the mirror. Will looks older too. How long?"

John glanced at Maureen, who stared back at him without any visible signal.

"Um, ah, maybe a few months? I can't say for sure," John said.

"If we were asleep for a really long time, who took care of

213

us?" persisted Penny. "Someone had to."

"That's a good question, Penny. No doubt it was the same people who covered up our windows. I just don't know. For now, we have to stay in the house. At least until this virus goes away."

"What's going to happen to us? Are we going to die?" asked Will.

"You're scaring them, John."

"I don't mean to, Maureen, but I don't think lying about our situation is going to help."

John turned to Will. "We're going to be fine, son. If we did sleep for that long, then someone took care of us. They know we're here, and they're not going to let anything bad happen. So we wait. We're all here, and we're doing fine. Let's finish our breakfast and we'll figure this out. Okay?"

"Okay, but I hope they show something else on TV. I don't like *Gilligan's Island*. Ginger's kind of creepy, and Mr. Howell sounds like Mr. Magoo."

Everyone laughed.

"More powdered eggs, anyone?" asked Maureen.

"Powdered eggs?" asked John. "I knew they tasted different. When did we buy those?"

"We didn't," Maureen said, fighting back tears.

Jesus, shut up, John, thought John.

After breakfast, everyone took turns in the shower, and John tried the kids' cell phones. As he expected, there was no phone signal or Internet connectivity on either one. The television continued to broadcast the *Gilligan's Island* marathon. It was the weirdest thing. They played one episode after the other, with no commercial messages in between.

John decided to see if he could break through one of the plastic coverings. If this was some kind of biohazard situation, he might get in trouble for doing it, but goddamn it—no one had asked *him* if it was okay to cover his house in shielding. He started down to the basement to get his toolbox, but when he opened the basement door, he discovered a sheet of that plastic crap right behind it, covering the entire entrance. It seemed to continue into the floor and wall.

"Shit!" he shouted. *Wait. I've still got a few tools upstairs for the shelving I was going to build in Penny's room.* He went up and retrieved what he had, then he returned to the basement door.

John started with the hammer and pounded on the plastic for several minutes. He didn't even scratch the surface. He tried the drill next. Nothing. The tip of the drill bit couldn't get any purchase on the smooth plastic wall and kept slipping off to either side. He tried prying at the sides with a screwdriver, succeeding in removing some wood, but the plastic just seemed to continue behind it. It wouldn't budge, and he couldn't cut it—at least not with the tools at his disposal.

What the hell is this stuff?

He thought for a moment. If he couldn't get through the plastic, he'd just punch a hole someplace that wasn't covered. The roof. He could patch it up later, but first he was going to break out of this prison and give those responsible a piece of his mind. If his family had to be quarantined, so be it, but they deserved an explanation at the very least.

He grabbed his tools and started for the attic, passing by the living room and noting that *Gillian's Island* was no longer on the television. Instead, there was a message. He dropped his tools and approached the screen.

On a white background in black lettering, it read, **"Stop what you are doing. It will not work, but it may damage your house."**

Someone is out there watching us, thought John. *Maybe they can hear us too.*

"What the hell do you want?" John shouted. "Why have you done this?"

"All in good time," read the screen. Then *Gilligan's Island* resumed.

John turned, picked up his tools, and climbed the stairs. He met Maureen coming the other way, drying her hair.

"What were you yelling for?" she asked.

"I'll tell you in a little while. I want to try something first."

Proceeding to the end of the hallway, he reached up for the trap-door rope and pulled it, causing the access ladder to swing down. He climbed up to the attic and flicked on the lights. It was dusty and warm. Scattered around were several boxes of Christmas decorations, memorabilia, and photo albums. There was also an old bicycle of Maureen's. He didn't remember hauling that thing up here and wondered why they hadn't stored it in the detached garage instead.

John thought about where he should make the hole and decided the southwest corner of the roof would be the easiest to climb down from. He proceeded to the spot, plugged in his electric drill, and started to penetrate the wood.

My circular saw would be very useful right now, he thought. *Unfortunately, it's in the basement. I'll just drill enough holes to weaken the wood. Once I get my hand saw into the gap, it'll go a lot quicker.*

The drill went through the board easily but stopped way too early. He tried another location, and the same thing happened.

Oh, no, he thought. *It couldn't be, could it?*

He drilled several more holes close to one another until he confirmed that yes, it could be.

That hard plastic was apparently covering the roof.

It surrounds the entire house, John realized. *The only way out is through the locked metal door in front.*

Deflated, John gathered his tools and descended the ladder. He found Maureen in the living room, standing in front of the TV screen.

"What does this mean?" she asked.

"We told you," the screen read.

"Why are you doing this to us?" John yelled. "Are we contagious? Is this virus going to kill us?"

"There is no need to shout. We can hear you," read the screen, then the letters disappeared and another message appeared. **"The shielding is for your protection, not ours. None of you have a virus."**

After a few seconds, the message continued.

"Supplies will be delivered and trash will be picked up in the front hatchway at 0900 each day. The inner door will be locked from 0830 to 0930. If you require anything in particular, just say so."

Then they were treated to *Gilligan's Island.*

Three weeks later, John and Maureen were still speculating about what was meant by the statement that the shielding was for their own benefit. Had there been a nuclear war? Some kind of deadly chemical release? A meteor strike? Was the atmosphere outside toxic or radioactive? Was the rest of the population infected with a lethal virus? Were their neighbors similarly trapped in their homes? How far did this problem extend? Was it city-wide? The whole United States? Global? And why had they seemingly aged by a year or so at the start of their confinement? Were they comatose? If so, how did they all manage to come out of it at the same time? Had they been drugged?

They had many more questions than answers, and the people on the other end of the television signal refused to give them any useful information. The response to each of their questions was "All in good time."

The children seemed to adapt to the situation much more easily than their parents. Thankfully, they were able to access more than *Gilligan's Island* on the television. They had only to request a specific show verbally, and it would be broadcast. They could even watch the news—as long as it was a rerun—and nothing later than the date of their quarantine was available. All programming after August 16, 2020, was off-limits. What happened that night? Did TV and cable stations no longer exist? John and Maureen had no way of knowing. They watched the August 16th news on every channel they could think of, and it all seemed completely normal. There was no hint of anything that might presage their current condition.

They received no mail. They couldn't check their investments. They didn't know who was paying their bills, or if they were even still getting any bills.

They had to be somewhat guarded in what they said because it soon became apparent that their keepers could hear even whispered conversations within the house. Frustrated and fearful, the family fought more than usual. Being cooped up in their home, as spacious as it was, grew old quickly.

One day, John decided he'd had enough. He was determined

to find out what was going on, even if it cost him his life. Just after 8:00 a.m., while Maureen was homeschooling the kids, he wrote her an explanatory note in case things went wrong and left it under a pile of books on the kitchen table. Then he snuck into the front hatchway and hid beneath some trash bags. When he heard the inner door lock as usual at eight-thirty, he sat quietly, waiting for the outer door to open at nine.

It never did. At 9:30 a.m., the inner door unlocked again. John gave up and went back into the house.

The television displayed this message: **"That was very foolish. You could have died. Deliveries and trash pickup will be withheld for two weeks. Please try to be more cooperative in the future."**

Maureen was distinctly unhappy when he told her what happened, and John slept on the couch for the next several weeks.

A month passed, and Maureen was finally speaking to John again following his failed attempt to leave the house. Besides the fact that he had put himself in physical danger, the two-week cessation of deliveries had turned out to be a real hardship, as their refrigerator and cupboard contained only about five to seven days' worth of backup. Even with rationing, they were running out of food by the tenth day. Repeated appeals to their keepers were ignored. It became painfully obvious just how dependent they were on the people outside—which was why, when the television screen gave them their next instructions, they decided not to object.

"In preparation for the grand opening, please remove all curtains, shades, and other window coverings and place them in the hatchway. An explanation will follow your compliance."

With the kids' help, they did as instructed. The plastic sheeting outside was translucent, so the window treatments didn't serve much of a purpose anyway.

"What do you think they mean by 'the grand opening'?" asked
218

Maureen as she removed the living room curtains from their hooks.

"Maybe we're finally getting out of here," said John.

"Oh God, wouldn't that be nice?"

"Yeah, but don't mention it to the kids in case I'm wrong."

When they finished the job, they placed everything in the front box, closed the inner door, and heard it lock. There was a tone from the television behind them.

"You may now ask three questions," the screen read.

"Let's consider this before responding, Maureen," said John. Then, for the benefit of their providers, he said, "We want to speak among ourselves for a few minutes. We'll tell you when we're ready to ask our questions."

"Understood," read the screen.

"Should we send the kids to their rooms?" asked Maureen.

"No, Mom, please!" said Penny.

"This affects them too," said John. "They should stay."

After a few minutes of discussion, John said, "We're ready. Question 1: How long must we remain locked inside our home?"

"For the remainder of your lives," read the screen.

Maureen screamed, then collapsed to the floor, crying. John stroked her hair and said, "Question 2: Why?" Maureen raised her head to read the answer.

"The outside atmosphere is toxic to humans."

John sat down heavily on the sofa. "How is that possible?" he asked.

"Because you are no longer on Earth. This is the planet you call Proxima B, circling the star you call Proxima Centauri. You are approximately 4.3 light-years from your birth planet. We welcome you to your new home."

"That's ridiculous! Do you think we're idiots? How can you expect us to believe such a thing?" John shouted.

The translucent plastic covering around their house suddenly cleared, and they could see out. This was not their neighborhood. The ground was reddish, and the alien structures around them were unlike any buildings humans had ever designed.

The stars were all wrong too.

But the main attractions in the night sky were the two moons, one of which was either very large or orbiting very close, as it dominated the horizon. It looked like Earth's moon, only twenty times bigger. Numerous craters dotted the landscape and a large mountain range stretched in a jagged line from top to bottom. A quarter of the moon was in shadow, but there were several points of light emanating from the dark portion.

The second moon hung in the opposite side of the sky. It was a small green disk dotted with lights.

Both of those moons have been colonized, John realized.

"Cool," said Will.

"Wow," exclaimed Penny.

Maureen stared open-mouthed and seemed unable to move.

John rushed into the kitchen and threw up into the sink.

The windows clouded over, and *Gilligan's Island* resumed.

Three days later, the screen read, "Are you prepared to ask more questions?"

"Yes," said John.

"Good. We know our guests need time to adjust, so we try not to overload them with information right away."

"How did we get here?"

"We brought you. Our ships travel at a maximum velocity of 20 percent of the speed of light, but they need considerable time to accelerate and decelerate. The journey took approximately 200 of your Earth-years."

Maureen put her arm around John for support. "Two hundred years? We'd be dead," said John.

"No. You were in stasis. Your body functions were slowed down. Physically, you only aged about one and a half Earth-years during the trip."

"I suppose that's why we felt sluggish and sore when we first got here."

"Yes. Also, our planet is about 30 percent more massive than Earth, so you no doubt had to struggle with the extra gravity. We are pleased that you have adapted so well."

"There's no going back, is there?"

"No. We do not intend to return you to Earth. Even if we did, you would not recognize it. It would be another 200-

year journey. Also, because of relativistic time-dilation effects at near-light speeds, clocks move slower while you are on the ship. By the time you got back to Earth, it would be approximately the year 3000."

The screen went blank for a moment, then this message appeared: **"And given the recent history of your species, we are not certain your planet would still be habitable by then."**

The screen blacked out again.

"I am told you may have found that last statement of fact insulting. My apologies."

"Why did you bring us here?"

"We collect species from our nearest celestial neighbors. Do not worry—we will care for you. Just act normally. Our people wish to observe you in your natural habitat."

"In other words, you've put us on display. In a zoo."

"Yes, your analogy is accurate. A zoo. The grand opening is tomorrow. Sleep well. And to prepare you, here is a picture of what we look like."

The picture appeared.

The kids screamed and ran from the room.

Maureen fainted.

John dashed for the sink.

"There is no need for alarm. We are your friends. Your keepers. We will take excellent care of you for the duration of your natural lives. Enjoy your stay with us."

22

The Adventure of the Vacant Rooms

o Sherlock, she was always *the* woman. I had seldom heard him mention her using any other name. In his eyes, she eclipsed and predominated the whole of her sex. I refer, of course, to the esteemed Courtney Sherlock, his wife and business partner. They had been happily married for over seven years when I decided to drop by their home on my way back from India. Little did I know of the mysterious and horrifying events about to unfold.

I met James Sherlock at college and had been impressed by his sharp intellect and keenly perceptive powers of deduction. While at Notre Dame, he pursued a major in engineering, another degree in Mandarin Chinese, and Courtney. I roomed with him for two years while engaged in my pre-medical studies. After graduation, he and Courtney married and started their successful residential property development business. They called it "Sherlock Homes."

Arriving at the intersection of Mover Boulevard and Shaker Street, I quickly found the address: 221b Shaker Street. I rang the bell, and a cat jumped up into the window. The door opened, and my friend James Sherlock peered out.

"My dear Dr. John Waddle! How nice to see you again. I hope your train ride from Chicago was enjoyable. You've just returned from India, I see. It's very good of you to stop by."

"It's great to see you as well, Sherlock," I said, "but how on earth did you know I had traveled from Chicago by train and was on my way back from India?"

"Elementary, my dear Waddle. Your jacket and pants are still a bit damp from the rain. It has not rained here in several days, but Chicago had a downpour this morning. The only way you could have arrived before your clothing had dried was if you had taken the 9:22 from Union Station. As for India, I simply noted the address tag on your luggage that lists a hotel in Mumbai. Since the fastest route to India requires one to cross the Pacific, you must either be going to or coming from California. Given that my humble abode in Cincinnati lies to the east of Chicago, it stands to reason that you are on your way back to your residence in New York."

"Amazing, Sherlock. Even after you have explained your logic, I am aghast."

"Tut-tut, Waddle. It is nothing but the application of observation and deduction. Anyone can do it if they focus their mind upon it. But why am I making you stand outside? Come in, come in. Courtney, look who just arrived at our door."

Courtney Sherlock emerged from the kitchen. "Dr. John Waddle! What a pleasure! We haven't seen you since you graduated from medical school."

"Yes, I've been quite busy with my residency. I just returned from a sabbatical trip to India where I volunteered my skills for a few months."

"That sounds amazing. Please sit down and I'll make us some tea. Artifice, you come here and I'll get you some nice kibble," said Courtney.

Artifice the cat ran straight into the kitchen.

I had just settled into my chair when there was a sharp rapping at the door. "Mr. Sherlock! Mr. Sherlock! Something is terribly wrong!"

Sherlock opened the door to admit an elderly Asian gentleman who was clearly in some distress. I stood, but Sherlock waved me back down.

"Waddle, Mr. Chin is one of my tenants. Mr. Chin, may I present Dr. Waddle. Now tell me, what seems to be the problem?"

"Apartment 101. Next to mine. I saw Mrs. Peabody last night and wished her a good evening."

"Yes?" Sherlock produced a pipe and placed it in his mouth.

To my knowledge, he never lit the thing. He simply liked the way it looked.

"This morning she is gone."

"And why is that so terribly wrong?" I asked.

"She is over ninety years old, as Mr. Sherlock knows. She never goes out. She didn't answer the door when I tried to deliver the morning paper to her, so I went outside and peeped through the window. Her apartment was empty!"

"So she changed her routine and went out. I still don't see—"

"No, you don't understand. The *entire* apartment was empty. No furniture. No pictures. No curtains. Nothing left but the carpeting, light fixtures, and appliances."

"Interesting," said Sherlock, puffing on his empty pipe. "I deduce that Mrs. Peabody's rent payment may not be forthcoming this month. You heard nothing last night?"

"Not a thing."

"Curious. Well, I think it's worth a visit, don't you all? Waddle? Courtney? Will you be so kind as to join me?"

Sherlock let himself into Apartment 101 with his passkey. As Mr. Chin had indicated, it was completely empty.

"She might have cleaned up a bit before leaving," said Courtney. "These countertops and windows are filthy, and I won't even begin to describe the mess she left in the refrigerator."

"I don't believe Mrs. Peabody had intended to vacate the apartment," said Sherlock. He removed a magnifying glass from his pocket and examined the floor. "This is scratched," he said. "I'll have to find someone to buff and polish it."

"Who else lives in this building?" I asked.

"It's a fourplex," said Courtney. "Mr. Hobble and Ms. Snip live in the apartments above."

"Good Lord, man, that was an excellent question," said Sherlock. "Let's check whether they heard anything last night."

We proceeded up the steps. Mr. Hobble answered the door looking somewhat the worse for wear, clearly annoyed that we had awoken him.

"Of course I didn't hear anything last night, Sherlock. You bloody well know I work nights. I only got home an hour and a half ago."

We apologized for disturbing him and walked across the hall. Sherlock knocked on Ms. Snip's door. There was no answer. He opened the door with his key to find … a completely empty apartment.

"This is very disturbing," said Courtney.

"Intriguing," said Sherlock.

I began to explore the apartment and stepped into the bedroom.

"My God!" I exclaimed. "Sherlock, come here!"

James and Courtney Sherlock quickly appeared in the doorway and gazed upon the spectacle I had just found.

There was a plastic *Twister* game mat spread across the middle of the floor, consisting of multicolored circles. The spinner was lying next to it, with the pointer set at "right foot – yellow."

A severed human foot lay upon one of the yellow circles.

Courtney screamed and left the room.

"The game is a foot, Waddle," said Sherlock, adding, "but that is certainly not Ms. Snip's foot."

I quickly agreed. It was a male appendage.

"But what is the meaning of this?" I gasped.

"Someone is sending a message, but I'm presently at a loss to explain what it might be. In any case, I suppose we should call the police."

The detective and his support staff arrived thirty minutes later. Inspector LePlodd had worked with Sherlock before and shook his hand warmly before I was introduced. After listening to the facts of the case and viewing both empty apartments, he stood over the foot.

I decided to give Inspector LePlodd the benefit of my preliminary medical observations. "This foot is that of a male adult. Based on the lack of significant tearing around the bone and blood vessels, I believe the foot was surgically removed from its owner. You will want to have your coroner confirm this, of course."

"I don't think I'll even mention it to him," said LePlodd. "The coroner and I don't get on very well. He will likely view your opinions as interference."

"Oh, I'm sure you can bring him to heel, LePlodd," said Sherlock. "Just don't start off on the wrong foot."

LePlodd let these remarks pass without comment. Instead, he asked me, "Any thoughts on how the man died, Doctor?"

"No. Unless something turns up in the blood analysis, I expect it will be impossible to determine the cause of death without finding the rest of the body. His death could well have been natural."

"Aren't both of you jumping to a premature conclusion?" asked Sherlock. "Isn't it possible that the man might still be alive? Footless and fancy-free, perhaps?"

"Well, yes, I suppose that is possible," I answered. "But why would someone remove a man's foot?"

"Did the two women who lived in these apartments know one another? Might they have jointly decided to leave for some reason?" suggested LePlodd.

"Not that I'm aware of," replied Sherlock. "No, I'm convinced that neither of them had planned to vacate their apartments so suddenly. We should consider these disappearances as suspicious."

"No shit, Sherlock," said LePlodd, with a wink.

Sherlock turned away, saying to me privately, "LePlodd slips in that comment every time we meet. It is becoming rather tiresome."

"I heard that," said LePlodd. "Sorry, Sherlock, just kidding. I'll do a thorough background check on these women. If it turns out they didn't know one another, then you and your wife are the only links between them. Can you think of any reason someone might do this?"

Sherlock seemed to become guarded. "I, um, want to do some investigation of my own before I make any accusations. Give me a few days, Inspector."

"Very well, James. If anyone other than you had given me such an evasive response, I'd haul them in for questioning, but I trust your judgment. Just bring me into the loop as soon as possible."

"Of course I will. Anyway, we'd best be off. Stay on your toes, LePlodd. Don't get caught flat-footed."

"Oh, put a sock in it, Sherlock," said LePlodd.

"Surely, you mean *on* it."

I couldn't get Sherlock to confide in me concerning his suspicions. All he would say was that he had made several inquiries and was waiting for a response.

Around ten the next morning, we heard the sound of the mailman at the door. Courtney collected the small pile of letters and leafed through the envelopes. "Bill. Bill. Rent check. Bill. Advertisement. Bank statement. Oh, this one is odd."

"What is it?" asked Sherlock.

"It's a postcard advertisement for a surgical procedure. Strange that they would do a mass mailing for this kind of thing."

Sherlock sat up straight. "What kind of surgical procedure?"

"It's for a receding chin. You can't see too many of those, I wouldn't think …"

Sherlock raced for the door. We followed in haste.

Of course, we were too late. Mr. Chin was gone, and his apartment was empty.

Empty, that is, except for a Monopoly game board in the bedroom. A hotel was placed upon the "St. James Place" square, and a title deed card for St. James was set in front of the board. The "shoe" game piece was also sitting on this square. There were no other cards or game pieces, and no Monopoly money.

But there was a pair of dice.

The dice were in the palm of a severed hand, positioned in the middle of the board. The hand looked considerably fresher than yesterday's foot. It was seeping blood.

"Fascinating," said Sherlock.

"Why is this happening?" asked Courtney.

Sherlock paced up and down the room. "Given the reference

to St. James Place, I expect we can safely assume that I am the target of this action, my dear. I believe this attack is all about property. The culprit is eliminating our rental income from this building and trying to scare us into selling. I think we all know who is behind this."

"Professor Mariachi!" Courtney and I exclaimed.

The solution was obvious, now that I thought about it. Mario Mariachi, doctor of forensic pathology, owned a chain of retail stores called "Professor Mariachi's Burrito House and Crematorium." One could attend a funeral service and have a meal in the same building without having to drive to a cemetery or a restaurant. He had contacted the Sherlocks on several occasions, expressing interest in purchasing the very property in which we stood. And because of his business, he had access to plenty of body parts.

"But how can we prove Mariachi is the criminal mastermind behind this?" I asked. "What evidence can we produce?"

"I spoke with LePlodd this morning. As I had expected, there were traces of embalming fluid in the veins of the severed foot. I am hopeful an analysis of the chemical elements of this fluid will match the type used in Mariachi's operation."

"Brilliant, Sherlock," I said.

"Elementary, my dear Waddle. Unfortunately, however, a chemical match may identify a possible source of the body parts, but it will not prove that Mariachi is the man behind these kidnappings."

"Kidnappings, you say. So you believe your tenants are still alive?"

"Undoubtedly. Murders bring far too much police attention. Mariachi is highly intelligent, and he wouldn't risk killing people unless there's a significant advantage to be obtained. In this case, there'd be none."

"So how will we find them?"

"The matter is in hand." Sherlock looked down at the Monopoly board. "So to speak. Yesterday I engaged the assistance of some boots on the ground. Happily, the feet inside those boots are still connected to other body parts."

"You mean ..."

"Yes. I called upon the Shaker Street Asymmetricals."

The Shaker Street Asymmetricals were a band of Cincinnati

street urchins and homeless people who acted as observers and informants. They had proven useful in some of Sherlock's previous cases and real estate development transactions. (Perhaps you have read my account of "The Mounds of the Baskervilles," in which Sherlock cleverly discovered who had stolen his neighbor's Halloween basket of chocolate-covered coconut candies. But I digress.)

Sherlock told me he had commissioned the Asymmetricals to watch the apartments last night, based on a suspicion that another tenant might be kidnapped. They were instructed not to interfere, but to instead track any suspicious characters back to their lair. His spies never reported back, however, and Sherlock was becoming concerned about their welfare.

Just then, there was a knock at the door. Two young boys were at the threshold and apologized for the lateness of their response. They gave their report.

"At three in the morning, two men showed up and began to move furniture out of the house onto a cart. The last thing they brought out was a rug that was making jerky movements on its own. We jumped on the back of the cart as it was leaving. It went to a house in Kentucky, just over the river. We hopped off just as the cart arrived and ran to some nearby bushes. We watched the men unload. Then we decided to take a short nap before walking back. We overslept, sir. We're very sorry."

"That's quite alright, boys. You did well. And what was the address of this house?" inquired Sherlock.

"555 Dubious Drive, in Coventry."

"Well, then, Sherlock, what are we waiting for? Let's call for LePlodd and go rescue your tenants," I said.

"In good time, Waddle. In good time. I will ask LePlodd to post a watch on the house. But if we go in now, we will give our hand away without capturing the man behind it all. Instead, I suggest we try to catch the culprits in the act. Tonight."

We waited in darkness and silence in the bedroom of Mr. Hobble's apartment. Sherlock sucked on his unlit pipe and occasionally nudged LePlodd, who looked as if he would fall asleep at any moment.

At 3:30 a.m., we heard a faint scratching at the hallway door. It opened, and we peered out to see two men quietly enter and approach the bedroom. When they crossed the threshold, we set upon them. One of the men was carrying a syringe, which LePlodd knocked out of his hands. We tackled the man, but his partner escaped back into the hallway.

"Don't worry," said LePlodd. "My man outside will stop him."

He didn't, as it turned out. The man had dodged the officer and was very fast on his feet.

But we had one of them anyway. Or so we thought. LePlodd cuffed the intruder with his hands behind his back and propped him up against the wall.

"Who are you working for?" demanded LePlodd.

"I'm not saying anything, screw. He'd kill me and he'd take his time doing it. There's no way I'm going out like that."

He turned his head quickly and bit down upon his shoulder.

"Stop him!" yelled Sherlock.

But it was too late. The man began to choke and convulse. In a few moments, he was dead. I examined his shoulder and found a small bag containing some form of poison taped beneath his T-shirt. I could guess what it was immediately, just by the smell. My eyes began to water.

"Concentrated ghost pepper," I said.

"What a terrible way to go," said LePlodd.

"He clearly thought it was better than the alternative," said Sherlock.

"This villain is a tough one to de-feet," said LePlodd.

"Things are certainly getting out of hand," replied James Sherlock. "Well, LePlodd, I suggest you direct your men to enter the Coventry house and recover my tenants. Unfortunately, I expect that Mariachi will have covered his tracks by now. If you need me, I will be at home."

"Tell Courtney I said hello," said LePlodd. Turning to me, he added, "I feel for that poor young woman, you know. She waits upon him hand and foot."

The police stormed the house where the three tenants and their furniture were being held. None of the kidnappers were present. The victims had been tied and gagged but were otherwise unharmed. Unfortunately, though, Ms. Snip's nightstand had been damaged, and she kept insisting that the moving company should pay for its repair. Everyone was transported back to their respective apartments.

The police left a guard at the house for another week, but Sherlock was convinced there'd be no further attempts. "Professor Mariachi knows when he's been beaten. He'll regroup and try something different," he opined.

A week later as I was preparing to leave for New York, a picture-postcard arrived in the mail from London, England. On the front was a picture of the large Ferris wheel called the "London Eye." The back contained a handwritten message.

"You win this round, Sherlock. But I've got my eye on you. We shall meet again. M."

23

Good Help Is Hard to Find

rince Milo awoke from a deep sleep and rubbed his eyes. *What new experiences does life have for me today?* he wondered. He considered calling for the servants but he decided just to relax in bed for a while. It being Saturday, he had no appointments and nothing in particular that he had to do. *It's great to be wealthy*, he thought.

He scanned the room. It looked the same as always. Tan walls. Clock and decorative lamp on the nightstand. Large wooden dresser (although truthfully, pretty much everything seemed large to him, being himself somewhat small in stature – apparently due to some genetic mishap.) Table off to the side. Small couch and comfortable chair. Bookshelf filled with some of the classics. Mobile with hanging dinosaurs. Immobile now, though. Milo loved that mobile. *It should be revolving*, he thought. He started to feel a twinge of displeasure. *Why isn't that thing moving? Did the maid switch it off? Someone will pay dearly for this!* He let out a deafening roar, knowing that one of the servants was always within earshot.

The pretty one entered and smiled. "Good morning, my little prince! And how is His Highness this fine morning?"

Milo looked up at her and wondered why he suffered this woman's daily insolence. *'Little' prince indeed! Does she seriously dare to make light of my unfortunate physique? But she seems not to bear me any malice, and I'm hungry.* Milo let the comment pass. As was his custom, he declined to speak with her and simply continued to scream. *Let her figure out what I want*, he thought. *It's her job, after all.*

233

"Hungry, are we?"

Prince Milo bellowed until the woman brought him breakfast. Then he quieted. One can't scream while simultaneously quaffing large quantities of milk. He had tried, and it only caused him to cough and choke.

When he was sated, he emitted a large burp.

"Well done, Milo!" the pretty one said.

Milo wasn't sure that his belch constituted a particularly great accomplishment, but he figured that she was simply currying favor with her employer, and there's certainly nothing wrong with that. He smiled wide and let out an approving laugh.

The pretty one seemed pleased and asked, "Shall we read a book?" Without waiting for a response, she walked over to the bookshelf and pulled out a thin volume. They sat together on the couch. She turned to the first page and read aloud.

"In the great green room …"

Ah, wonderful, thought Milo. *One of my favorites. A classic piece of literature.*

"There was a telephone …"

Is there? Where is it, then? I don't see a single smartphone in this picture. And what is that weird-looking black thing with a string going down to the floor?

"And a red balloon …"

Yes. Right there.

"And a picture of …"

Yes, yes, the cow jumping over the moon. I know, I know. Now ask about the mouse! Ask me about the blasted mouse!

"Where's the mouse, Milo?"

There! There! By the fireplace! Are you blind, woman?

"There it is," said the servant, pointing.

Ah, yes. Indeed. Well done. Milo relaxed and laughed.

The story was interrupted at that point by the arrival of Milo's other primary minion.

"Hey, y'all. How's my little man this morning?" the large man asked.

Grrr. No need to rub it in.

"He's been very happy, once he'd eaten," said the woman.

"Bruh. Bruh," Milo added for emphasis.

Without warning, the large man grabbed Milo and tossed him up in the air.

234

"Aiiii!" Milo screamed. And he spit a white viscous substance onto the man's shoulder.

Oh, shoot. Missed his head again, thought Milo as gravity brought him down and he was caught. *More!*

"Say 'Papa'," the servant said.

"Bruh. Bruh," Milo replied.

"Close enough," said the underling. "Plenty of time for that. Well done, Milo!"

Milo gurgled and thought, *These servants aren't so bad, even though they can be less than accommodating on occasion. I guess I'll keep them. After all, good help is hard to find.*

24

Uncooperative Characters

T he author stared at the blank screen and willed himself to think of a storyline. Any storyline would do. He could patch it up later, but he couldn't take another hour of this idiotic writer's block, this painful constipation of words. He was going to pen something today if it killed him. So what if it sounded like a bad idea at first? Many great works of fiction began with a stupid premise. A man wakes up to find he has turned into a gigantic insect, for example. Or some young boys get stranded on a desert island and start to kill one another. Or an evil ring must be destroyed. (Tolkien managed to get three large books out of that one.)

"Death is always a good character," suggested Death.

The author turned to find a black-robed figure sitting in the La-Z-Boy recliner and a black-handled scythe leaning against the grandfather clock. The Grim Reaper held a can of hard cider in one bony hand and some peanuts in the other. Every few seconds, he'd toss a peanut into the dark void of his cowl where it disappeared, never to return. The remaining nuts trembled with fear.

"I already wrote a short story about Death," said the author. "You were on a beach, remember? And stop eating my peanuts."

"Write another one about me. I'm telling you, Death never gets old. I could even SPEAK IN ALL CAPITAL LETTERS if you like."

"No. Terry Pratchett already played that card, and much

better than I ever could. Besides, I kind of maxed out on capital letters in my first novel, *The Coyote*. I'm afraid my computer will run out of them if I keep it up."

"How about a different font then? Something spooky and ominous?" Death suggested.

"Better, but I dunno … I was thinking more along the lines of a romantic comedy/magical pirate Western, with maybe a sci-fi teenage slasher vibe. Something with plenty of gratuitous sex and violence but conveying a compassionate message that all mankind can embrace."

Death delivered eternal rest to the remaining peanuts in his hand and grabbed another bunch from the bowl. "In other words, you don't have a clue what to write about, do you?"

"No."

"Well, in that case, I see only one option," said Death.

"You don't mean …?"

"Yes. You must hold a Zoom meeting of the stock characters."

It only took a few hours to organize. Naturally, due to the short notice, many of the more popular stock characters were unavailable. Prince Charming, Girl Next Door, Sleazy Politician, and Wise Old Man had prior commitments. Mad Scientist, Dark Lord, Tiger Mom, and Bug-Eyed Monster were in locations without Internet connectivity, and Humorous Drunk Guy was "indisposed," having never gotten over the damage his reputation sustained thanks to the movie *Arthur* several decades ago.

However, plenty of stereotypes were online when the author entered in his Zoom meeting ID and password. The computer screen was filled with little rectangular boxes, each containing a small video image of a standard fictional character.

"Good evening, everyone. I'm the author, and I'd like to welcome you to tonight's Zoom meeting on the topic of my new short story, as yet unnamed. I'm hoping to get some inspiration and insights from each of you as we brainstorm possible plots. Remember, there are no bad ideas on this call, so please don't criticize other characters' suggestions. To minimize unnecessary embarrassment, I will quietly discard all the crappy concepts after the Zoom call is over. Death is here with me, and he'll be taking notes during these proceedings. Who'd like to begin?"

"Well, I guess I'll run this up the flagpole and see who salutes it," said Hard-As-Nails-Gunslinger-With-A-Heart-Of-Gold. "How's about Femme Fatale and I get together to investigate the disappearance of her husband, for starters?" Femme Fatale signaled her agreement by crossing her legs and raising a coquettish eyelash.

"Yeah, okay," seconded Evil Clown, "but it turns out the husband's dead, killed by yours truly, and I go on to kill his Sleazy Lawyer and Sleazy Banker as well. Of course, the reader won't know that it's me at first."

"Sounds like a good start to me," said Death.

"I thought Sleazy Lawyer had another commitment tonight," said the author.

"No, I'm here," said Sleazy Lawyer. "It was my friend, Sleazy Politician, who had the conflict."

"Oh, my mistake."

"I'd like to volunteer my services at this juncture," said Red Herring. "You can direct the initial attention to me as the likely assassin."

"But then I'll have to kill you," said Evil Clown.

"Of course," replied Red Herring. "But not too soon."

Evil Clown rolled his painted eyes. "Please. Give me some credit. I'm a professional."

"No offense meant, Your Clownship."

"None taken, Red. It'll be great working with you again."

"Hang on a minute. This plot seems too male-oriented," said the Female Chosen One. "Maybe I should get in on the action."

"Okay, point taken, but isn't the Chosen One a vampire slayer? I don't think we require your services since there are no vampires in this tale," said the author.

"That can be fixed," said Bloodsucking Vampire.

"Not so fast. This is a short story, not a five-book epic series," replied the author.

"Tut-tut. No criticisms. Remember the ground rules," said Death.

"Oops. My bad," said the author.

Female Chosen One put on her pouty face. "The Chosen One is not limited to fighting vampires. I've slain many an Evil Clown in my day."

"I can attest to that," said Evil Clown.

"Very well," said the author. "That's good for starters. I'll consider it. But let's get a few more ideas on the board for me to choose from. Anyone else?"

"How about if a cockroach named Gregor were to wake up one morning to find he had been transformed into a tiny human?" said Tiny Human.

"Yes, and then he is shunned by his fellow bugs," said Monster-Eyed Bug.

"You're here? I thought—" started the author.

"*Bug-Eyed Monster* is out of town. I'm *Monster-Eyed Bug*," clarified the bug.

"Oh, right."

"Or how about a horror story about a bloodsucking vampire?" suggested Bloodsucking Vampire. "Although I should point out right away that I'm a dues-paying member of the Stock Characters Union and your usage of my character will need to comply with all union rules."

"Um, I'm not sure if I'm completely familiar with—"

"I can help with that," said Sleazy Lawyer. "I'm employed by the union. A full description of the rules would take too long to provide on this call, but just let me highlight the biggies. I'm available for consultation to discuss the rest, at reasonable rates of course. First, union members must be afforded frequent coffee and relaxation breaks. Therefore, my client can only appear on odd-numbered pages of your story. You're perfectly welcome to have other characters talk about him on the even pages, as long as he isn't present."

"That sounds unduly restrictive," said the author.

'You'll figure it out. Second, you cannot defame my client's character, and you must always defend his honor during your narration."

"But he's a bloodsucking vampire!" exclaimed the author.

"That's *Honorable Bloodsucking Vampire* to you and your readers. Third, my client can only die at the hands of another member of the union. Fourth, he is not permitted to utter any words beginning with the letters q, v, x, and z because all such words have been deemed silly and inappropriate."

"You mean, like *vampire*?" queried the author.

Sleazy Lawyer stopped for a moment. "I take your point. We may be able to get a waiver of that particular rule in this case. If you would prepare a written list of the words you would need, I could seek the necessary approvals for a small fee."

"None of this is going to make me particularly inclined to hire a union member, is it?" asked the author.

Sleazy Lawyer frowned and said, "I hope your last comment doesn't imply a bias against the union because refusal to hire one of our members solely because he, she, or it belongs to the union is illegal, and we would prosecute you to the fullest extent of the law. Perhaps I should have mentioned earlier that I am recording this entire Zoom call for possible legal use. You may expect a court summons if your next short story doesn't include Honorable Bloodsucking Vampire."

There was a long silence.

"Just out of curiosity, how many of you are union members?" asked the author.

Everyone raised their hand except for Death and the Monster-Eyed Bug.

"Oh my God!" exclaimed the author.

"Ahem," said Honorable Bloodsucking Vampire. "In addition to the union rules, I will also have one condition of my own."

"And what might that be?" asked the author.

"It's nothing much. I simply don't want to work opposite Female Chosen One again. Frankly, her holier-than-thou attitude gets on my nerves."

"Now just a darn minute, you bloodsucking—" began Female Chosen One.

"*Honorable* Bloodsucking," corrected Sleazy Lawyer.

"People, people, let's keep this civil, please," said Death.

"We're just putting together ideas here, folks. There's no need to mark your territory," said the author. "Please continue, Honorable Bloodsucking Vampire. If Female Chosen One is not your nemesis, then who is?"

"That's your decision; you're the writer. Perhaps Old Wise Man?"

"He's not available right now due to a prior commitment," said the author.

"Not so fast, sonny. I *am* available," said Old Wise Man.

"But—"

"Look, it's *Wise Old Man* who's absent. I'm *Old Wise Man*."

"But ... what's the difference?"

"Are you daft, Author? It's self-evident. He's an old man who happens to be wise. I, on the other hand, am a wise man who happens to be old."

"I see."

"And you call yourself a wordsmith," Old Wise Man scoffed.

Ignoring the slight, the author said, "Why don't we hear from some of the stock characters who have remained silent thus far? You there, in the red shirt. What's your name?"

"Who, me? I'm Joe Redshirt."

"Um, help me out here. What exactly is your role?"

"Well, I'm the guy who gets very little introduction and is the first to die. You know, like in the original *Star Trek* episodes? There'd always be some young ensign who beams down to the planet and gets killed by Bug-Eyed Monster before the first commercial. He's usually wearing a red shirt. That was me," Joe Redshirt said proudly.

"Oh, I see. Thank you, Mr. Redshirt. Now, I'd like to find out about the person or thing to your right. What's your deal, sir or madam?"

"I am Terrifying Space Alien. I generally don't have a speaking part."

"Yes, your slime-dripping tentacles certainly are intimidating, I'll grant you that. What's your particular specialty?"

"May I demonstrate?"

"Of course. That's what we're here for."

Terrifying Space Alien suddenly dissolved into nothingness, then rematerialized right behind Joe Redshirt. He wrapped his tentacles around the man and squeezed until Joe's head exploded, covering his box with blood.

Teenage Scream Queen looked up from the box directly below and screamed.

"Well done, Terrifying Space Alien," said Death. "I give you nine points for style but minus two points for excessive gore. The author wishes to remain unnamed, but I *can* disclose that he is *not* Quentin Tarantino."

Terrifying Space Alien rematerialized inside his own box and said, "I'm sorry to hear that, Death. But if you happen to bump into Mr. Tarantino in the future, I'd really appreciate it if you could put in a good word for me."

"I certainly will," said Death. "I do some consulting for him fairly frequently."

"I was pretty good too, wasn't I, Mr. Death?" fawned Teenage Scream Queen.

"Oh, yes," said Death. "It was a very nice scream, my dear. Ear-piercing, I should say."

Teenage Scream Queen blushed.

"OH MY GOD! WE'RE ALL GOING TO DIE!!!" shouted Delayed-Reaction Pessimist.

"Hey, watch it with those capital letters," cautioned the author. "They don't grow on trees."

"What about you, Evil Henchman?" prodded Death. "You've been unusually quiet this evening."

"Oh, just call me Igor. Everyone does," said Evil Henchman. "But honestly, I don't even know why I logged onto this call. I never work solo, you see, and Mad Scientist is vacationing in Peru. Thus, I'm not currently in a position to hench."

"Maybe you should reconsider your solo prohibition policy, Igor. You don't always have to be paired up with Mad Scientist. What if I featured you in a story with Absentminded Professor? It could create an interesting dynamic," suggested the author.

"I'd be up for that," said Absentminded Professor.

"Hmm. It could be interesting to hench for a good guy. But would I still be evil?" asked Evil Henchman, a.k.a. Igor.

"Of course," said the author. "That's what I mean about the dynamic. Absentminded Professor could *think* he's doing good, but you steer him toward evil without his knowledge."

"I'd be up for that," said Absentminded Professor. "What were we talking about again?"

"Very interesting," said Evil Henchman. "Igor will consider this suggestion. Thank you, Master. I mean *Author*."

"sorry," said Delayed-Reaction Pessimist. "i didn't mean to speak in all capital letters before. i just got carried away. i hope i didn't blow my chances for a spot, but i know i probably did. this kind of thing is always happening to me. my life sucks."

"Really, Delayed-Reaction Pessimist, don't worry about it," said the author. Then addressing the entire group, he said, "Well, everyone, our time limit on Zoom is almost up."

"Only because you're too cheap to buy the version without a time limit," muttered Old Wise Man.

The author continued undeterred. "I'd like to thank you for

participating in today's video call. It's been very instructive, and you've given me lots to think about. Once I've decided upon an appropriate plot, I'll contact you directly if you're a potential fit for my story."

"I'll be holding my breath with anticipation," said Old Wise Man.

"Again, thank you for—"

The screen went blank, and a small message box appeared. "Your Zoom meeting has ended."

"Well, did you find that helpful?" asked Death.

"I don't know. They weren't exactly the most cooperative bunch of characters I've ever worked with."

"But it gave you some ideas to consider, I hope?"

"Perhaps. A few."

"Anyway, I must be going. I have an appointment in Samarra tonight. Toodles," Death said, suddenly disappearing from the La-Z-Boy with a small "pop."

Author With Writer's Block turned back to his computer and stared at the blank screen.

25

Epilogue

In the end, there was nothing left but God and a few of His angels. Time still technically existed, but no one cared anymore so it didn't bother being very precise.

The last star had burned out a long, long, long, long while ago. Even the black holes had stopped emitting Hawking radiation. Now there was only infinite darkness and silence. The darkness would have been evil if it had cared. But no one was watching, so it didn't see the point.

At least there was plenty of room to stretch out, assuming you were comfortable with a uniform vacuum and a temperature of minus 273.15 degrees Celsius, which is minus 459.67 degrees Fahrenheit for you fellow Americans. But of course, no one was around to stretch, because nothing can be alive at a temperature of absolute zero when even the atoms stop partying and call it a night.

Eventually, God turned to Satan and said, "Well, that was interesting."

"You owe me five bucks," replied Satan

God coughed. "Do I?"

"Yes. We made a bet about man turning out to be good or evil. He was clearly evil, so I won. Pay up."

"Um, I don't know. Surely, man wasn't all that bad, was he?"

"Mankind destroyed every world that he ever inhabited through mismanagement or aggression—not to mention a host of planets populated by a multitude of Your other intelligent creations. I think that fits the definition of 'bad'."

"Yes, well, he really didn't mean it, though. Cooperation was never one of man's strong suits."

Satan frowned and crossed his arms. You couldn't possibly have seen it because of all the darkness. But God took notice.

"Oh, don't pout about it, Satan. I suppose you're right. You won this time."

God reached for His wallet. But just as He was about to hand over the cash, He cast an inquiring gaze upon Satan.

"Best two out of three?" He asked.

"Sure. Why not?" replied Satan.

And God said, "Let there be light."

Thanks for reading my book!
Please help me out by posting
your rating on Amazom and/or
Goodreads!

Postscript

Many thanks to those who provided feedback on this work, including Elizabeth Carrico and Sharon Honeycutt.

A special thanks to my daughter Rosie for the cover design, and to my daughter-in-law Courtney for her work on the website.

For descriptions of my other books and some fun links and information, please visit my website at www.PeteSimonsAuthor.com.

Photographs of some of the places, objects, and scenes described in my books may be found on my Pinterest page at www.pinterest.com/PeteSimons0323/overview.

About Us

The Author

Pete Simons grew up in Saddle Brook, New Jersey and graduated from Brown University. His dad helped him drive his rock-and-roll record collection and other meager belongings down to McAllen, Texas, where he toiled for a few years as an oil field engineer. When he'd had enough of that, he earned an MBA from The Wharton School and joined Amoco Corporation, holding various positions in Chicago, Houston, London, and Stavanger, Norway, somehow picking up a wife and four kids along the way. When British Petroleum devoured Amoco in 1998, he escaped to Minnesota and became VP and Treasurer of Land O'Lakes, the agricultural cooperative. Their butter really is the best. They're no longer paying him to say that, although if someone from the company reads this and wants to mail him a check, he won't refuse.

After retiring from Land O'Lakes, he joined Teach for America and briefly taught high school physics, gaining a new appreciation for the educational profession. When he had sufficiently recovered from this experience he started writing. *Uncooperative Characters* is his third work of fiction. His previous two novels, called *The Coyote* and *White as Snow*, are also good. If you liked this book, you should try them. If you didn't like this one, I can't imagine you're taking the time to read about the author. Unless you *really* hated it, I guess, and wanted to know who would write such dribble. That would suck.

249

The Cover Designer

Rosie Simonse is responsible for the awesome cover of this book. She is a graduate of Thomas Aquinas College in Santa Paula, California, where she earned a bachelor's degree in liberal arts. She is currently working on a Master of Fine Arts degree in graphic design at the California College of the Arts in San Francisco. In the interest of full disclosure, she happens to be the author's daughter. But that isn't her fault. Nor are the terrible internal illustrations in each story, for which Pete Simons bears the blame.

Also by Pete Simons

The Coyote

As the story begins, the cranium of retired NYPD detective Don Quincy has an unfortunate encounter with a heavy falling object. In his delusional state, Don believes that he has been recruited to be a superhero. Adopting the moniker of "The Coyote," he sets out to fight evil, generally making things worse in the process.

The Coyote's main quest is to find a woman known as 'Dull Cindi,' with whom he has fallen in love. Unfortunately, Cindi is also being sought by a drug kingpin and his two unusually intelligent henchmen, because they believe she may have witnessed a murder they committed. Along the way, The Coyote meets a homeless man named Pancho Sanchez, who helps him in his quest.

Any similarities to the tale of *Don Quixote* by Miguel de Cervantes are purely coincidental. Or not.

White as Snow
A Rock & Roll Fairytale Murder Mystery

White as Snow is a tongue-in-cheek murder mystery that uses the story of Snow White as a very loose backdrop.

While walking back to her dormitory one winter's night, Brown University college-sophomore Bianca Snowden collapses and expires in the snow. Her friends, who exhibit character traits oddly similar to those of the seven dwarfs, are devastated by the revelation that Bianca died from an overdose of drugs and alcohol. Twenty years later, one of the group is murdered. And then another. The culprit leaves a musical calling card at each crime scene, consisting of a song related to the manner of the killing. One of the friends, Detective Charles "Chip" Munck, seeks to determine who is bumping off the other members of the "Heigh-ho Supper Club" and why.

For sample chapters, sale links, and more, please visit my website at www.PeteSimonsAuthor.com.

Made in the USA
Middletown, DE
16 May 2022

65822267R00156